TO HEAVEN BY WATER

JUSTIN CARTWRIGHT's novels include the Booker-shortlisted *In Every Face I Meet*, the Whitbread Novel Award-winner *Leading the Cheers*, *White Lightning*, shortlisted for the 2002 Whitbread Novel Award, *The Promise of Happiness*, winner of the 2005 Hawthornden Prize and, most recently, the acclaimed *The Song Before It Is Sung*. Justin Cartwright was born in South Africa and lives in London.

TO HEAVEN BY WATER

JUSTIN CARTWRIGHT

BLOOMSBURY

LONDON · BERLIN · NEW YORK

First published in Great Britain 2009
This paperback edition published 2010

Bloomsbury Publishing Plc
36 Soho Square
London W1D 3QY

www.bloomsbury.com/justincartwright

Bloomsbury Publishing, London, New York and Berlin

A CIP catalogue record for this book is available from the British Library

ISBN 978 1 4088 0103 1
10 9 8 7 6 5 4 3 2 1

Typeset by Hewer Text UK Ltd, Edinburgh
Printed in Great Britain by Clays Ltd, St Ives plc

Praise for *To Heaven by Water*

'Perceptive and frequently moving new novel ... As ever, Cartwright juggles hefty themes (the function of art, the nature of divinity) without losing sight of his characters or the demands of the narrative ... thrillingly agreeable' *The Times*

'What distinguishes *To Heaven by Water* and turns it into a convincing take on the English (or rather London) early 21st century is the eye for detail and the sheer brio of the writing' *Independent*

'Many things make this such a good novel. Cartwright's prose is ironic, crisp and beautifully crafted without ever seeming effortful. The characters of all sizes are carefully portrayed ... the writing can be exquisitely touching. A fine work, one which could well emulate the achievement of his 1995 novel *In Every Face I Meet*, by being shortlisted for the Booker Prize' *Literary Review*

'There are sharp pictures of modern London, often captured in brusquely pitiless formulae ... These unworldly abstractions don't cancel the slowly accumulating power of the many small scenes in which the realities of friendship, love, ageing and the approach of death are brought believably onto the page' *Sunday Times*

'Never less than sophisticated literary entertainment and Cartwright maintains complete control, without being too obviously a puppet-master in the way of Ian McEwan' *Sunday Telegraph*

'Devilishly good . . . Has the keen eye for detail of everyday life (slang, adverts, fashion, even politics) in Noughties London that will one day make it required reading for social historians' *Scotsman*

'Cartwright is particularly good on how people accommodate such destructive events if it suits them ... Cartwright, with often startling imagery, offers a glorious range of minor characters'
Independent on Sunday

'A harsh, funny, affecting portrait of a man through his relationships. The writing is astoundingly good' Kate Saunders, *Saga*

For Geza Vermes

James M'Cann's hobby to row me o'er the ferry ...
To heaven by water.

Ulysses
– James Joyce

'Such,' he said, 'O King, seems to me the present life
of men on earth, in comparison with that time which
to us is uncertain, as if when on a winter's night you
sit feasting with your earls and thanes, a single sparrow
should fly swiftly into the hall, and coming in at one
door, instantly fly out through another. In that time
in which it is indoors it is indeed not touched by the
fury of the winter, but yet, this smallest space of calm-
ness being passed almost in a flash, from winter going
into winter again, it is lost to your eyes. Somewhat
like this appears the life of a man; but of what follows
or what went before, we are utterly ignorant.

Ecclesiastical History of the English People
– The Venerable Bede, 731 AD

PROLOGUE

DEEP IN THE Kalahari, two brothers, Guy and David Cross, no longer young, are sitting by a campfire. The sun as it descends is setting light – in an act of mindless arson – to the cirrus clouds that appeared unexpectedly in the middle of the afternoon, so that for a few minutes these clouds look like the flags of a medieval army. The brothers have long and unkempt – pilgrim – hair. The older brother, Guy Cross, is reciting, staring upwards at forty-five degrees, as he is inclined to do when smoking dope:

> *I caught this morning morning's minion, kingdom of*
> *daylight's dauphin, dapple-dawn-drawn Falcon, in his*
> *riding*
> * Of the rolling level underneath him steady air, and*
> *striding*
> *High there, how he rung upon the rein of a wimpling wing*
> * In his ecstasy! then off, off forth on swing,*
> * As a skate's heel sweeps smooth on a bow-bend: the hurl and*
> * gliding*
> * Rebuffed the big wind. My heart in hiding*
> *Stirred for a bird, — the achieve of; the mastery of the*
> *thing!*

Brute beauty and valour and act, oh, air, pride, plume, here
  Buckle! AND the fire that breaks from thee then, a
  billion
Times told lovelier, more dangerous, O my chevalier!

  No wonder of it: shéer plód makes plough down sillion
Shine, and blue-bleak embers, ah my dear,
  Fall, gall themselves, and gash gold vermillion.

And indeed the embers of the brothers' own little fire are unstable beneath the blackened, cherished kettle, and occasionally crumble and fall, to release for a moment from their depths gold vermilion, curiously free of smoke.

Guy Cross has tears in his eyes. He is easily moved.

'Shit, that's beautiful. Sorry, it gets me every time,' he says.

'No problem,' says David Cross. 'I am in my ecstasy.'

He feels a rushing, unstoppable love for his older brother, whom he has barely seen in the last forty years.

The stars are appearing as the lurid sunset subsides, soaking away beneath the rim of the vast, flat, inscrutable earth.

David Cross mouths: *L'amor che muove il sole e l'altre stelle.* The love that moves the sun and the other stars.

And the stars are now implausibly bright, scattered carelessly like lustrous seed across the southern sky.

I

THE TRUTH IS, David thinks, that none of us has a clue, although Brian, who lived in Hong Kong twenty years ago, believes he does. We are all losing our hold on small things; the world we were brought up in, and we thought belonged to us, is losing us in the dense, moving panorama which surrounds us. Our forms are still here but they are short on substance.

Brian is ordering. He knows a few words of Cantonese, or maybe it's Mandarin, and he believes he is charming the waitress, who wears a cheongsam of that shiny silky brocade material the Chinese favour. Woven into the cerulean sheen are little pictograms of herons. When you look at them closely you see that there are only two herons, flying around or standing knee-deep in water, endlessly repeated. The buttons, you discover, are frogs.

Some time ago David gave up on Chinese food and took up Japanese for its undoubted health advantages. But for these lunches — once or twice a year — they always meet here, in Lisle Street, and they all know that it is a ritual which must be closely observed, even down to the taking of the monosodium glutamate.

The waitress has very sturdy legs, which are at odds with her small, delicately porcelain face, the face of a child, perhaps sent here from some poor rural town in the north of China. These people are anyway going to inherit the earth; they have a certain steeliness, and they don't need or want our understanding or sympathy.

Brian has the bit between his teeth. He's ordering soup and sesame toasts and char siu pau, which – every time – he tells them is bread dough with barbecue-pork stuffing, and most times he recommends something Szechuan, which, he reminds them, is hot. The people in Szechuan, he says, not only like chilli but are very tall. He orders something called Man and Wife Offal Slices, which will undoubtedly bring sweat to their scalps. The waitress smiles at his witticisms, but her eyes are as glassy as a heron's. One of the first poetic images David remembers is *the mussel pooled and the heron Priested shore* in Dylan Thomas. He no longer asks himself why he suddenly remembers things without warning. Or why he finds emotion rising in gusts, unbidden: that child missing in the Algarve; Tony Blair saying my hand on my heart, I have done what I thought was right; a cheetah cub being killed by a lion on TV. In recent days all these had caused that treacherous welling from the depths.

He suddenly gets a strong gust of a forgotten fragrance. It is urgently rushing in to fill a space that he has unconsciously kept vacant. He remembers the small takeaway, decorated with two tasselled lanterns, on the high street near his parents' house in Ewell, where they sometimes ordered sweet-and-sour pork, in those days, small hard kernels of a deep-fried porky batter in a sweet sticky sauce. The recollection is inexplicably pleasurable, like the emotions you have in the cinema, which have no real consequences. When those boys in the Territorial Army complain about serving in Iraq and about how badly they are being treated, it's because up until now they had only been play-acting, without expecting to see real death or to experience real pain. Nobody signs up for that. When he reported from war zones, David always felt mysteriously protected from what was going on around him, although in his rational mind he knew it was an illusion.

He looks round in the direction of this scent, which dates from the time of carbolic soap, and sees, in robustly threaded garments, an elderly couple – not that much older than he is, but from another era – tucking in. The man's tweed hat rests on the table. His hair is grey although stained the colour of nicotine at the tips of the wings, which are trained over the tops of his ears. The woman, pinched by years of disappointment – so David imagines – wears a pale-blue quilted waistcoat.

He smiles at them.

'Sorry to peer. That smells lovely. I wish we had chosen it.'

'It's our favourite,' she says, smiling warmly. 'We live in Cornwall.'

'Marvellous, enjoy.'

Even as he says it, he knows that the man, who looks annoyed by this spontaneous bonhomie, will hate that metropolitan injunction: *enjoy*.

'You still know how to talk to the common people, I see,' says Julian.

'Nice couple. Up from Cornwall. They were pleased to find someone in London who can speak English. How's old Brian getting on?'

'Old Brian's well away. Speaking in tongues.'

'Yes, I am,' says Brian, breaking off for a moment. 'I plead guilty to being more worldly and cosmopolitan than the rest of you.'

'You are. No question. Are you engaged to Tiger Lil yet?'

'I've given her the deposit for a house. She's just off to ring the agent.'

Here we are again: Brian officiating, Julian quiet and watchful. Adam half drunk already, a pinkish aureole on each cheek, Simon looking subdued; Simon always starts quietly, as though it has been difficult for him to accept that these are his friends, friends of the inalienable sort, not necessarily the people he would have chosen in an ideal world, but ones with, as the police say, previous.

'I've ordered Peking duck for the traditionalists.'

'Brilliant. As you know, we would eat bogies with sesame seed if you ordered them. Where you go on any culinary voyage, we follow.'

'Oh shit.'

'What?'

'Adam's already drunk half a bottle and the Jiaozi dumplings and soup haven't even arrived.'

Adam raises his glass.

'Chill. Here's to that nice Mr Brown, our new leader.'

David still believes Blair is a fine person and prime minister and that the new man will flounder. Politics has changed: Brown is from a different time, like something discovered when a glacier moves, and nobody will like him when they discover the truth. The waitress now brings the dumplings, the soup, the char siu pau and some other unspecified bits in little baskets stacked one on top of the other. Brian opens the baskets, glances inside, and closes the lids quickly, as though he is expecting small creatures to pop out if he isn't quick.

'He's bonkers,' says Simon.

'I don't think he's bonkers. He's overly rational,' says Julian.

'Sadly, politics is not rational. You remember what Macmillan said when he was asked what the pitfalls of a political career were: *Events, my boy, events.*'

Of course they all know what Macmillan said, and they also remember him, the prime minister of their boyhood, a bewhiskered old grandee, with sagging eye pouches like empty purses, defiantly Edwardian. Even then it was a mystery how he came to be cast as leader. The memory of Macmillan touches David: it seems so distant. He's beginning to see his childhood as his children see it: lost somewhere, stranded in an age of mist. The black-and-white family photographs, with their donkeys and beaches and your mother in a one-piece Jantzen swimsuit, help create the impression that the wheel turns pretty quickly. When he sees pictures of himself at the age of eight or ten, he sees an imposter, some little stranger who has come through the wainscot. *The Water-Babies* was his favourite book and the feeling that his childhood may not have happened as he remembers it is fostered by that book: for a few years he wasn't sure if he was real or a creature of the sea. And of course he hadn't realised that it was a tract against child exploitation; Tom was, as Blake wrote in *Songs of Innocence, a little black thing among the snow* – exploited labour.

Ed, at thirty-two, thinks of me as encumbered by my past. To him I am a Bactrian camel, staggering along laden with all sorts of goods which nobody needs or wants any longer. In fact all of us here are in some way trying to prepare ourselves for what is to come.

Adam is ordering another bottle; he hopes, and he has every possibility of succeeding, to be drunk when his end comes. Although none of them talks about their own deaths, these meetings have a subtext: we may be ridiculous and out of time, but we represent something, even if it is something our children don't see and the world doesn't require. When Nancy died nearly a year ago, many friends came, some from far away. They hadn't come to mourn Nancy, so much as to show themselves, like those forest people in the upper reaches of the Amazon who occasionally appear mysteriously from nowhere, in a diffident but defiant sort of way, saying yes, we are here.

There's a capacious, unused look to Gordon Brown, like an old rectory with too many rooms. God knows what he looks like without his clothes on: he's way too fat, unlike Blair who keeps himself pretty trim. More and more the role of the politician is to provide the people with an excuse to air their own banal and inaccurate opinions. Politicians' lives only have meaning in relation to how they are perceived; in fact Berkeley's saying, *To be is to be perceived*, seems to have been stood on its head. David finds his friends strangely eager to make themselves heard, as though this is their last hurrah, the last chance to catch the ear of the heedless. It's only when they are gathered like this that they can believe that their youth and their vitality and their recklessness and their indiscretions and their sexual and sporting and creative achievements are not forgotten. They like to be reminded of these, because they are inclined to think that they have invented their pasts. It's an unsettling feeling.

The fact that many people still recognise him, and often come up to speak to him, doesn't lessen David's sense of insubstantiality. And sometimes in the middle of the night when he wakes up and finds to his surprise that Nancy is not there, he feels a little resentment towards his children for treating her death as an excuse to peg him down: he should, in their view, feel himself diminished and his posture in the family should be one of gratitude. Their own lives are not so perfect, of course, but then families have unreal expectations of their blood relations; the family is a sort of Platonic ideal, floating way above the real facts, the facts on the ground.

'You look thin,' says Adam. 'You're getting to be gaunt; are you OK?'

'Funny, isn't it, when you lose weight, I mean deliberately, everyone thinks you are about to kick the bucket. No, Adam, I haven't got anything terrible. I'm just trying to get fit.'

'For what?'

'Well, yes. That is the question.'

The rest of the food arrives. Adam's cheeks have anticipatory highlights. When he gets drunk he simply becomes more amiable. His curly hair, only slightly grey, falls over his face; he wears a red T-shirt that displays his rather soft chest too frankly. Written on it are the words: *The meek shall inherit the earth, after we have finished with it*. He has absolutely no dress sense: he is wearing camouflage trousers with many zips and buckles, and huge black trainers, which he almost certainly borrowed from one of his sons. The whole family goes to restaurants together and they eat and drink prodigious amounts. Sometimes they sing. In his heyday as a scriptwriter, Adam once confessed that he had spent forty thousand pounds on eating out in a single year.

David is getting thinner and stronger by the week, and eating less and less. The gym has become a ritual; endorphins make him happy. (Although scientists are undecided on how endorphins relate to happiness.) This morning there were three fat women on the running machines, wearing headscarves, but with their abundantly feminine bottoms clearly outlined in tracksuits. None of the women jogged, they walked slowly. On the monitors facing them was a music channel, which shows videos of black male singers attended by gyrating girls bumping and grinding, tits on display, legs spread wide, booty undulating, in a kind of shivering motion, which David thinks is demeaning, suggesting they are all dying to have sex with these gold-swagged potentates. He wondered how these Muslim women saw these videos; perhaps from within their headscarves they felt immune to evil impulses. He would have liked to ask them, but he thought that this might be a transgression. Maybe they simply took this video nonsense as lightly as everyone else.

Over to the right from the cross-trainer, where he was simulating the art of skiing across the snowy tundra, is the weight-lifting section where unemployed men, white and black, lift weights sporadically and then stare at the mirror to see if their muscles are responding to order. They have a curious way of walking from one apparatus to another, stately, self-regarding, profoundly pleased with their bodies, seeing or imagining that something beautiful and significant is emerging.

As I do.

The Muslim women never broke into a run; they walked on the treadmill just a little faster than they would on the street. Their bodies probably have a softness and roundness that their husbands like, but now they want to be lean. It is going to take some time at this pace: he could see the LCD display and they were walking at 5.2 km per hour.

Most days there are also three middle-aged taxi drivers who have had heart attacks, or *events*, and who arrive together for a workout before their breakfast near Mount Pleasant. All three are shaven-headed and jocular, with legs that look like Mediterranean tree stumps. Cardiac problems have brought them close; illness has become a badge of honour. Sometimes they do runs for a cardiac charity called My Heart is in the Right Place. He wonders if this suggests transplants, but he doesn't ask. He admires them: a little younger than him, jovial, ironic and clutching at straws. Or perhaps they are Jewish, making bricks without straw. They assume he is also here for his heart: *How's the old ticker this morning, Dave? Still working when I last looked*.

Simon is cheering up as the restaurant becomes foggier and more aromatic. There is a tropical mist of soy and ginger, invisible but closing. It's always the same with Simon: he starts slowly but eventually remembers what camaraderie and friendship are, so that he is usually the last to leave the restaurant at four in the afternoon, plumped up with human feeling, full of plans which presage a retreat. This is what getting old produces in some people, a deliberate withdrawal from the hurts and insults – the acknowledgement of lack of presence. Germans call it *Dasein*, being. Being is what we lack.

Last night he went to the Royal Opera House to see one of Darcey Bussell's farewell performances. He can't stand ballet, but it seemed churlish to refuse Ed and Rosalie's invitation. For Rosalie this leave-taking is something highly significant: his daughter-in-law belongs to that small but clearly identifiable class of pleasantly melodramatic young women who love dance. Dance to them is life, and they wish they could all have been Darcey Bussell. Ed has told him that they are trying to have a child. (How hard would you need to try with Rosalie, he wonders, only mildly ashamed.) If they produce a girl, Rosalie will clothe her in soft airborne materials so that she will look like Edmund

11

Dulac's fairy drawings in his mother's calendar. He keeps this calendar in his desk; with its notes about meals and recipes, it summons her more directly than the picture on the piano taken during the war of her in a floral dress, a tea dress, beside his father, who is dapper in naval uniform.

He likes Rosalie. In the Floral Hall at Covent Garden, where delicate smoked-salmon sandwiches – the food of choice for the dancing and theatrical classes – were pre-ordered, he was proud to be with her as she walked elegantly to find their table, toes placed in classical fashion, her clothes, endowed with mysterious lightness and subtle colours, swirling behind her like the Northern Lights. Waiting with her for Ed gave him a pleasurable sense of complicity. As always, Ed was late, arriving just in time, slightly moist, strangely serious in his dark office suit, but still the rumpled child he had loved.

He just had time to swallow a glass of the Pol Roger his dear old dad had ordered for him.

'Fucking clients,' he said. 'Sorry, Rosie. What's she doing?'

'*Das Lied von der Erde*. Her favourite piece.'

She said this as though it was a widely known fact.

David remembered *Das Lied von der Erde* only from Tom Lehrer's 'Alma', about Mahler's wife:

> *Their marriage, however, was murder.*
> *He'd scream to the heavens above:*
> *'I'm writing* Das Lied von der Erde
> *'And she only wants to make love.'*

But when Darcey Bussell danced, skipping away en pointe, and the soprano moaned the last line, ' "For ever . . . for ever," ' he recognised the power of art and accepted that it could be found in ballet, even in this sustained cruelty to Darcey Bussell's toes. Ed was concerned, perhaps embarrassed, when he saw his father in tears. Those treacherous tears. More and more David sees in art a desperate urge to fix ourselves in the universe – which he finds moving.

'You OK, Dad?'

There was something a little peremptory about the words.

'I'm fine.'

All his life he had been under the impression that ballet was a sort of high-class vaudeville, full of gesture but signifying nothing much, the tortured bodies and the extravagant costume and the camp sets, a homosexual fantasy, the sort of thing you see writ large in hairdressing salons, but last night he understood – a fact he had in reality always known – that art comes in many guises. And maybe he has been wrong about many other things, he thinks. When Nancy was alive he seemed in some way to be channelled, so that his thoughts and his values butted up against hers and became more rigid. If she had been there last night she would have said how beautiful Darcey Bussell was and he would immediately have reacted poorly to this suburban thought and condemned the whole enterprise. Without Nancy, he is both more uncertain and more free. Darcey Bussell reminds him of Jean Shrimpton, and of his youth. How could he tell Ed this?

'I'm OK, big boy, just sentimental.'

'Is it because of Mum?'

'In a way.'

But not in the way that Ed imagines and desires. Children crave conventionality in their parents' affairs. What Ed dreads most, he knows, although they have never discussed it, is the possibility that his father will take up with some gold-digging, well-upholstered forty-two-year-old. The bereaved must live quietly and modestly, forsaking sex, of course, until their time is up.

And here we are again. We are sitting at this round table, a little battered, but each of us in our own way with a rich history that is not apparent to the other customers and is utterly inscrutable to their waitress, with her enamelled features and functional legs, legs which end in, he sees, pigeon toes. Strange – ballerinas splaying their feet outwards, Chinese waitresses making dutiful, inverted steps with theirs. The waitress is being supervised from a distance by a thin, older man who wears a clip-on bow tie. His face is benevolent but in the course of a slow process of subsiding into a folded-linen shape, as if his upper features are becoming heavy and pressing on the lower section, causing it to crease. And in the rising humidity and quickening tempo of the restaurant, David has the sense of a crowded world composed of infinite numbers of expressions and beliefs and delusions – some of them organised into little groups, like the Noodle Club – which have a central gravitational pull. This pull is to counteract the vortex effect of mortality, which drags on everybody. It all seems arbitrary and unfathomable to David now.

Nancy sometimes accused him of having autistic tendencies, by which she meant that he often took no interest in her views and judgements, because, she said, he was incapable of understanding other people's deep feelings. Of course he could not say, *I don't have Asperger's, I am genuinely not interested in what most people say most of the time*. Marriage is not a forum designed for discussing each other's shortcomings; to work at all, it requires restraint. *Now Ed wants me to start digging my own grave*. As he grows more plump and corporate, he is suspicious of his father's leanness. He suspects me of being on the lookout, which, in a sense, I am and always have been, but it is not for some desperately signalling divorcée.

Adam orders more wine. There is nothing furtive about this, the way it is with some big drinkers; he just can't conceive of a day or a meal without alcohol and he can't allow his friends to miss out.

'Are you drinking, Davey boy?'

'Just a beer. For Chrissakes don't take it as any kind of affront.'

'I won't. How's things, generally?'

'Same old, same old.'

'All the better. That's why we are here. To acclaim the same old.'

'You're quite a philosophical old bastard these days.'

Adam's face has a softness, through which the underlying blood vessels, particularly at the cheeks, are visible, creating a blush like the skin of an apple. He looks unnaturally young, a child with a fever, the curls falling downwards and his small, delicate mouth already stained by red wine.

'How's the writing? I read about you all the time.'

'Oh shit, David. Don't go there. Every time somebody comes to me with a script proposal I want to tell them to fuck off. But we spend so much money I can never say no. Now I am running through the Tudor monarchs. I am specialising in cod Elizabethan dialogue, prithee.'

'And winning an Emmy,' says Simon, who owns a bookshop in Sussex.

'Oh that. Yes, for best dialogue spoken by an actor in a ruff this year. Actually, I am getting the work because they think I was alive in 1589.'

Adam always has a book in his pocket. He reads, walking

down escalators to the tube or waiting at the dentist, but he claims to hate almost every known writer apart from P.G. Wodehouse and Jerome K. Jerome, whom he reveres. David doesn't read either of them.

'And you, are you over Nancy's death, in so far as old cunts like us can ever get over that sort of thing?'

'That sort of thing?'

But he's not really reproaching Adam.

'You know what I mean. No offence.'

'I am not unhappy. No. My son asked me the same question only yesterday. The children, of course, would like me to be pottering around the garden and falling asleep in front of the television at six-thirty. I miss her in the sense that you would miss a piece of your body if it fell off.'

'What, like your cock?'

'I wouldn't necessarily miss that.'

'Do you know what Richard Harris said to me about his dick?'

David remembers the story, about the need to have a woman to hand at all times because his erections were so infrequent. As he listens again, he sees that there are various ways of dealing with approaching old age: the Anglo-Saxon way is to be ironic. Adam's life is anyway a kind of performance; he's always complaining about producers, agents, the BBC – where countless harridans have stabbed him in the back – and publishing, while at the same time being in constant demand to speak on radio or do an adaptation of Jane Austen or write a drama about the Tudors or speak at a school or college. His one successful novel, written eighteen years ago, *The Wise Women of Wandsworth*, is a comedy classic, although no longer read. David loves him unreservedly; he loves his kindness and his openness and his willingness – his compulsion – to wear his heart on his sleeve. The strange thing is that his apparent defencelessness hides a very shrewd understanding of how things work. It's not given to many, not even captains of industry or lawyers, to really understand how things work, the important things like art and politics and love, but Adam understands. This understanding comes mostly from books, but then that is what books are for, although many people believe that books, like politics, are there to confirm their prejudices or to flatter them.

But now, David thinks, here we are, the ones who scrambled into the lifeboat together, and yet we never allow our intensity of feeling to show except in small considerations which stand proxy for love. Probably it's just that in the normal course of a life you find you have few friends left who share a kind of intimacy: you need shared experience for intimate understanding. And the English of our age, David thinks, keep that sort of stuff at a distance with little ironic asides and jokes, a difficult habit to break. And perhaps we don't really have the intimacy that I imagine, but only a kind of resignation: these are the ones I am yoked to and I may as well accept it.

Adam is drunk. David loves it when he gets that slightly crazy look, combative and crafty, but always benign.

Adam kisses David on his cheek.

'You look great. If I was a homosexual, I would want to fuck you.'

'Thanks. And you still look like a debauched choirboy.'

'As the *Guardian* said in 1981.'

He turns to Brian.

'Brian, Brian, the food is the dog's bollocks. Well done, mate. A fucking triumph.'

'It could actually be dog's bollocks, I suppose.'

'A dog's not just for Christmas, Brian. There should be

some left over for Boxing Day. No, fabulous, Brian, I mean it. And so tall, the people from Szechuan. Big buggers. Huge. Didn't you say that the women are like Douglas firs? Swaying in the breeze? No, Brian, you're a pro.'

'I'll take that as a compliment.'

They're loosening up as they always do before they regress cheerfully.

'Did I tell you how Richard Burton asked David if he wanted to fuck his wife?'

'Yes, Adam, about fifty times.'

'And did I tell you he said no?'

'Yes, Adam.'

'Oh all right. To the Noodle Club.'

'The Noodle Club.'

David sips his Tsingtao beer. He once filed a report from the brewery, which was founded by Germans in Qingdao in about 1907. He knows many largely useless facts and he wonders on what basis his brain chooses to preserve them. His training doesn't really permit him to drink, but he doesn't want to cast a pall over the Noodle Club, which has come together again from London and the countryside – never all the same people each time – and it is his job to lend wholehearted support. Julian's minor stroke – this is his first appearance since being declared fully recovered – has left him with a frosted appearance. His Foreign Office hair and his features seem to have acquired a fine coating, barely visible – maybe even imagined – of pale, mycological filaments, almost a mould. After the stroke they spoke on the phone often and David knows all the details: the numbness and the blinding headache, the inability to move his mouth for a week, the sense of utter helplessness.

'It was a wake-up call,' said Julian, in his new tired

voice, directed, it seemed, through the wrong chambers of his head, to emerge with an unfamiliar timbre.

For the last three months he has been very active. He invited David to play tennis at Queen's. After they played, David saw that his chest hairs had taken on this ephemeral, spun-sugar look and that his circumcised penis poked out of a snowy nest, like a fledgling. Surprisingly, his tennis was as good as ever, neat with plenty of slice, but the permafrost look, perhaps visible only to David, was unsettling. Julian told him in the bar that one of his sons had never discussed his stroke: he attributed this to hypersensitivity. David wondered if it wasn't the reaction to incarceration in boarding school while his father carried the flag to foreign lands, eating a million canapés for Queen and commerce in the process. Julian is on various committees. He takes a special interest in the Sudan. And he also takes a lot of interest in his three grandchildren, all under five. David wonders if he doesn't frighten them. Everyone says that having grandchildren wakens very deep family feelings and ties. They also say the best thing about grandchildren is that they go home. David is looking forward to having a grandchild. Julian, for all his detached upper-class English sangfroid, a quality that has largely left the earth, is a Jew. Maybe in his heart he believes that he would have been given one of the big embassies if he hadn't been Jewish.

'It's good to have you back, Jules.'

'The wandering Jew returns.'

'Yes, for a moment there we thought you might be wandering off.'

'No such luck. We went to see Darcey Bussell the other night.'

'So did I. Last night, in fact. With Ed and his wife,' he

adds in case Julian thinks he has been exploring his feminine side.

'Wasn't it wonderful?'

'Utterly fantastic. She reminded me of the girls we used to shag.'

'Or wished we were shagging.'

'Ballet is bollocks, total fucking bollocks,' says Adam. 'Poofs' football, as Osborne called it. What was that girl's name you had in Rome? She looked just like Jean Shrimpton.'

'Jenni.'

'Sex on a stick.'

Julian probably thinks this conversation is insensitive, just eleven months after Nancy's death. But sometimes when he is alone in his bed, David thinks of the girls he fucked – a word still strangely evocative to him – and he can remember with clarity many tiny details. It seems important to him to remember these things, as though they contain something vital about the nature of being human. The thoughts that more and more keep him awake at night are really a kind of assurance that he has been alive, although he is not sure how it works. Nancy used to go to yoga classes for a while and could sometimes be heard chanting – actually, it was more like the background electronic muttering of an old and raucous fridge – *Om, om, om, om* – which was designed to allow the disciples, like Nancy, to have a handy condensed version of the guru's teaching. David sometimes wondered if you could concentrate all this wisdom into one word – if it was a word rather than notes or a chord – but he understood that it produced a profound meditation. *Cheaper than crack*, as he once said. Even when Nancy switched to Pilates at Rosalie's suggestion, David never enquired whether she had felt any regret at ditching the wisdom of millennia concentrated in that chant. Pilates was pioneered by Joseph Hubertus Pilates, who understood the strains dance imposed on the bodies of ballet dancers: faith in mystic forces has been replaced by a belief in quack science. But David didn't mock Pilates either: he understood that everyone needs a sense of worth. Often extreme credulity is applied to far more high-minded nonsense than Pilates. For instance the love of freedom, as understood by George Bush.

Jenni Cole. He met her in a discotheque called Sabrina. She was working in the wardrobe department on the film of *Dr Faustus*. He borrowed the Fiat Seicento from Adam and they drove down to Ostia, where they made love behind a fisherman's boat until the sun came up. She had straight, jet-black hair and she uttered charming bat squeaks to the rosy-fingered dawn rising from the direction of Yugoslavia. It was the same classical dawn that had risen on Ovid in exile and on the Argonauts on their journeys, a dawn which turned quickly to a white and furred light. Mercilessly illuminating Ostia, it revealed to the hungover and exhausted young couple that the beach was not clean. Unspeakable things lay about, and Jenni's very short dress, which he had been so keen to remove – it was a sort of provocation rather than a garment – was heavily stained with tar and oil, and some other substances, possibly the excrement of seabirds.

His memories of former blitheness are crowding Nancy out, as if they are rushing to fill a vacuum. While Nancy was alive he always felt a buzz of unease; this version of himself was burdened by the sense that he was never quite able to make her happy. Yet he knows that almost all his friends – male and female – believe that in some way they have been diminished by marriage. The people who say that their wife or husband is their best friend are deceived; and the reason is that love and friendship are different. Coleridge prized friendship very highly, but it was male friendship: *the unspeakable comfort to a good man's mind, nay even to a criminal, to be understood – to have someone who understands one. The hope of this, always more or less disappointed, gives the passion to friendship.*

He can't tell Ed or Lucy that their father is in some ways happier now that their mother is dead. But to his own mind he is more himself than he has been for nearly forty years, and he has friends, a little ravaged it is true, who understand him. As far as that is possible. When Nancy was alive, he had secrets that he kept from her. Now that she is dead he has a secret that he must keep from his children: he is not unhappy.

But he knows that, for example, he will never be as happy as he was that summer in Rome.

The restaurant is now warmly alive; the rich fog of Hunan chilli and Szechuan pickle and dark soy and faintly medicinal sesame and hot peppercorns has swirled into every corner, and into this suspension the warmth of human bodies has infiltrated itself. From behind their table David can still smell, he imagines, the scent of sweet-and-sour pork. He looks round to see that the man with the nicotine hair is wiping his face with a hot towel while his wife looks on. She smiles at David, who winks, absurdly and conspiratorially.

Simon, who is now fully animated, asks Adam about his new novel.

Adam understands that this is his cue.

'Which fucking novel would that be? I don't write novels. I gave it up. I hate all novels written since 1940. But mostly I hate novels which describe the awful problems of being a writer and novels about a mysterious legacy of papers found in a trunk which may explain the meaning of the Gnostic gospels, and I hate novels which tell you the real story of William Shakespeare, who was secretly a Catholic priest, as you can tell from a small carving on a pew in a chapel in Stratford, and I hate novels about magic and elves and the lost arts of necromancy, and even worse – much fucking worse – I hate novels about fairies and guardian angels and novels about sensitive people who have autistic children touched by fucking genius and I also hate novels of suspense where the writer withholds from the reader details that he knows perfectly fucking well in order to make it suspenseful and, even worse than having my nuts passed through the grinder, I hate reading novels about time travel and what is called – can you believe this? – fantasy, which turns out to be fucking bollocks on a Homeric scale about people dressed in plastic armour with silly names like Snarfbucket of Zadok, Lord of the Fens and the Mountains.'

David is laughing uncontrollably. He fears that particles of Szechuan pickle will come out of his nose.

'And I hate fucking novels where everybody says that family is a tyranny and I hate novels where people remember child abuse and . . .'

The couple from Cornwall are off, hurrying not too ostentatiously, as if this rant is just the sort of thing they were afraid of, a kind of urban anarchy, all restraint lost.

'And it explains everything about why they are hopeless parents and I hate novels where the father finds he has an illegitimate daughter and people go on a long journey and discover they are somebody else or that they are bisexual or fall in love with a gondolier or a horse or move to the country, where everybody is fantastically fucking wonderful – or awful, take your pick – or move to another country where it takes them a while to discover that they can't really understand the locals who hate them, and even worse, much worse, I hate novels where the author says oh gosh, aren't we all weak and pathetic but likeable with our immense collections of seventies records and our moody librarian girlfriends, so frankly there's very little left to read, fuck all in fact, except for Jerome K. Jerome. Fucking masterpiece. Brian, can you ask your mail-order bride to bring some more wine?'

David applauds. Adam has done what he had hoped for by delivering one of his rants. It's a relatively subdued performance: in private he can go on for half an hour and strip to his Y-fronts to expose his lightly furred, speckled legs and his strangely unstable chest, which is as pale and unformed as it was when they met as schoolboys. He has no muscular definition at all, but there is something miraculous about the fact that in a sense he is the only one among them who hasn't aged: he still looks soft and infantile. He loves his drunken children immoderately; a dinner with them in some Italian restaurant, where the owner adores the whole family, is all he aspires to in a social life. He likes to be with the boys and their girlfriends, although that subplot is becoming more difficult, as adulthood begins to take a hold and the boys discover to their surprise that they are subject to the dead weight of responsibility and the drag of expectation. It has happened to Ed, too: his newly critical tone is probably explained by disappointment. He would have preferred to remain a student with his carefree friends. But the friends all began to pair off or move into the City and he found himself with the gravity-defying Rosalie, who had a very clear idea of how things should proceed and David wonders if Ed doesn't feel constricted, although the law is treating him fine. There is something about women like Rosalie, women with deep instincts, which gives them the edge in the marital dialectic.

And this may be one of the defining characteristics of our restless age, that all of us believe that our lives could have been better or different. Unlike the cattle-obsessed Masai or the horsemen of the Mongolian Steppe, who derive satisfaction from undying ritual and can imagine nothing better. Stasis is not something you see in the political parties' manifestos. Why not? This Gordon Brown, this rumpled old political wheeler-dealer, with the coelacanth mouth and just the one eye, is always talking about radical change and reform as if that is what we want politicians for, to change everything. What politicians don't understand is that a lot of the electorate want them to put things back how they were – at some unspecified time. For example, they would like migrants to go home. David sometimes thinks that he would, too, but at the same time he knows that this is not possible. He can't even imagine how many times he has read the words *asylum seekers* and *immigrants* off the autocue. Anyway, who says everyone should stay in their place of birth? Why don't the Alps belong to me just as much as to someone who was born there? And then there were the British-born bombers. The whole multicultural conceit fell apart after that. The Muslims seem to think that Iraq and Israel are unbearable provocations, which we are deliberately fostering. But as Blair said, it's not we who are blowing up mosques and innocent children in Iraq. It wasn't us who attacked the Twin Towers.

David feels a kind of contentment settling over them.

Nobody accepts Brian's suggestion of fruit or ginger ice cream; they don't believe the Chinese know how to do dessert. Brian rather stubbornly orders fresh mango, which comes neatly sliced and laid out in a wagon-wheel. Brian made a lot of money in Hong Kong in the eighties working for a merchant bank, where he became entitled to special treatment from waiters. Somehow they all did, all these English public-school boys who went out there. Simon is the only one among them who has no children. He is not gay, but he once told David that he feels the assumption rearing up whenever he says he has not been married. Sometimes he tells strangers he is widowed. He's got plans – he's talking about them now – to put his bookshop on the web, but David suspects that by the time he gets back to Sussex he will have lost heart. Brian recently offered to put money into the bookshop for new computers but Simon never went further than talking about it. He said to David, 'I can't really see the point. Do you find that? You wonder why you would make plans to paint the house or visit the pyramids.' And David knew what he meant, although he has half-formed plans.

Lucy, too, has taken some time to adjust, but now she seems to have found a niche with the auction house. He worries more about her than he does about Ed. Before he took his law-conversion course, Ed had an idea for a television game show and then for a web project offering interactive tutoring. What he wanted was a way of making money fast so that he could put that behind him and live a carefree life. Now, three years after qualifying, he is working for Robin Fennell, a friend of David's, near the British Museum. Ed's doing well as a solicitor, while his soul, David suspects, is seldom present.

Simon says he wants Adam to come and read in his

bookshop: there will be quails' eggs and celery salt. The bookshop is panelled and pleasantly chaotic. Simon is excited by the idea of Adam reading; he can picture the plates being handed around by his volunteers from the village; he can feel the literary excitement rising as Adam staggers to the podium, which they erect in the widest part of the shop, effectively blocking access to the lavatory.

'Jesus, Simon, I love you, but I haven't written anything for eighteen years.'

'Of course you have. Scripts, all kinds of things. You've written all kinds of things. You've just won an Emmy.'

Simon has a curious voice, slightly over-articulated, as if a fondness for books produces a kind of prissiness.

'Simon, my old bibliophile, your audience out in Wibbly-Wobbly-Wood wants a genuine celebrity novelist or biographer. They don't want an old hack like me. Anyway, I could never find the bookshop.'

'Come on the train and stay overnight.'

'I hate trains. I hate travel.'

'Oh shit. You are such an awkward bastard.'

'Give me another glass of the old Chateau Beijing 1929 and I may reconsider. Maybe I could sing. I know, I'll set my radio play about Baden-Powell to music. What do you think? Could it work?'

'Perfect.'

'I'll drive you down,' says David.

'OK. Agreed. You can be my Ifor Jenkins.'

Adam, too, had never forgotten that summer in Rome with Richard Burton, the summer that formed their lives, and David knows that Adam is thinking of how Ifor often had to lift his drunken brother Richard into the Bentley.

*　　*　　*

Julian is the first to leave. As a diplomat he was always expected somewhere urgently and David thinks he finds it hard to shake off the habit, now that he has almost nothing to do. He offers Brian some money, but Brian says, holding up a flat palm, 'Next time.' In drink Brian becomes their prince-patron, but he does it with grace. They watch Julian exit and stand outside looking around for a few seconds, perhaps expecting the mujahedin, before striding off to the tube. Only David notices that one of Julian's legs is a little reluctant to march in step.

A little later the remaining four gather for a few minutes next to some giant wheelie bins at the back of a cinema. It's becoming dark and a gust of popcorn from a duct on the blank wall of the cinema rushes out into the heavily laden Soho air. They don't really want to separate. Who knows how much strain the weakening links can stand? Eventually they go – Adam kisses everybody to wish them Godspeed on their almost-elderly way. David is very aware that for each of them these separations have a kind of poignancy, hinting at something more final. He notices, as he walks up Wardour Street, that Chez Victor, the last of the old Soho restaurants, is now boarded up. His father once took him there and they ate rump steak and thin *frites*, which his father said were authentically French. Victor himself sat grumpily drinking absinthe.

David loves Soho. In the sixties when he was working here, he felt that it was in some way his secret. Right in the middle of London and untouched. Once Francis Bacon offered him a drink in the French House. Frank, the heavily bearded theatre critic, who looked like a mariner off a tobacco pouch, said that if you let him bugger you he would give you a painting. That would be worth a few million now. Old Compton Street is alive with gays. It's become their boulevard, the scene of their febrile passeggiata. And they think they have discovered Soho, just as I did. Camisa is still there, even though the Spanish deli opposite, Delmonico, with barrels of sardines in oil standing on the pavement, has long gone, to be replaced by an unnaturally youthful selection of men's clothing. The currency of homosexuality which once stood for something brave and noble, has, he thinks, become debased. A bottle of sherry cost seven shillings and sixpence. He can see the hand-lettered sign: *Amontillado 7/6*.

He walks fast. He wants to get to the gym.

2

'YOUR DAD'S BECOME very thin,' says Rosalie. She says it in a way that alerts Ed.

'I know. But he says there's nothing wrong with him, if that is what you meant.'

'No, I just wondered. Do you think he enjoyed last night?'

'You never really know with Dad, but yes, I think he did. He was in tears during Part Six.'

'So was I.'

'Ah, but you're a girlie. You love puppies and embroidery. You can't help yourself.'

'The old jokes are the best. No, I think he's probably got a girlfriend and that's why he's working out. But he doesn't want to tell you.'

'You've got the most amazing talent for fitting the facts to your own theories.'

'What are you saying?'

'I'm not saying anything.'

'Are you saying I am crazy?'

'No, of course not.'

'So, if he's not ill, why's he working out?'

'Firstly, I don't know if he is working out and secondly if he is he may just be doing it because he likes it.'

'He doesn't drink much any more.'

'No, but I'm not sure that's such a bad thing. On the contrary, it's good.'

Rosalie looks at him coolly, as if she has never seen him before.

'You know, you have begun to sound like a lawyer. On the contrary, m'lud, I think that, on the balance of the evidence, any reasonable person would conclude that the defendant could not have committed the crime. He is a person of good character.'

'Rosie, Rosie. A few years ago we were in deep shit. I couldn't get a decent job, and you couldn't get into a ballet company. Now I've got a proper job, and you are accusing me of becoming pompous. I must say in your defence that at least you are very adaptable in your criticism.'

'Yes, you've gone from poor and interesting to quite prosperous and boring. Does this happen to all lawyers?'

'Probably. Here's the thing, in order to be a good lawyer you have to fake a kind of seriousness. As you know I am really deeply frivolous.'

'You used to be. So you don't think he's got a girlfriend?'

'No. But he told me last night when you nipped off to the loo that you are wonderful. He loves you. He likes the way you walk.'

'He said those exact words?'

'"Lovely mover," he said. He notices odd things like the way your feet come down, ballet-style, at forty-five degrees. "Lovely little mover." '

'Why do you say "Lovely little mover" in that silly accent? He doesn't speak like that at all.'

'It's my Peter Cook.'

'Lawyers shouldn't tell jokes or do voices. They think they can, but they can't.'

This is becoming too pointed. Rosalie is oppressed by their inability to have a child. So is he, of course, but her troubled state is oppressing him far more than the prospect of being childless for ever. He knows how desperately she wants a little acolyte following her into the magical world of dance and he knows that she longs to dress her up for children's parties, perhaps as an angel or a fairy. Often when he looks at Rosalie these days he sees the blithe girl he fell in love with five years ago. But also, just occasionally, although he's reluctant to acknowledge it, as that would spell the end of innocence, he sees that a shadow has fallen on her. When her dance career ended — she knew that she was never quite good enough — she had a clear idea of how things would turn out: she would live through her children and induct them into this larger world of dance and music and colour. Last night at the ballet she looked mostly happy, but there was, he thought, a manic edge to her happiness, a hint of desperation. Dad didn't notice, of course, but Ed was wary.

'Darling Rosie, it will be all right.'

'How can you be sure?'

'It will be, I know.'

'How long is it now? I make it eighteen months.'

'Nearly, but that's not unusual.'

'Some people have babies after a one-night stand.'

He can see that she thinks this is a gross unfairness.

'Mr Smythson said we should relax. There's nothing wrong with us.'

'The more they tell you to relax, the harder it gets.'

'I know what you are thinking.'

'And that is?'

'That is that you begin to wonder if you're doing it because you want to or because you don't want the other person to wonder if you're doing it because you want to appear unconcerned.'

'And do you know?'

'Honestly? Not always.'

'Nor do I, so that could be a relief.'

'Maybe.'

They are sitting in their tiny courtyard garden. It is in deep evening shade. In truth, it has the sun for only one hour a day, somewhere between four and six in summer. For the rest of the time it has a dark, lichenous quality. They have a small, slate-topped table and four chairs of wrought iron, which Rosalie has painted a green-blue, the colour of Italian beans. On the table is a bottle of New Zealand Chardonnay, half empty: the label has a picture of a hawk in flight and the wine comes from Sophie's Vineyard, her 2002 vintage. Wines have become cheerful and user-friendly; the mystique has been banished, along with the old dour wine makers with nose-hair. They drink a wine called Rickety Bridge and sometimes a red called Chocolate Block, and another called Big Ass Zinfandel. The baby business is encouraging them to drink, because alone together they find that their conversation stalls. He can see why serious drinkers long for that first deep gulp: the wine, for all the fancy adjectives about fruit and nose and so on – Sophie's Vintage – is just an excuse for surrendering the troublesome self.

Rosalie has decorated the walls which enclose their garden with Moroccan lamps, which she now switches on, so that the little garden is romantically lit – theatrically lit – through the fretwork of the lamps, which were once used in a production of *Carmen*. Rosalie kisses him: the vinous interiors of their mouths, the warm viscous wetness of their saliva, become one and he feels calm again, as if by turning on the lights Rosalie has caused everything to change. He thinks of Darcey Bussell en pointe in *Das Lied von der Erde* as he puts his arms around her hips – she is still standing – and he feels reassured by holding them and pressing his face to her flat – reprovingly flat – stomach.

'It will be all right, won't it?' she says. 'Do you promise me?'

'I promise, darling.'

'You know I get anxious. I'm sorry. I say stupid things.'

'You don't have to apologise. Neither of us does.'

It's strange to him that this little intimacy, this kiss and the feel of her hips, should suddenly put the doubts to flight. Now he feels guilty for his secret fears about all those ballet exercises and their effect on her hormones. When Mum died, he wondered how much Dad had loved her after thirty-eight years; recently he has been wondering if you can sustain love in marriage for ever. Rosalie thinks Dad has a girlfriend, but Ed doubts it. Whatever his reasons for becoming so thin and wearing the African bangles his brother sent him on his wrists, it's nothing to do with wanting to have a girlfriend. Ed thinks – he has intimations already – that marriage can impose a sort of heaviness that never lifts, a sort of muting of the senses, and perhaps this has lifted in Dad's case.

When he had lunch with him a couple of weeks ago, he asked Dad if he was happy.

'Everyone asks me that.'

'It's a natural enough question.'

'Ed, the happiest I have ever been was in Rome in 1966.'

'Oh, you and Richard and Liz.'

'Yes, me and Dickie and Liz, and Adam, of course.'

'And Mum?'

'What about your mother?'

34

'Do you miss her?'

'Darling, of course I miss her. I miss her terribly. One thing I think you should know, in case you haven't guessed it, is that, like most people who have been married for years, we weren't what somebody of your age would think of as in love.'

He emphasised the last two words and gave them a slight country-and-western edge – *in lurve* – which Ed found irritating. But of course it's a habit he has inherited, and perhaps a lot more, too. They were sitting in the covered courtyard of the British Museum, Dad in a T-shirt and jeans with his Masai or whatever bracelets, and Ed in his lawyer's suit, as though they had changed roles. Dad may have dressed deliberately in this way for their lunch date.

'How's Rosalie?' Dad asked, perhaps switching the attack. He had told his father that they were – awkward phrase – trying for a baby.

'OK.'

'No luck?'

'Not yet.'

'It'll happen, trust me.'

'Jesus, you've really become a bit of a hippy guru, haven't you, with your T-shirt and bracelets? As well as being the oldest gap-year student in the world, you've become an amateur gynaecologist.'

'And you think, Ed, that it is somehow related to Mum's death?'

'Is it?'

'In a way it is. But not in any way you would understand.'

'Try me.'

'It's not really explicable.'

'You've had your teeth whitened.'

'It's part of my retirement deal. Yearly whitening. What

are you accusing me of, Ed? Insufficient grief? Lack of dignity? Inappropriately glowing teeth?'

'No, just that you look like a bit of a twat.'

'You're saying I'm embarrassing?'

'A little.'

They laughed. Dad was suddenly caught in the grid created as the sun fell on the glass roof above; the whole courtyard was divided geometrically into celestial graph paper. His face was instantly more deeply furrowed, demonstrating that the weight-loss came with a retributive cost.

'But you're OK, aren't you? You're so thin.'

'When you were a little boy you used to worry I was going to kick the bucket or be shot or kidnapped. The irony, the cruel irony, actually, is that everyone, including me, thought your mum would go on for ever. But, yes, I'm fine. And believe me, I am deeply touched that you worry about me.'

'That's OK then. Got to go now, Dad. Take care.'

'And you.'

Last night at the ballet, Dad seemed to have entered a trance. He leaned towards the stage – a long way off – every time Darcey Bussell appeared. His features were in close sympathy with what was going on, as if he could extract meaning from every moment and every step. It was surprising.

Ed lets go of Rosalie, and removes his cheek from her stomach. Maybe she thinks he has been listening out for developments. As he looks up, he sees the bougainvillea in its death throes, which have gone on for six months. Although Rosalie warned him it could never grow here, he decided that with huge doses of fertiliser it might triumph. It became a minor battle of wills, which he has lost. It has only one coppery flower. It is a reproach to him but he's resisting the temptation to see something symbolic about its condition.

'Did you hear anything down there?'

Rosalie, half drunk, is cheerful again.

'I thought I heard the pitter-patter of tiny feet. But perhaps it was your blood going round.'

'Or my lunch.'

'Yes, it could have been that.'

He's always found her stomach and the hinterland lying between her slim hips erotic. It's the confluence of everything sexual. It's an odd thing: his sexual desire is urged on by small details – the way, for instance, Rosalie's long strong legs form a little delta as they join her hips, which creates a crease when she sits. Now, under the snake-charmer light and shadow, which is given movement by a light breeze in the moribund bougainvillea, she pulls up her skirt and sits astride him. He takes his cock out, and, easily bypassing her panties, he enters her.

'I'm going for twins,' he says, feeling his face congested – it may not be visible from the outside – with a strange mixture of regret, lust and happiness.

'Why stop at twins?'

'It will be fine, Rosalie.'

But even as he says it, even as he marvels at the effortless suppleness she brings to sex, he wonders if it is true. Her face, so close to his, is out of focus, so that he only sees patches of skin or an earlobe or one eye or a few hanks of her dark-red, almost russet hair or her moist, ribbed lips. It's like one of those French movies he loves, where lovemaking is composed in a series of arty hand-held shots.

She breathes warm scented wine on him, which makes a communion with his own breath. He thinks, as he always does, that fucking is a way of trying to become one flesh. Their mouths are now – too urgently – attached, as if they are searching, like Dad's chum Faustus, for the alchemy that will make a baby, the baby which she will dress all in gossamer material and which will learn to run, toes strangely springy and angled, after her ethereal mother, who is now beginning to utter, which makes him giggle, because this courtyard is only one course of bricks away from the neighbours on three sides.

When she finally stands up and pulls down her skirt, he feels a deep warmth for her, which is actually, he knows, self-serving: he is released from the anxiety which has plagued him all day at the office. Dad and I, he thinks, are similar in this respect: even our relations to those closest to us are subject to our fascinated interest in our own feelings and states of mind. But then maybe everybody is the same and it's just a question of degree.

Rosalie sits sideways across his lap now, and puts her elegant arm around his shoulder and her head on his shoulder, like a reposing swan.

'Don't say anything,' she says: and he knows that she doesn't want him to spoil the moment. She is a believer in moments – intense, meaningful, fateful, numinous, although he doubts if she knows the word – and he has long ago realised that she sees the world in an intensely romantic fashion: she believes you must listen to your inner self and you must leave this self open to the unexpected and the spiritual. She thinks that too many people have closed themselves off to the transformative. For example, she believes in the magic of theatre. And it seems that his father, judging by his catatonia when Darcey Bussell was on stage – the little intense forward movements of his head, almost as if he were gulping down some nourishment only art can produce – also shares in this idea of magic.

He holds Rosalie very close as he contemplates the moment. He looks at the changing filigreed light on the walls and up at the London sky, still retaining some if its underbelly gleam, with the orange of the sodium lights catching the undersides of the clouds, and he listens out for that rumble which never goes away, a rumble, a moan you don't hear unless you make a conscious effort. It is cut by sirens and even helicopters and, at this time of year, by disputatious cats, but it's always there for a city boy like me, he thinks, to provide comfort, the sound of humanity. It seems to have a kind of consistency, the noise of machines and the more intimate noises – Rosie's choked cries, the clatter of crockery, fractious babies, music (including the deep throb of hip hop from passing cars) – all contributing minutely to this unorchestrated symphony.

To him this sort of thing is pleasingly random. But Mum was always preparing herself for greater understanding. Her Pilates and her yoga were the five-finger exercises in this cause. In fact her attention span was quite short: she said herself she had a butterfly mind. He finds that he misses her still every morning when he wakes. For the last year before she died he rang her promptly as he set off for work on the short walk between this little house and the underground. He knew these conversations were precious to her, but he didn't realise until she died how much they meant to him, too. She had given them some money for the house and when she died she left them enough in her will to pay off the mortgage. Dad in the meanwhile is talking of selling their house – the family home – and buying a flat. When people are bereaved they seem to need to make radical adjustments. Why not stay where you are? Or does that suggest you can't move on? There is something strangely adamantine about Dad these days, as though he's happy to go through the motions for the moment, but seems to have plans of a personal nature: nothing is settled, his life isn't over. Perhaps he thinks that Lucy and I want him to subside into quietude, like an extinct volcano. Lucy is the one who imagines that some opportunist with re-inflated tits is going to snaffle him. Like Rosalie, she is sure he is working out in order to be ready to take his clothes off when the moment arrives. Rosalie says that men believe their cocks look bigger when they are thin. Women think like this: they are often more basic and more direct, which goes against the popular mythology. *Counter-intuitive* is the phrase the senior partner Robin Fennell, Dad's pal, favours. After nearly three years as a lawyer, Ed sees that successful people in the law and in corporations have an urge to acquire a philosophy, which conveniently explains why they are entitled to such a large portion of the world's riches, and that is because they understand human nature and the springs of action in a way that politicians and journalists and commentators don't. Robin writes letters to the paper.

Now Rosalie is in the tiny kitchen. She has put on some world music, which comes from countries where the musicians have an enviable ease with their cultural traditions and run-down landscape. He quite likes it: it goes with the Ali Baba feel of the tiny courtyard. He pours himself another deep glass of Sophie's – excellent – 2002, and swallows it. Barely concealed in the straw-coloured and oaky wine is an advance warning of a headache. Judging by the anarchic clamour coming from the kitchen – it reminds him of the sudden, violent and unexpected timpani of world music – Rosalie, normally very deft, is a little drunk, too. He can see their future as replicating *Who's Afraid of Virginia Woolf?* Robin Fennell is slightly in love with Rosalie; three times when they had him to dinner a week ago he said what a great cook she was. He made it sound as though he believed there is a direct line between being good in the kitchen and being good in the sack. Perhaps this is part of his life philosophy, developed in his climb up the greasy pole. Matrimonially, it hasn't all been plain sailing for him: his third wife has just left him, which is why he asked himself to dinner. He is listed as a patron of Covent Garden, *starter tier*, but it turns out – Ed looked at the records – that the money actually comes from the partners' fund. They don't give enough to warrant a box, but they do have an unobstructed view and, under the terms of their membership of the Artists' Circle, the opportunity to go to rehearsals. This, Ed sees, is another aspect of the financially successful male's world view, his urge to appropriate some creative clothing by giving money or by buying art, because surely to be so rich means that he has understood how the world works and has applied some creativity. Even if it's only in accounting, he thinks.

Fuck them. Wine can do this: it can help you see how things really work. A lawyer can join the Artists' Circle. Christ is risen.

3

ON THE TRAIN Lucy sees a group from the near suburbs, mothers and daughters probably heading for Oxford Street to shop together. They sit tightly grouped, occupying facing benches. The daughters' hair is a little more relaxed than their mothers'; still, it is streaked and crimped and bleached. It's as if outside a fairly tight cordon around central London you arrive in a world of white-leather sofas and fast food and criminal hairdressing. The mothers' hair has been tormented, sometimes into strange butch cuts, sometimes in a waved carapace like a walnut, sometimes streaked with pink or blue. The mothers and daughters are all fat. This fatness comes in cheerfully displayed rolls in the young, in slabs of marbled fat on the upper arms of the mothers, like clothes hanging from a washing line. Their backsides are formless in different ways, but the common theme is that the motive force has departed. What is missing from these bottoms is muscle.

The older women in the group are in high spirits; their voices are harsh, almost metallic, corroded by smoking. They are not old: none of their daughters is more than twenty and the mothers are only in their late thirties or early forties. The mothers favour comfortable suits of terylene. The girls go for pink, white belts, leggings and dangly earrings. No sign of their men: no Darrens or Jasons with the girls, no Steves or Kevins with their mums. The girls hold their mobiles as if even down here under London they are likely at any minute to receive a message that will change their lives. Lucy wonders what they are hoping for. They talk in a new hybrid dialect, partly Afro-Caribbean, partly cockney: one of the girls says, *No, I nevah dunnit*. Another says, *You ain't listenin' to what I's sayin'*. Strangely, Lucy envies them. They move in chattering, uninhibited flocks, like parakeets. By contrast, Lucy sees an image of herself very clearly: she's alone. It's not that she believes that every girl should always have a boyfriend, it's the sense she has had since Mum died and she broke up with Josh that she has become isolated. Ed is wrapped up in the abstracted Rosalie, Dad is trying to recapture his youth in some way, and she, Lucy, at twenty-six, is wary and abandoned. She misses the Sunday lunches Mum produced, attendance virtually compulsory, even with the underlying tensions and pretence. In retrospect, she sees these lunches as beacons in her featureless landscape. Dad shows no sign of introducing any kind of form into their lives, and really, why should he?

She gets out at Piccadilly Circus not far from where those doctors tried to blow up a nightclub and she wonders, as she shuffles through the huge gallery of the station, whether they had any idea that almost nobody in this part of town is from here; they are Arab, Chinese, African, Eastern European and various other denominations of Asian. The sink of Western decadence they were proposing to send sky-high would probably have contained as many believers as infidels, certainly more foreigners than English. Doctors! And then they tried to blow up Glasgow Airport and one of them was incinerated. As she walks down Haymarket, she hopes her feeling of isolation isn't making her seem a little weird to her colleagues at Grimaldi. There's only so much understanding available; she never mentions her mother's death and she fends off questions about Josh lightly, but she thinks that her friends are becoming a little wary of her. This, of course, makes her behave in a more self-conscious fashion. It's a spiral, downwards, which will end with her eating quantities of chocolate and looking after a cat.

While her mother was alive, Lucy had the feeling that she wasted her time in pointless telephone conversations and in writing letters – she refused all offers of email – and choosing presents for godchildren and nieces, planning to renew a bit of the kitchen or recover a few cushions or searching through gardening catalogues in a hopeless quest to make the unimpressionable London clay at the back of the house bloom. These pursuits, Lucy thought, were too trivial, too timid for a woman who had studied English at university. But recently she has realised, with all the force of a revelation, that every family needs one parent who is dependable and unselfish. And that certainly could not be said of Dad. He's of the old school that thinks – although of course he would deny it – that men are made of finer material, which excuses them from the constraints of the trivial and the tedious. In fact they are obliged to avoid anything that will keep them from their higher pursuits, their *grands projets*, which turn out to be largely about the nourishing of self-worth.

Josh is certainly one of these men. He took up fishing: if by chance a big trout takes his fly it is because Josh has chosen exactly the right fly – you must match the hatch – and has positioned it with uncanny knowledge of the fishy mind, just where a monster is lying up. It's not, of course, that trout are terminally dim and easily deceived – at times suicidal – but because of Josh's intuitive understanding of certain mysteries, susceptible only to the male mind. Others are the meaning of sport and the underlying logic of the stock market. In fact, as she approaches the restaurant, which is, she knows, wildly fashionable, she has cheered herself up with the thought that men are, in a way, to be pitied. And thank God she will never have to walk a riverbank again, watching the Izaak Walton *de nos jours* snag trees and thrash the water while explaining his next brilliant ruse to confuse the trout.

Ed is waiting. She spies him across rows of upholstered banquettes. She has a certain restaurant presence, and despite herself takes a little pleasure in how happy the maître d'hôtel is to shepherd her to her brother's table, where he is waiting in his new light-grey suit.

He stands up to kiss her, which she finds pleasantly formal.

'Only twenty minutes late, but hey, who's counting?' he says.

'You are, obviously. By the way, coming from someone who will be late for his own funeral, it's a little uncalled for. This is pretty damn swish, my bro.'

'I like it. And it's far enough from the office not to see too many fucking lawyers. You look great, Luce.'

'Thank you. You look fit in your suit, sort of right. I think you like being a lawyer really, but for the sake of your cred, you have to pretend you hate it. What's to eat?'

'It's all good. It's the same people who did the Ivy and the Wolseley. I'm going to have a rib-eye steak. I am desperately short of protein. Rosalie, of course, doesn't eat meat.'

'Good for her. How is she?'

'She's OK, but worried about the baby business.'

'What are you doing wrong? Can I give you some advice? Feel free to ask.'

'Oh Jesus, don't start. We are not doing anything wrong, as far as I know.'

But she can see that the baby business is bearing down on him, too. He's too easy to read.

'It'll happen,' she says.

'And if it doesn't?'

'I guess it's the glass jar and the porn mags for you.'

'Jesus, Lucy.'

'Is that so bad?'

'Yes, it is. I've been there already for the fertility tests, and I certainly don't want to make a baby looking at porn.'

'I don't think it will come out deformed or anything just because you were spanking the monkey.'

'Oh good. That's a relief. What are you going to have?'

'I'll have the tuna sashimi and a Caesar salad.'

'Two starters?'

'Anything wrong with that?'

'No, fine. I am having six oysters and the rib-eye.'

'Ah, I see the subplot: lead in the pencil.'

'You're beginning to annoy me.'

'Already?'

'Yes.'

But it's not true: they are always delighted to see each other. He's ordering two glasses of champagne.

'Any clients this afternoon?'

'Fuck them.'

'What are we celebrating, by the way?'

'We're not celebrating. We're remembering. It's Mum's birthday.'

'Oh shit, so it is. I'm so sorry.'

'You've forgotten her so soon.'

'You know I haven't. I was thinking of her on the way here. I really only properly appreciate her now.'

'Me, too. It's odd. And also, it's like when someone dies you are more or less bound to feel guilty for all the things you didn't do at the time.'

'Yup. And the problem is you can't tell her or explain what you really thought.'

'Josh rang me this morning, Luce.'

'Which Josh?'

'Your former boyfriend.'

'Oh, that one. What did he want?'

'He wondered if I thought he could ask you out.'

'Why didn't he ask me if he could ask me out?'

'It was like maybe she is so pissed off she won't take my call. I didn't tell him that you have been sitting by the phone hopefully for six weeks.'

'I haven't.'

'Can he call you?'

'Of course, we're both adults, except for him.'

'He's scared you'll raise the question of the one-night stand.'

'Oh, so it was a one-night stand?'

'I don't know. I'm just using a generic term. Maybe it was two nights.'

'Which is worse?'

'Look, Luce, can I be brutally honest with you? Other people's affairs are not that interesting to the bystander. I'm just relaying a message. He's terribly sorry, et cetera, et cetera, and misses you – blah, blah. Can he call?'

'He can. No big deal.'

In fact she's delighted. She will not take the moral high

ground and anyway she's since had a one-night stand, too. She's banked that one against a rainy day.

They drink to their mother and she whispers, just above the level of audibility, *Happy birthday, Mum*. She feels a familiar surge of desolation for a moment, as Ed squeezes her hand. *Happy birthday, Mum*, he whispers.

For a moment they sit silent. She drinks half of her champagne in a gulp.

'We both miss her, but . . .'

'But what?' she asks.

'Dad. I'm not sure about him.'

'In what way?'

'Do you think he's behaving normally?'

'What's normal when your wife has died?'

'I'm not sure. I really don't know, but it is a fact that he seems a little detached.'

The oysters arrive. God knows what it is with men and oysters It seems to be a manly thing to do, to slurp down, raw, suggestively shaped molluscs, a very primitive life form. They arrive sitting seductively on their shells, which, in turn, are placed on top of a Gallic silver holder, apparently designed specially for the job. The French have made a fetish of food. Last time she ate an oyster she was horribly sick. Maybe it's the Russian roulette element that appeals to men: every sixth oyster could kill you. In the knowledge that Josh is pining for her, she tries to forget that he is fantastically stupid, despite his misleading good looks, and that he is sexually disturbed, chronically promiscuous and vicious when drunk. *Apart from that, Mrs Lincoln*. . . . Her mind is racing cheerfully. Her sashimi is beautiful, five thin slices of a very pale tuna laid out in a fan and doused in lime, soy and ginger. You could eat the *Yellow Pages* marinated in this stuff. She looks at Ed as he swallows the first oyster, tossing his head back like a burgher in a Dutch painting. A moment of very male satisfaction, which of course is accompanied by a bit of self-congratulation.

'Fantastic,' he says. 'They fly them in from Ireland.'

'I'm glad for your sake they didn't make them walk.'

'You're hilarious.'

'Yes, I am. You think women shouldn't make jokes, don't you?'

'You shouldn't.'

'You know what happened this morning? I was just leaving the flat when I heard this wonderful whistling from round the corner. It was "My Way", and whoever was whistling was in a bad way. Very emotional, lots of wobbly vibrato. Anyway, a dog comes around the corner, which I recognise, a boxer, and then a bloke of about Dad's age appears whistling away. Each note was pin sharp and packed with feeling.'

'And your point is?'

'He is the bloke from the newsagent, George, who sold it to the nice Bangladeshis when his wife died last year.'

'And?'

'And I spoke to him and asked him how he was, and he said, "Devastated, I've got nothing to live for." '

'And?'

'And nothing. I found it very poignant.'

'Because of Mum?'

'Yes, I suppose so. He's a big fat bloke, sort of unhealthy the way some of these older geezers are – gold chain, cheap sports clothes, large clapped-out dog, wheezing, and he's whistling "My Way". I was moved. That's what happened to me. Little things get to me. I don't have much control.'

'Me neither.'

He swallows another oyster, and then another. Lucy

imagines a faint marine sound – water slapping on a jetty
– as they slide away.

'Ed, do you think Dad's got another woman?'

'That's what Rosalie thinks. But she would.'

'And you?'

'I don't know.'

'Would you mind?'

'On a theoretical level, no, I wouldn't. In practice I think
I would.'

'Has he ever hinted to you, you know, man to man,
about nookie?'

'Nookie? What sort of a word is that? But no, to be fair
he hasn't. What's he said to you? He always tells you first.'

'Nothing. I asked him why he was so thin and he said
he liked working out. He's going to the gym every day.'

'Let's just accept it, for the moment.'

'We don't have a whole lot of choice.'

'True.'

She sees that Ed thinks he is carrying the burden now,
as the one in the family who has to keep the ship steady,
what with Dad running around wearing those cheap
bracelets and distancing himself from his children. We have
suddenly been promoted beyond our competence, handed
the responsibility for tending the family flame. This flame,
she thinks, is love, even though she can't possibly say that
to Ed, whose head is tilted back to receive the last oyster.
He swallows and his eyes perform a brief, ecstatic victory
roll.

'Do you mind if I ask you a direct question, Ed?'

'Go on,' he says, without enthusiasm.

'Do you think he loved Mum?'

'You'll have to ask him.'

'Of course I can't ask him. And, why would I? What's

he going to say? No, I didn't? What I mean is, do you think there's a kind of love which survives a marriage?'

'Yes. I suppose I do. I hope so. Christ, I hope so. Otherwise, what's the point?'

Maybe Ed is thinking ahead: what if he and Rosalie can't produce a child? What if he does have a sperm problem? And maybe she was insensitive talking about wanking into a glass jar. Rosalie could be too formed a personality for Ed. There's a sort of woman with very definite standards and expectations which don't allow for too much divergence. Rosalie is one of those. Her airily sweet and elegant exterior – Lucy thinks – hides a rigid and conventional sense of her due. Her due is to be the mother of beautiful and similarly elegant children, who will run charmingly – like the von Trapps – after her, employing only ballet steps. Ed is definitely under pressure.

'My sperm count is high, just in case you were wondering.'

'I didn't ask.'

'No, but you were wondering.'

'How did you know?'

'So you were wondering.'

His steak arrives. She looks at it, oozing thin and watery blood, like the blood that appears in your mouth at the dentist.

'But you're not taking any chances, I see.'

'Oh Jesus, Lucy, it's a steak. Boys like steak. Trust me, I've got enough healthy sperm to impregnate the whole of a small country. Men, women and livestock. I wanted to talk about Dad.'

'We have.'

'Yes, but do you want me to talk to him properly? About money and so on? He's planning to sell the house.'

'Why?'

'I don't really know. He says he's cutting back. I think he's trying to go minimalist.'

'What about the cats?'

'Are you turning into the sort of fruitloop who worries about cats?'

'No, but you and I could each take one.'

'Rosalie's allergic to cats.'

'Oh so, so sorry. *Pardonnez-moi*.'

'You don't really like her, do you?'

'Of course I do. What's happening to her, in fact to all of us, is that life has begun to get serious. We're supposed to be grown-up. Look at you in your suit with your big-balls steak. And look at me, pathetically pleased that the lowlife wants me back, even though I know he's a total flake, and look at poor Rosie, thwarted in her ambition to be the loveliest young mother on the planet, the lead in a ballet where she dances all the solo roles surrounded by charming little ankle-biters in dirndls, and then there's Dad the minimalist gym rat, opting out of all responsibility. Fuck me, what's happening to us? And finally, there's you obsessing about your sperm count. A whole small country! Wow.'

'I'm not obsessing about my sperm count. You're a bit like Mum – whatever anybody told her she adapted for her own use.'

'That is actually true. She sort of fitted everything to her world view.'

'And now you are doing it. My sperm – I will say this once, and only once – are fine. Oh look, your rabbit food has arrived.'

'When did you last see a rabbit eating Parmesan and raw eggs?'

'Good choice, Madame,' says the waiter suavely, as he places the salad on the brilliantly white cloth.

'I've come to seize your salad, not praise it,' says Lucy.

'Ah, the old jokes.'

There is blood oozing down one side of Ed's mouth.

On the way to the tube she wonders whether she should call Josh or wait. She decides to wait. On the train she wonders why her father is proposing to sell up. There's something disturbingly nihilistic about him these days. She spent most of her life in the house and, although she has had her own small rented flat for two years, she still thinks of the house as home. She feels she must be consulted before it is sold. It is a betrayal. What has caused him to become so insensitive? So much has happened in this house, in a quiet back street of Camden. Her parents, in their telling, were pioneers arriving in the first covered wagon to this wild, unknown place in the sixties. Her small room is up three floors under the roof, where she looks out over the dreary disarray and failed endeavours of Camden's sodden gardens towards a heavily salted Gothic church. She can sometimes hear the Greek Orthodox service on Sunday evenings. She can sometimes smell the censers, which the plump priests and their acolytes – she believes – swing about with terrific vigour, like gauchos hunting rheas. Her mother used to read to her in that little room before sleep. Most of these books, early on, had animal heroes, which in a way formed her own world view. She had sex there for the first time, not frightening at all, but strange and reassuring that two human beings could merge in this way. And when you think about it, it is a peculiar business, this connection of expressly designed bits of the body, a connection that seems to convey so much human significance.

The sky outside that window is never dark. The London sky is rarely vivid, but always distempered and suffused, and always, like the sea, in flux. Christ's blood does not stream in the firmament; nothing that dramatic takes place in the muted, crawling sky of Camden. But framed by her window, by her ex-window, the view is dear to Lucy. A view, she thinks, is personal property.

4

DAVID ROWS AWAY. It's far from certain where he is heading. The upper body is something new, a sort of unexplored region attached by the isthmus of the waist to the lower body, which houses the restless sex organs and is also the terminus for the legs. The rowing machine is good for the upper body and the legs. Straightening his back, using his legs (all of the power in rowing comes from the legs), imagining the water flying by, ducks happy to get away unscathed. Ahead of him, staring at the video screens, the three Muslim women walk on the treadmills. He notices that today they are walking more slowly, because they have the machines inclined slightly upwards and they hold on as though they are being towed, in danger of being left behind, in fact. He looks at their bottoms to see if there is any sign of improvement in definition. So far – it's about five weeks since they first appeared – there is no obvious change. He rows on for half an hour until he has floated free of the gym and on to a sea of tranquillity.

He whispers to himself, *To heaven by water*.

He remembers Burton's face so vividly, the pockmarks above the beard clearly visible in the side lighting, like a reminder of pestilence, his eyes glistening with anguish: he is caught in a terrible tragedy:

O I'll leap up to my God! Who pulls me down?
See, see, where Christ's blood streams in the firmament!
One drop would save my soul, half a drop. Ah my
   Christ!

And now as he rows he thinks of Darcey Bussell ignoring gravity, while the singer standing by the side of the stage moaned, *For ever, for ever*. Darcey Bussell, who reminds him so keenly of Jenni.

So much has passed me by in all those years since I stood with Jenni and Adam watching Burton.

They found a space for themselves on the set behind a huge arc lamp that hid them with its intense radiance. As he rows he wonders how he lost his faith in transcendence: film entranced him then, but somehow, over the following forty years, he lost that ecstasy. At times – treacherously – he has blamed Nancy in his heart, but he knows that this is unfair, even repugnant. It was her sensible – how demeaning that sounds – and clear understanding that provided the stability a family needs. It is just that there is no libretto for how the world really works: it might work entirely differently. Now, a single man, he feels entitled, even obliged, to live on a higher plane. When Lucy asked him why he was thinking of selling the house, he muttered evasively about releasing money for her and Ed and about downsizing, but he couldn't tell her the truth: he was going to spend his remaining years in some way free of the material: how crazy, how absurd that would have sounded. It isn't an idea you can easily discuss. And yet he has an urgent need to get rid of everything and to tread lightly on the surface of the earth. It's nothing ecological, it's entirely personal: to strip himself bare of distraction, to make himself naked, to open himself to . . . to what, exactly?

The Muslim women leave. They are tired. He looks at the wall clock: Christ, he has been rowing for nearly an hour. He has won the boat race single-handed. He glances at himself in the huge mirrors where the weight-lifters preen. He never uses their equipment. He looks drawn, his hair damp with sweat and his grey T-shirt stained to resemble those dark patches on the moon landscape.

One night they raced Adam's Fiat Seicento around the Piazza Navona. They were drunk. When the carabinieri stopped them on the second lap, Adam spoke to them in Italian and demanded a pardon. We were commemorating, he said, the fact that this was once the site of Domitian's chariot races. We were honouring Bernini's fountain. We were celebrating Italy. Italians love youth and vitality; now the carabinieri would probably lock you up and throw the key into the Tiber, but then they let them go with a warning that contained more than a hint of complicit admiration for the English; they were young and glamorous, and scholar gypsies. Now David wonders why they never considered what would have happened if they had crashed into Tre Scalini or Gian Lorenzo Bernini's Fountain of the Four Rivers. In those days Rome had a makeshift quality: the lesser ruins were unvisited, the back streets had a rundown rural feel and lunch could be had for a pound in any number of trattorias near their flat in Trastevere. They were free of the Brussels sprout and the brown sauce. It's difficult for the children to believe how unspeakable British food was back then.

Once he and Adam watched a cardinal, a prince of the church, take lunch in solitary splendour at a Jewish restaurant known for its deep-fried baby artichokes. The cardinal followed the artichokes with a whole fish, very biblical, deftly filleted under his imperious gaze, and last, a fresh orange, which was peeled reverentially by a waiter to form one long and complete scroll of skin. Finally the orange was neatly sliced so that it lay on the plate, a perfect rose window. *Try asking for that in Joe Lyons'*, said Adam. The cardinal had a medieval manner: these Jewish waiters seemed concerned that the richly attired old boy should be afforded every dignity. His cloak was brought to him at the end of the meal and there was bowing and abasement. This cloak was lined in a clamorous red, which perhaps had for the waiters a sense of menace after two thousand years, a lethal warning like the colouring of a toadstool. David, too, ordered an orange, *Una arancia, per favore* – and it was brought to him whole and unpeeled on a plate. Adam thought it was hilarious and celebrated with a third sambuca topped with a pale-blue flame. To this day he still occasionally asks David if he would like an orange.

He suddenly remembers the name of the restaurant, Il Giardino Romano. He finds it harder every year to remember names. That first night in Rome – he can't be certain, time is collapsing in on itself – Adam introduced him to Jenni at a huge aircraft-hangar disco and by morning he was in love. Adam was acting in the film of *Dr Faustus*, directed by Burton, and David had followed his friend to Rome. When *Dr Faustus* was at the Playhouse, Adam and Burton became drinking companions at the Bear in Woodstock. Burton saw Adam as an innocent, living a life he could have lived in Oxford, and in Rome he invited him to the villa, and then David joined the circle and Jenni, too.

Those few weeks have loomed far too large in their lives; it is their defining myth.

David starts to run, in his nostrils and deep in his

head the resin scent of umbrella pines and the slightly mineral taste of Frascati rise. His legs feel light. He soon begins to float. He is more closely familiar with this bland room – this machinery, these hip hop images on the screens, this blare of a music station, this strangely assorted cast of fellow supplicants – than he is with his own house and certainly with the natural world. He feels at home here, although he seldom talks to anyone and he never attends any of the offered classes, most of which seem to suggest a back door to enlightenment. You can do stretching, yoga, aerobic dance, and – these are new – courses in assertiveness and anger-management through meditation.

As he runs, David cannot lose the picture of Burton's intense, utterly absorbed face against the background of Faustus' study in Württemberg – bound volumes, phials, a memento mori, quill pens – all positioned unnaturally perfectly by the art department.

The face, which had been made so familiar, a public property, was now just a few yards away, in the grip of an acting seizure:

One drop would save my soul, half a drop. Ah my Christ!
Ah, rend not my heart for naming of my Christ!
Yet will I call on him . . .

As David watched him and heard that astonishing voice swelling to fill the huge stage in Dinocittà with its anguish, he found himself shaking: a forty-two-year-old Welsh miner's son had dissolved the barriers between the immanent and the transcendent worlds. When it was done, Burton stood on the spot. He nodded finally to the assistant director, who called *Cut*. He was the director but still he was waiting for a word from his mentor and honorary co-director, Nevill Coghill. Coghill was mute. They embraced briefly and then the quotidian activity started again as the crew, burdened with tape and lamps and props, prepared for the next scene.

Burton winked at Jenni as he passed on his way to his dressing room for a drink.

'Strange bloody life, isn't it?'

'You were wonderful, Mr Burton,' she whispered.

'Thank you, luv. Just doing my job, actually.'

But it was far from true. He was living out his life as though it was a morality play. Or so David thought. As he walked off, David saw that he was in thrall to something else, a fame which caused people to lie and fawn and disparage, sometimes in the same breath: *One drop would save my soul*. His soul was already lost on the journey from a miner's cottage, where thirteen children were conceived, to an enormous villa in Rome, staffed by many including a chef, a valet, two drivers and a minder for Elizabeth's children. His brother, Ifor, was his personal assistant. What Burton had was unimaginable, almost supernatural, power. And that is what celebrity means to ordinary people, the power to escape the constraints of daily life. Burton had enormous amounts of money, the most beautiful woman in the world, and a voice which contained all the promise and possibility of human endeavour. What a burden for a miner's son with a drink problem. Elizabeth was his reward: *Her lips suck forth my soul: see where it flies.*

But he had left his first love and his children in Wales and in his heart he knew that he had committed a crime against nature.

David and Adam are older now than when Burton died. Yet while Adam has retained his essence, David thinks he has lost his. He thinks that he has been thinned out by too many compromises. Still, he is running effortlessly, feeling no tiredness and no heaviness in the legs. His breathing is even. He is licensed to think whatever he likes without being constrained by the rational: he will follow his instincts. He plans to buy a small flat in Soho. Lucy is upset but he has told her that she will have more than enough to buy her flat. What she imagines is a kind of destructiveness – she thinks he is turning his back on the family, the shared myths and comforts, but that is not nihilism at all, it is an attempt to move on to the higher plane. You couldn't actually use that phrase: his children are attuned to all the ironies, so that almost any phrase can be derided: *higher plane* would fare very badly.

He increases the speed. He is now running at 15.5 km per hour. His feet are hammering on the rubber conveyor. The screens ahead are a confusion of football, videos and rolling news. He sees a ticker-tape caption: *Breaking news . . . 12-year-old boy shot dead in Manchester*. When it first came in, twenty-four-hour news demanded that the same few items be hyped up and repeated every half an hour. If news broke suddenly, he was required to flannel away for as long as necessary while they edited the incoming pictures and changed the running order. He became a master of the sonorous platitude, a safe pair of hands, but also someone who graced the news with a kind of bogus gravitas. He wondered if they were living in a time of madness or merely the same world charged by the clamour for sensation. The areas of agreement in society are shrinking; it's not possible to prescribe behaviour or belief. Adam said, 'The genie is out of the bottle.' Adam loves the sense of chaos. Maybe it suits drinkers to believe that there is no constancy in the world.

One of the staff, a black man called Ashley, who has two glittering diamond ear-studs, comes up to the treadmill. David slows down.

'You OK, mate?'

'Yes, I'm fine, Ash.'

He uses the shortened name to show that he's chilled.

'No, it's just like there's a few people what wants to get on this machine.'

At first David doesn't understand him.

'What?'

'You bin on 'ere more than 'alf hour.'

'Is there a time limit?'

'No, only like when it's busy and that.'

'OK. I'll stop. I've probably overdone it.'

'No, you was goin' great. For real.'

David looks at the display: he has run 9 km. His heartbeat is 160 per minute.

'I'm outta here,' he says, overdoing it, in his desire to be unremarkable.

He showers and changes into his jeans and starts walking down towards the Museum to see Robin Fennell. Since he took up walking he believes his life has acquired a new, more reflective pace. He believes that he is more attuned to the city, its actual materials, the bricks and the paving stones and the decoration of buildings. He finds himself looking at these things closely as if in some way the human effort that went into making them and placing them will reveal itself to him. The granite kerbs that line every street – originally from Caernarvon but increasingly from Portugal – seem to him miraculous. He loves the sense of continuity and the elemental labour that goes into getting these blocks here; he thinks about the days when the farmers drove turkeys along the road all the way from

Norfolk to London. Strange thoughts, random thoughts, bearing little connection to the life he has lived so far, engage him.

He has asked Robin to meet him at a café near the Museum. He doesn't want his son to be embarrassed at his place of work by his casually attired father, nor does he want him to be reminded that he only got his job here because of his father's long friendship with Robin Fennell. Since Robin's third wife, Valerie, left him, he has been agitated. Last time they met David listened to his troubles and still paid a legal bill for what proved to be two hours of his overpriced friend's therapy.

By the time he arrives at the café, between a souvenir shop selling teddy bears and a shop selling prints of olde London, he realises that he is exhausted. His legs are vibrating, as if the tendons are playing some gentle chamber music. Robin may be the last of his friends to wear a silk pocket scarf; it matches his tie, the colour of Dijon mustard. He has put on weight since Valerie's defection and his clothes are under pressure. As he stands up – the old-fashioned manners – he has the shape of a garden bird. He probably thinks that he is dapper, but the effect is dispiriting.

'Old chum, welcome. How nice to see you looking so, so thin,' he says.

'Oh Jesus, yes, I am thin and before you ask again, yes, I wanted to be thin and no, I am not ill. How are you? Are you over Valerie?'

'More or less. I had dinner the other night with your Eddie and the lovely Rosalie. Cor, what a stunner.'

He has an obsolete sense of irony, of the same vintage as his pocket handkerchief. Also, David thinks it is a little crass to mention his daughter-in-law, but he couldn't justify the feeling.

'How's Ed doing?'

'Terrific. Yes, he's really doing well. We have some business in Geneva, and he's handled the first assignment well. I'm going to make him a partner, although I haven't told him yet. I have to run it past the others. Not that they can disagree, but one is obliged to observe the protocols.'

'That's great. That's incredibly good of you, Robin. No nepotism, I hope.'

'He's up to it, believe me. I just need to ask you a question, Dave, before we get down to business. Is everything OK at home with Eddie and Rosie?'

Why does he take every name and turn it into a diminutive? He feels a stab of irritation.

'Why do you ask?'

'He seems to be very close to a young trainee we have taken on.'

'How close?'

'I'm not saying they're shagging or anything, but I would hate to think there's anything serious going on.'

Coming from Robin, who over the years has seen the trainee solicitors as his personal preserve, this is offensive. At the same time he hopes Ed isn't looking for some refuge from Rosalie's unhappiness.

'I hope not.'

'Times have changed. Inappropriate behaviour is the cant phrase these days.'

'Can we get on with business? Last time I saw you, there seemed to be some role reversal.'

'Sorry if I unloaded on you.'

'And you sent me a bill.'

'Did we? We'll send you a credit. Sorry. Anyway I have, as you would expect, lots of papers for you to sign – the

64

trust deeds, the standing orders, the power of attorney, the appointment of agents.'

David looks at Robin. It's a little late to be asking himself, but does he trust him? In the sexual arena he has been devious. Often it amazes David just how susceptible women can be to these implausible men, the sort of men who wear coloured pocket handkerchiefs and order expensive bottles of wine in restaurants to impress their underlings. Valerie was an eager trainee fifteen years ago. Now, aged forty-two, she has gone off with a thirty-one-year-old Australian scuba-diving instructor she met in the Maldives. Robin admitted it has undermined his sexual confidence. He has tormented himself with visions of his wife having athletic Antipodean sex on the deck of a dive boat, moored to a palm tree. The rickety foundations of this kind of doomed relationship will be propped up for a while by the large amount of money Robin was forced to give Valerie. Inappropriate behaviour, with a scuba-diving instructor, does not weigh in the financial negotiations. When they discussed it, Robin said the scuba-diving instructor was stupid: 'As thick as pig shit,' were his exact words. But then maybe he was a sex instructor, too. And it was that possibility, he guessed, which was troubling Robin, rather than the Aussie Cousteau's low IQ.

'Robin, what happens if you pop your clogs before I do?'

'Decease is the word you will find in the deeds. It's all very straightforward. But if I do pop my clogs first, I have nominated an alternative trustee, also a partner here, Annie Morris, and she will keep things going.'

'And if the firm goes tits up?'

'Goes into liquidation, you mean. But yes, if we were to go tits up you have full control of your trust fund. It wouldn't go with us. The trustees only operate at your discretion. It won't fall through the cracks or anything.'

David signs various bits of paper where indicated. As Robin shuffles the papers, marked with tabs placed there by a secretary, or a trainee, David looks at him. His face is utterly, utterly bored, with the cosmic weariness you see on the faces of the higher primates. God knows how many thousands of times he has shuffled papers, helping people to ditch their spouses, embrace bankruptcy, set up dummy companies, sell their businesses, convey their houses. All these kinds of transaction demand a lawyer's presence, but what are lawyers actually contributing to the sum of human happiness? When his wife left him, no legal redress was available to ease Robin's heart. Ed told him that Robin had more or less invited himself to dinner at their place; perhaps Robin was on a secret mission to see if Ed's wife was a suitable consort for a partner in his firm. Or perhaps Robin is just lonely. None of his children speaks to him, and maybe he can't bear to be alone thinking about his wife and the Australian Lothario going through their sexual repertoire. We are all disappearing, beaten to airy thinness.

'Where are you going to live?' Robin asks.

'Soho,' David says.

'Batting for the other side?'

'Robin, Robin. That's not worthy of you.'

David thinks that Robin, in his agony, is becoming bitter. He is losing his humanity. This seems to David to be the most important quality required if he is going to live on a higher plane: the ability to be open and sympathetic. After all, this great play, this maelstrom, of humanity all around us is a miracle, a phenomenon and really the only thing there is. But Robin, chubby, bored, prurient and

66

dressed in this self-regarding way, has pulled down the shutters.

'All done,' says Robin, closing the folders. 'Another coffee?'

'Rob, do you want me to talk to Ed?'

'No. I'll speak to the girl if I find the right moment.'

'What's she like?'

'Young. Pretty. Bright. They're all bright, but not all of them have what it takes.'

'I don't suppose so. No.'

'Eddie's got it. You have to grasp the essentials very quickly. It's no good faffing about with the side issues. That's really all it takes in the end. And Eddie is as sharp as a tack.'

David wonders what he is talking about and in what way his son has acquired the ability to home in on the essentials. Robin is drawing some comfort from this opportunity to explain his philosophy, a need which grows more pressing as his essences drain away. When he looks at Robin again he reproaches himself. He remembers him when they first met, doing a holiday job at Allders in Clapham: he was cheerful, irreverent and ambitious. He is still going on about the law and the essentials and the requisite understanding of human nature that good lawyers have, but David sees fear, the realisation that his time is up. *Send not to know for whom the bell tolls*.

More and more he finds himself remembering lines of poetry, long forgotten.

'What I have always found, quite frankly, is that not everyone can see the wood for the trees. They think the law is about pompous language and rootling about in obscure precedents. No, it's not. It's really intuitive. This is what most people, sadly, don't get. They don't see that it's all about stripping away the . . .'

'Jesus, Robin.'

'What?'

He looks up, surprised, unused to being interrupted.

'We were young once. What's happened to us?'

'Sorry, old chum, I've become a fantastic fucking bore, haven't I?'

'I'm not saying that.'

'I am. I'm a fantastic fucking bore. Let's go and have a drink.'

As they walk to the pub, David takes Robin's arm for a moment, feeling a need to reassure him.

'Why not?'

'I'm sorry, Davey; when Val left me it hit me hard.'

David squeezes his arm again briefly.

'I understand.'

The sun is shining through the Edwardian glass in the windows of the pub, so that the light divides into discrete and variegated shafts, which strike the beer glasses, causing them to glow or brood, depending on the depth of the remaining beer; the refracted light from the glasses falls, in turn, on the scuffed and world-weary tables. The whole thing forms a chiaroscuro, familiar at a very low level to anyone who has ever been in a pub. The place is empty, apart from three young men in those slightly too small and slightly too rumpled business suits that make them look as though they sleep in their cars. They are talking about football.

David wonders, as the barman pulls two pints, if it's worse to be left by your wife than to be widowed. Being left probably casts a retrospective doubt on your abilities as a lover, or even as a human being, whereas bereavement attracts sympathy and a certain ambiguous respect, as if death is in this way a test of mettle.

He wants to talk to Robin frankly, but he cannot because Robin is holding his son Ed hostage.

5

ROBIN'S SECRETARY, MANDY, is about fifty-five, devoted to him, of course, but prone to a little ironic eyebrow twitching when he is too demanding. These facial antics suggest that she sees him as a lovable baby, although she once told Ed that he had a very short fuse – tantrums, throws his toys out of the pram, that sort of thing.

'He wants to see you at eleven,' she says.

'What's it about?'

'He didn't say.'

Ed feels a deep unease. He's probably protected in some way by the fact that Robin and Dad go back a long way, but still he passes the next hour unable to concentrate on the material facts of Fineman versus Brent Council. He is supposed to be preparing the brief for counsel, one of those barristers who is happy to paddle in very shallow waters. In this case Julius Fineman has refused to pay increased rates to Brent on a point of principle. The barrister is to get an injunction from the High Court to stop the Council distraining his goods. It's pathetically small beer. But Ed likes Mr Fineman, a pharmacist, who has been deprived of business because of a needless traffic rerouting which prevents his elderly clientele reaching him, for fear of their Zimmer frames and disabled buggies being crushed by twelve-wheeler trucks. His shop, now isolated on a sort of island in the North Circular, has a very old-fashioned smell as though Mr Fineman is making his own potions, practising alchemy. Also, Ed likes his Romanian assistant, whose face is an advertisement of lasciviousness, and whose very thin legs appearing from beneath a white coat proclaim a miracle in their ability to support the lavish superstructure. Her name is Olla and she is a flagrantly ambitious economic migrant. She has asked him about resident status. Every time she talks to him in her liquid, confident approximation of English, he feels his cock stirring. He has visited Mr Fineman – only narrowly avoiding becoming road kill – more often than strictly necessary. Mr Fineman has what Ed thinks of as a Jewish characteristic, a willingness, even a compulsion, to steer their conversations into a warm familial direction. He has twice told Ed that he reminds him of his son Erhud, who was only a few streets from a Hizbollah rocket in the town of Haifa two years ago; the rocket, which blew in his son's windows, is living proof that there is evil out there. Olla hovers in the background of these conversations and they exchange complicit glances. Should he be encouraging Mr Fineman in his windmill tilting because he likes seeing Olla? Obviously not. But Mr Fineman is resolutely determined on a showdown with the council, and Ed feels exonerated.

At eleven he crosses to the reception where Gloria rings through. He may proceed. He knocks on the heavy door that guards Robin's office.

'Come.'

Robin looks up briefly. He takes at least half a minute going through his papers. Then he removes his reading glasses and motions Ed to a buttoned chair. His desk is vast, like the desk of an aircraft carrier, and covered in red rococo leather; objects from golf tournaments and legal conferences litter the surface. On the walls are botanical prints of anonymous fruits and flowers and, in some dark shelves, leather-bound legal books. He reaches behind him and produces a cut-glass decanter and two glasses. He places them on the desk, as if he is conferring a sacrament.

'We're celebrating,' he says finally.

'Oh good. What are we celebrating?'

'Eddie, I am today, on behalf of the partners, offering you a partnership in this firm.'

'Good God. How amazing, thank you.'

Robin passes him a glass of sherry.

'It's traditional. I take it you accept?'

'Absolutely. Yuh, yuh. Thank you. I'm sorry if I don't sound grateful; I'm stunned. Thank you.'

'Here's to our newest and youngest partner. Rosalie will be pleased, I hope.'

'Yes, she will. She'll be really chuffed.'

'That's good. You had better warn her that you'll be working hard.'

The sherry contains a kind of oily gravitas, as though its sole purpose is to solemnise. You wouldn't actually drink the stuff for fun. *I have been transubstantiated by taking a sip.* Robin explains to him how the partnership accounts work. He is a non-equity partner at the moment, possibly for a year. He will receive one per cent of the profits in the meanwhile and he will receive a large increase in his basic salary. Robin speaks on the phone. In a few moments the other partners file in. They congratulate him. They are not rowdy people – there are six of them, two of whom are women – and he wonders if he hasn't been inducted into some kind of sect: they all look mad. Now

Robin is standing; he beckons to Mandy, who brings in two bottles of champagne; she seems to be wonderfully and naturally delighted, which chastens him. She takes charge of bringing in some chairs. When she says, 'Somebody's got to sit on the pouffe,' there is nervous hilarity. It's all so fucking English and stultified. Still, he is delighted, although he wonders if he hasn't had preferential treatment: Robin reveres Dad. Many people do, although it's hard to know exactly why. When he was on television he acquired a certain fame, but it was clear to the young Ed that the people out there saw him as far more than a newsreader and occasional correspondent: they believed that he knew things about the inner workings, although if he did he never let on. Women liked him, too, and it was difficult for Mum. She told him once that when they went out to any television occasion woman would stand right in front of her in their eagerness to talk to him. There is no sisterhood, she said.

He's drunk two or three glasses of champagne by the time the partners are shown out again: Fineman versus Brent will have to be put on hold.

'Will you ring Rosalie?' Robin asks.

'Of course.'

'Use my phone.'

'OK, thanks.'

Robin steps out in the direction of reception.

Rosalie sounds a little flat. She's on her way to the gynaecologist again, to discuss IVF, which they now think is their only hope.

'I've been made a partner.'

'Good God. Congratulations. Are we rich?'

'Not yet. But we're doing well.'

'Why are you whispering, baby?'

'I'm in Robin's office.'

She's taken to calling him baby, which he finds a little strange. But he hears lots of people doing it; the language of endearments changes fast.

'Can we celebrate?'

'Let's do it tomorrow. I have to go with my new colleagues for a few drinks.'

'Lovely. All right. You are a star.'

He feels his deceit clamp heavily on his heart. He and Alice are having a quick drink; it's always described as a quick drink as if to take the sexual possibilities out of play, but both of them know where this is heading. Back at his desk he signs various bits of paper, without really knowing what he's signing, and then goes back to the Fineman papers, which Alice has prepared for him. She emails: *CONGRATULATIONS. You've joined the grown-ups. Hope you can still come out to play*. He replies: *Quick meeting at six-thirty as arranged, Miss Dugdale*. She replies: *Yes, sir. I will report for duty at the Coach and Horses, ready for action*.

He deletes everything from his screen as fast as possible.

Soho has always had anonymity and tolerance. He thinks, with gratitude, that the people walking up Old Compton Street couldn't be less interested in him and Alice. He cuts through past Foyle's and under the arch and into Soho itself. The pub is always busy at this time with a democratic mixture of post-production folk and graphic folk and folk who work in publishing, as well as a few film technicians, comedy writers, actors and voice-over people. You sometimes see well-known old actors and weather-beaten directors who haven't worked for years. They never quite lose their brittle vivacity, at least in public. He takes off his tie as he enters the pub. Alice is sitting in a booth and he slides in next to her. She has loosened her dress in some way so that the thin straps of her bra are visible on her shoulders. Her lips have a lot more shine than when she was sitting in her hutch at the office and her dark hair is a little tousled, so that a few artfully stray locks, previously under strict legal control, fall over her left eye.

She kisses him formally on the cheek.

'Congratulations. A partner, wow. How does it feel?'

'I feel a little queasy. I should, of course, be overjoyed. Maybe I am. What's that fizzy stuff?'

'I ordered a bottle of champagne.'

'I thought it looked a bit like champagne. I'll pay.'

'Don't be silly. It's my treat.'

They clink glasses. Already half drunk he looks at her and decides to kiss her. His new importance impels him. Her tongue enters his mouth briefly and her hand goes to his thigh.

'When we've finished this, will you come to my place?'

'What for?'

'To fuck me.'

'Fine, as long as it doesn't go any further.'

She holds his thigh firmly now, her fingers working insistently. He has a disturbing thought: this partnership and the promise of money has tipped him over the edge. He would never have kissed her if he hadn't felt a surge of approbation. He understands why hideous oligarchs have beautiful women in tow; the power of money admits them into other people's lives. Alice, he realised some time ago, is fully conversant with the male sensibility. Strange that all the male words for sex are transitive: fuck, hump, screw, shag, while all the polite ones are intransitive: make love, sleep together, go to bed. *To fuck me*, she said, declaring herself the object. In this mood of elation, caused by the unjustifiable sense of entitlement, he can't wait to go and be utterly transitive. And he needn't feel too guilty about it, because there are no finer feelings involved. So he tells himself. As they look for a taxi outside in this late-summer evening, the street is busy: everybody is young and boisterous and untroubled. A party of young women in short black skirts, suspenders and policewomen's hats goes by, bursting with a chubby, hysterical cheerfulness. He and Alice, off to fuck at her flat in Stoke Newington, are, he is happily aware, in no way remarkable. The sky is cooling to a sort of surly, gaseous unease. When he goes to the country he is always surprised by how dark it gets at night, and pleasantly aware that he is a city boy.

By then time he arrives home it is nearly two in the morning. Rosalie is asleep and he creeps in beside her. He has a headache and is sobering up. She stirs.

'Hello, darling.'

'Oh Ed, congratulations. I'm so pleased for you.'

She is sleepy and her body is warm, exhaling her own familiar scent, which he loves. He is suddenly deeply ashamed and frightened.

'I'm so sorry. We got horribly drunk. It's the tradition, apparently. The big man forced sherry on me and then we went out for a drink. Sorry, sorry, sorry.'

'He rang.'

'Who?'

'Robin.'

'What did he say?'

'He wanted to tell me your news himself.'

'He would. He's got a bit of a thing for you.'

'Bit of a thing?'

'He's a lonely old geezer since his missus ran off.'

'He didn't say you were going out to celebrate.'

'No, it was just some of the younger folk. We didn't tell him. To be honest, nobody wanted to ask him.'

'What time is it?'

'I think it's about one, one-thirty.'

'You stink of booze.'

'I know. I'm a disgrace. But then I may never be made a partner again.'

She kisses him and closes her eyes, perhaps in distaste. He can feel her body's tension, or he thinks he can.

'I know. You are a smelly, disgraceful legal eagle.'

'Sorry.'

He's longing for the end of this, dying to sink into quietude.

'I went to see Mr Smythson.'

'Oh shit, I forgot you were going.'

'He told me that we should not go for IVF yet. He says it's too soon to panic.'

'Are you panicking?'

'Sometimes.'

'I'm not.'

She opens her eyes briefly.

'Good. Well done, darling. Shall we sleep?'

He's tempted to make love to her now, but then he thinks that he may have depleted his sperm reserves. He closes his eyes: they feel as if there is some grit in the mechanism. By rights, lying next to the woman he loves, the woman who is going through hell trying to produce his baby, he should be feeling ashamed and penitent. But now that he has negotiated his way without mishap into

77

bed, next to the sleeping beauty, he feels exhilarated, vindicated. Sex with Alice is uncomplicated, it's fun, it's natural! Without his really noticing, sex with Rosalie has become something different. It's become a sort of rite, a marital rite, even an obligation. And – he now sees – it is this sense of obligation which has been playing havoc with their fertility. He has heard many stories of people having difficulty with conceiving children freeing themselves up by having extramarital sex. He sees it as a plank in his defence, if he has to justify himself: I was bonking Alice for my wife's sake, Your Honour. He laughs. He's drunk. He's a man of consequence and Alice is a perk. A friend in the City told him of a theory going round that successful people in business are insatiable in their demand for perks, because it's the perks that reassure them they are valued.

He can't sleep. He gets out of bed as quietly as he can and goes into the spare room – soon to be the nursery, he feels sure, as a consequence of his new potency – and lies down there. Adultery, after three years of marriage. It's not something to be proud of. Through the wall Rosalie is sleeping in her graceful, composed fashion, as though modelling for Millais, and through here in the future nursery her adulterous husband has a headache and an alarmingly chafed penis. He was sober enough to remember a tip he had read in *GQ* magazine: always shower after extramarital sex, but never use soap. The alien soapy aroma is the number one mistake, according to *GQ*.

Alice was all business, amused and eager. Despite himself he is a little disappointed that she never once said she loved him. If it's true that the male words for sex convey the sense of motion, Alice achieved terminal velocity very quickly. Perhaps the connection between love and sex has been lost in the five years he has been with Rosalie. Certainly Alice at twenty-four is far more accustomed to casual sex than he is. And he knows that, for all their propaganda about men being only a notch or two above the animal, many women seem to be rapt during the act of sex, possessed. Now he feels an ache for Alice, and he wonders if she is thinking of him. There was a moment as she was sitting astride him when he felt she was more or less unaware of him, engaged on a personal journey. But when the moment of ejaculation, that strange transmission of fluid to another body, arrived, it brought him to tears. She kissed him tenderly, and now he takes some comfort from that.

'Why are you crying?' she asked.

'I'm not really crying. I'm just overwhelmed.'

'Do you do this often?'

'Cry?'

'No, sleep with other women.'

He noticed that, post-coitus, she had gone intransitive and he took this as a good sign.

'You're the first.'

'I'm honoured. Why did you hit on me?'

'Did I hit on you? Is that what happened?'

'Well, no, I admit, not exactly, but you were obviously up for it.'

Her lips were slightly bruised, perhaps just the gloss or whatever smearing, but it looked erotic to him. Abandoned. As he was leaving her flat, ridiculously clad in his suit again, with tie, she was sitting on the bed cross-legged in a T-shirt eating a raspberry yoghurt.

'See you in the morning, hotshot.'

'Alice.'

'You don't need to say anything special. It was a fuck. A lovely fuck.'

'OK.'

In fact he wanted to say something special, something deeper, but he saw that this was not the moment.

Other lives. We all believe we could have lived other lives. Dad, he thinks, has been prey to this delusion. Sometimes he talks about Richard Burton: he says Burton consciously lived a life that he knew was ridiculous and dangerous, but at the same time heroic. He sold himself knowingly, like Faustus, says Dad. Now, still drunk, Ed thinks this is profound. Perhaps I have sold myself, too, in more ways than one. And it has taken Alice to make it plain that he could have lived another life. He remembers details as though he had been having sex for the first time: the drops of sweat between her breasts; where her thighs joined the pelvis a little runnel. There was no air in her flat. I have sold myself to Fennell, Dunston and Bickerstaff and perhaps also to the idea of a perfect marriage. Yet it's sadly predictable: I'm a partner in a law firm and shagging a trainee. But he finds to his surprise that he feels happy, while his wife is only a few feet away, dreaming perhaps of their balletic children. People's lives, when you get to know them well, are infinitely more complex than you could ever have imagined. And now, even though I have done something reprehensible, morally inexcusable and possibly ruinous, I feel perversely happy.

As he remembers Alice's surprisingly rough hand on his cock, he has a crazy certainty that he will father a child. Alice, without intending it, has lifted the weight that was constricting his seminal vesicles.

The last thing he sees as he drifts – staggers – into sleep is a picture of Ophelia he saw on the side of a bus, advertising an exhibition at the Tate. She looks just like Rosalie, lying on her back, floating downstream. Her face is strangely calm for someone soon to drown in his hotshot lawyer's potent semen.

6

LUCY WONDERS IF she has a self. A self is not just a sort of serviceable act which can be applied to life, an imitative process of appearing – for example – upbeat and enthusiastic, or pretending to like Renaissance art or knowing about books; it's not having in your head a lot of voices you can call on. It is most likely having solid values and firm beliefs about the world that are not subject to fashion. In our family, only Mum has ever had a clearly defined self. A self – a real self – would not require constant examination; it would be firmly moored.

Below them on the pond two small boys are operating radio-controlled boats. One of the boys steers his boat viciously into the other's.

'Fuck you, you wanker,' the second boy screams. It is hard to know if they are friends, as children routinely scream abuse at each other.

Dad loves the Heath. He says he has never liked Camden, but knowing that the Heath is just a few minutes up the road has made living there bearable for him. And it is still a revelation every time he goes for one of his walks, that you come upon this small country perched up here, not far from the mean streets. Up here, Dad says, the air is fresher. The freshness he imagines is probably moral as much as real. You can still see the hedgerows of the home farm that the Mansfield family used to own, he says. And he loves the ponds they created to provide a vista from the house. But he can't resist adding, 'Of course if the last owners knew that there would be a thousand gays in thongs lying about on a sunny day, they would never have left the place to the nation.'

'Dad, do you think we have a self?'

They are walking up from the model-boat pond on a sweep that leads past the swimming ponds. He turns to her and looks at her silently for a few moments. When he was on television he was known for his listening, or his appearance of listening.

'I don't know,' he says finally. 'In my job I had a kind of cultivated self which wasn't me, really. Why?'

'Why do I ask? I feel like I'm a shadow.'

'Since Mum died?'

'Maybe even before.'

'I've thought about this, too, my darling. My conclusion, for what it's worth, which is probably bugger all, is that your self exists only in relation to other people. And as other people see you, you sort of adapt yourself and gradually you settle into this self. Obviously in my business it was more extreme. But I don't think there is a permanent, unchanging self. In the Army, for example, we were expected to be something completely different, and we adapted. Except for Adam. He hasn't changed. Is that the question you were asking?'

'So what do the Masai bracelets say about your self?'

'Don't be worried, darling. I'm not going to run off with a bimbo or take to crack in a big way. I see a future of purely recreational crack use, actually.'

He still walks fast, in fact faster since he's been working

out. He is wearing shorts, with lots of pockets, and leopard-print trainers. His wire and elephant-twine bracelets gleam and occasionally jangle. He's treading a fine line on the edge of the ridiculous. They rise up to the top of the hill, passing the men's bathing pool behind the bushes. Often in summer if they go this way they see men striding briskly, towels over their shoulders, heads often cropped, heading back to the straight world. She wonders if these men are plagued by erotomania, flirtation with danger and the addiction to novelty. She also wonders if it isn't the transgressive nature of gay sex that is a big part of the excitement. She thinks but, of course, has never said it, that gay men have somehow elevated sexual behaviour into an aesthetic principle. Despite his weight-loss, bracelets, baggy shorts and the bizarre trainers, Dad would never be taken for gay.

'No,' she says. 'It's been brought on by Mum dying, but I just wonder if we aren't all three of us a little over-conscious. With Mum what you got was a kind of mooring. Grounded is the word, I think. She wasn't swayed this way and that. Am I making sense?'

'Yes, absolute sense. Darling, is this really a way of asking me where we're going now?'

'No, no. I was thinking about myself and Josh, actually. When he dumped me, I was devastated, but now that he's back and eager I keep thinking what a creep he is. If he's a creep, why did I want him back, and now that I have him back, why do I find him so deadly? It's me. I don't have a fixed personality.'

'That's showbiz.'

'Oh thanks. I'll try and remember that.'

'You may not have a fixed personality, but you're the best-looking of us all. I wonder who your father was?'

He doesn't want to talk about Josh, who, of course, reveres him. He has this effect, that people instantly believe they have a rapport with him. They are passing a huge, sprawling oak, which she used to think must be like the oaks in Sherwood Forest. Mum believed firmly in the old children's books.

'Dad, why are you so evasive these days?'

'Am I?'

He stops and hugs her.

'You're bony,' she says.

'Pleasantly bony or emaciated?'

'Different. You used to be chubby. This is a little strange.'

'I hope I am not being evasive.'

'Maybe evasive was too strong. But you are distant. It's worrying. Ed and I both think so.'

'Let's walk up through the wood to the tea room. What do you say?'

They enter the dark, leafy, damp and fungal woods that lead down to the concert bowl on the lake, where once they heard the *1812* performed with cannon effects that sent startled fowl crashing into the heavy foliage.

'Lucy, you know I can't replace Mum. We are what we are now, three individuals. Our family has shrunk. And what you say is true – she provided the mooring. I was sort of on the periphery. I had a busy life, obviously. And she was in charge at home, but I didn't think of myself as detached. And I don't want to be distant either but to tell the truth I don't really know how, without Mum, to re-create what we were. If I tried to do Sunday chicken and so on it would be false.'

His voice is reasonable and measured as though he is reporting from Darfur, but she is distressed now because he has confirmed what she feared most, that they can't go back, and that is what she wants most, even as she knows it is impossible.

'Don't cry, darling.'

That face which was famous for its concern, its manly compassion, its reassuring intelligence, is now directed to her.

'All I can tell you, Lucy, is that you and Ed are everything to me. I have nothing else. And I don't want anything else.'

She quietens in his embrace now. She feels suddenly calm. Perhaps that's all I need, she thinks, his declaration of unequivocal love, something that was always obvious with Mum.

'Do you mean that?'

'I don't want anything, except maybe to use the time, the empty spaces, to think a bit. You can't really think in television, except in a sort of "how's this going to play" fashion.'

'I'm sorry, Daddy. I am being boring and self-obsessed. Let's walk.'

The water on the lake is leaden, moving slowly and heavily. It's a strange effect on such a small stretch of water, a wrinkled sea, more appropriate to the North Sea. By the lake, grimly cheerful couples hover around their children and encourage them to run about and express themselves in this little paradise. There's a competition for excellent parenthood going on in subtle ways, fathers being unusually active, mothers being showily caring, and so on. When she was a child Dad would sit under a tree as she ran after Ed. In those days, not so long ago, there was no fence around the lake. One day Ed was pecked by a swan. Swans are malevolent creatures, not easily placated. Dad laughed, which sent Ed into a tantrum until Mum calmed him.

'Do you remember the swan?' Lucy asks.

'Ed and the swan. Oh yes. You and Ed ran and the swan pecked Ed right on his bum. It was hilarious.'

'We were terrified.'

'It's good to be terrified. My brother and I were often terrified.'

'Yes, I know, you and Uncle Guy didn't have any toys and you made your own puppets out of conkers and old tyres and you shared a spinning top and you both had a paper round. And we were spoilt and over-protected.'

'Yup. That's more or less the way it was. And, by the way, we only had brown bread.'

'And that's why you loved white Wonderloaf. Sad. So, so sad.'

'Oh – my – God, it's soooh, soooh sad,' he says in a teenage voice.

She hates to admit it, but he is a good mimic.

'Are you mocking your only daughter?'

'Not really.'

They walk on up the steep path to the house.

'Am I going to get over it?'

'Mum? You will, although at a deep level I think your parents' death is always there somewhere. Actually I think peripheral things will trigger your memories. Whenever I want to remember my father, I think first of his brown brogues, always polished, and if I ever smell shoe polish I think of him without meaning to. Ox blood. That was the colour of the polish. I don't think Guy ever got over our mother's death, and I'm sure that he went to Africa to get away from the memories, but that may be a bit glib, I know. Although a Freudian might say his problems with women all go back to that.'

'And your point is?'

'My point is that you will always be reminded of Mum, by unexpected things. But the pain will subside.'

'How's Uncle Guy?'

'He's not well, according to his son.'

'Lovely man, Uncle Guy.'

'I may have to go out to see him sometime. He has all sorts of problems.'

But at the moment she is not really interested in Uncle Guy's problems. The tea room puts an end to this unexpectedly reassuring conversation. It's not possible in a tea room in London, in contrast – she imagines – to the Closerie des Lilas in Paris – to have a serious conversation. If you are middle class you are obliged to be glib and humorous in public, as though the people around you are scoring you for knowingness and irony. When you want to talk seriously and bitterly, you whisper and lean forward. The other day in the restaurant with Ed, she saw a man and a woman leaning close; the veins on their foreheads bulged alarmingly, the hatred was spewing noxiously in terse, half-heard sentences, like the telegrams in old films. It's a different matter out on the streets: since Mum died she seems to see women threatening their children every day: *I'll give you a slap. I told you once, and now you're gonna get it.* The young children have frightened, feral eyes. The older children have developed a kind of sullenness. Their time is coming.

After tea – Dad refuses a biscuit – they walk on a long loop across a meadow scuffed by rabbits, and on through a tangled forest. After a while they realise that they are being followed meekly by a hairy dog, possibly a wolfhound. It appears to be lost and comes up to them when called. Dad looks at the tag around its neck. He reads: *Wolfowitz* and a phone number.

'A Jewish dog,' he says.

He calls the number. Lucy listens.

'OK, fine. By the model-boat pond. Oh, it's a girl. She's a girl. Wolfie. I see. OK, no, she looks calm enough. Red boots. OK, and we will have the dog, of course.'

'Right,' he says to Lucy, 'it's a girl and its owner will head for the boat pond. And we will know her by her red boots. Come, Wolfie, you are going home.'

He takes the Australian jackeroo belt from his shorts and slips it under the dog's collar. They march along up to the high point of the wood; Lucy thinks the dog looks like the one that accompanied the soldiers at the funeral of some Irish Guards recently. It has a subdued demeanour; like an undertaker's, easily assumed. Returning the dog to its unknown owner has given them a little mission. The dog may be depressed, but she and Dad have a new lift in their step.

As they descend the path towards the pond, they see the red boots before they can make out the figure of the dog's owner. They hear her calling, *Wolfie, Wolfie* as she sees them cresting the hill and the dog begins to whimper. Dad slips the leash and the dog gallops with huge strides deliriously towards its owner, who is kneeling to welcome it. By the time they reach her, she has the dog on a lead; as they approach, the dog growls at them.

'Oh thank you, thank you,' says the woman.

She's in her late thirties, with wild, dark, streaked-blonde hair and a tight pair of jeans tucked into red cowboy boots. She wears an embroidered waistcoat. Overall she is faintly rosy, in a Celtic sort of way.

'I'm Sylvie, by the way, and you've met Wolfie. She's my baby. I can't thank you enough. Oh my goodness, you're the TV person. I didn't recognise you in shorts.'

'Yes, I'm the TV person, and this is my daughter Lucy.'

'Thank you so much for finding Wolfie.'

'We didn't actually find her, she surrendered to us,' says Lucy.

Lucy is used to the shock of recognition that assails people when they see her father. Sometimes they seem to believe they have a personal relationship with him as though in their minds they have for years been conducting a conversation, a Socratic dialogue, about world issues with him. Lucy watches her: she is one of those women who light up in front of men and employ a whole range of coquettish devices; her hands run through her hair and she adjusts a bra strap, subconsciously – perhaps deliberately – drawing attention to her best features. The deployment of breasts, as most women know, is a kind of semaphore.

'Sorry, I didn't introduce myself properly. My name is Sylvie Mellors, and this is Wolfowitz. Wolfie for short.'

Sylvie has very white teeth, and there is something vulpine about her, too, with all that brindled blonde hair.

'Well, thanks, lovely to meet you,' says Dad. 'We must be on our way. Bye, Sylvie. Bye, Wolfie.'

Wolfie growls, her funeral director's mien now abandoned.

'Nympho,' says Lucy as they begin the homeward trudge.

'Do you think so?'

'Absolutely. Trust me. Women who make up sexy names for themselves are nymphos. Or desperate.'

'Not really stepmother material, then?'

'Don't even joke.'

As she has done all her life, she looks at Dad and tries to see him as the public sees him, a national figure, whose voice and mannerisms and honest-broker questioning are still known to millions.

'She was jiggling her tits, Dad.'

'Didn't see a thing.'

'So you say.'

'I do.'

He's smiling as they walk up the hill towards the row of grand houses where Sting once lived. They never knew which house it was, but they always said, 'Sting lives here.' In families you develop certain phrases, certain lyrics, which enter the family songbook. As children, every time they drove up Highgate Hill, Ed would say, 'Whittington's cat. Fuck, you missed it.' For years Lucy never saw the bronze cat on the pavement. In his teens Ed said *fuck* to annoy Mum. In families you take up positions to distinguish yourself from the others, but also to cement the family rituals. Rituals in families – she thinks – are no different from religious rituals: they dispel anxiety with repetition. Dad has become something of an Islamophobe – although of course he sees himself as part of the liberal elite – but he doesn't understand that fear and anxiety are what are driving Muslims to the rituals of Islam.

'Dad, do you think people like Ms Jiggly Tits love you because you are familiar and reassuring?'

'It could be. Mostly, they seem to think I know what's really going on. I realised a long time ago that celebrity is something other people project on to you.'

'And a few of them think you owe them something, because they made you.'

'That's true, too.'

But she doesn't want the conversation to go this way into generalities. She wants him to say something more to put her mind at rest, something to explain himself, something that goes beyond reason. She wants to feel as though she is properly attached to the world again. She wonders if it's true what Dad said, that little things will for ever remind her of Mum. Far worse would be to forget her bit by bit until she faded right away to the status of a postcard from the other side. Already she sees that she is remembering her mother in short and random scenes – her love of the sea, her near veneration of the linen cupboard, her insatiable and indiscriminate reading and the way she folded clothes carefully before putting them away at the dictate of the seasons – summer clothes, winter clothes: they were distinct categories in her mind. And she remembers how she looked absolutely serene in bed. Sleeping, she looked like a child. She was always very interested in Lucy's schoolfriends, and they loved her because they knew instinctively that her interest was genuine; and she remembers her driving – erratic, impulsive and even comical. But it's becoming an edited version of her mother's life. And this is what memory seems to do: it abridges and condenses as the object distances itself through separation or death. She was listening to a radio programme the other day and some expert said that we are the only animals that sing. He said that tunes remain embedded in the brain for ever, whatever happens to the powers of reasoning. Mum hummed tunefully around the house. But she stopped humming when the cancer was diagnosed. Perhaps the cancer had invaded that part of the brain which houses musicality.

'Ah there's the car,' says Dad, as if he's found it by chance.

Under Dad's care, the Jaguar has been neglected: paper cups, discarded mail, wedges of grass and mud, a sandwich wrapper, a broken pair of sunglasses, a torn road atlas, and an empty tennis-racquet bag lie about, suffering wilt and damp.

'Dad, this car is a tip.'

'Is it?'

'Yes, it's disgusting. Look, that paper cup's like almost alive.'

'Your mother was the tidy one.'

'I'll clean it for you.'

'You don't have to. It doesn't worry me that it's gone a bit ecological.'

'It's not ecological, it's a health hazard.'

'You're taking on your mum's role.'

'Meaning?'

'Meaning she always believed she had a duty to some higher power to point out my failings.'

'You're saying I am a nag.'

'She wasn't a nag. And nor are you. It was just a way of reminding me of my human frailties.'

'But that's what families are for, to remind you of what you really are.'

He ponders this as he reverses his Jaguar, almost running over a cat, possibly Sting's cat.

'Do you believe that? I think that the real you, the one the family sees, is actually the you that suits them. But there's no point in fighting it because it's unavoidable.'

'You're quite perceptive for a geriatric.'

'Am I a geriatric?'

'Yes. Nobody's fooled by the whacky trainers, I'm afraid.'

She looks at him as he drives. His skin and his hair have a kind of hue, as though they have been tinted by long exposure to the television lights. Or perhaps the daily application of make-up has dyed him indelibly. The girls at school who played the flute, the oboe or the clarinet seemed to have taken on the appropriately pale, other-worldly look as though the music itself – thin, reedy, haunting – had sapped their vitality, leaving them pupa-like and vulnerable. With Dad there has been a more robust effect: television has given him a sort of matured-in-old-oak-barrels look. People in television are often said to be chameleon-like, but those who say it aren't talking about skin colour. In this bright light Dad looks as though he has been lightly embalmed.

'Have you spoken to Ed recently?' he asks.

'We had lunch the other day, and I rang him this morning to thank him.'

'He's been made a partner at his firm.'

'When?'

'Yesterday.'

'He didn't mention it. He sounded a bit rough. You know how he goes when he's had a few drinks, a little like tentative.'

'I think we should take him to dinner or something. What do you say, you and Josh, Ed and Rosalie? And me.'

'And you with Ms Jiggly Wiggly.'

'Ho ho.'

'Can I stay at our house tonight?'

'Of course you can, sweetheart. I would love you to.'

Now the streets of Camden are embracing them reproachfully, as they return from the higher regions.

Later in her own bed – her real bed – she feels calm. Josh was scornful, even vicious, about her spending the night at home, but she says her father needs her, just occasionally, which may not be strictly true. Josh is out with his friends watching some football match in a pub, but he would still prefer her to be at her flat waiting for him to return smelling of hops and flatulence. The little room under the eaves where the roof slopes down towards the soggy back garden – it needs work urgently – not only calms her, it makes her optimistic. She can hear Dad downstairs somewhere still moving about. (Little tasks seem to take him some time.) The lime tree is whipping the back wall of the house, showering yellow seed balls on to the dark-green, algae-coated, heaving brick terrace; the neighbourhood cats are out on the noisy prowl; the susurration from Camden Road rises and falls gently, and everything is familiar. She wears one of her mother's nighties. She thinks yes, maybe I do have a self of a sort.

Much later her phone rings and wakes her. It's Josh. He says he wants to come round. He's drunk.

'No, Josh, you can't come.'

'Why not?'

'My father's here.'

'Oh, are we a little prudish or what?'

'Are you trying to be funny? Because you're not.'

'I'm coming anyway.'

'Don't. Please don't. My father's asleep and so was I.'

He rings off. A few minutes later there's a knock on her door. For a moment she thinks it might be Josh.

'Hello, darling. It's me, Dad,' he adds as if she might not recognise his voice.

'Come in.'

'I heard your phone. I was awake anyway. Why are you laughing?'

His hair, his television hair, hangs over his brow at the front and sticks up at the back.

'Your hair looks odd.'

'I can see where this is heading. I am becoming a figure of fun, an eccentric old goat with crazy hair.'

He wants to say something to me. But for the moment he can't express exactly what it is he has on his mind.

She sees the two of them, Dad sitting on the end of her bed, close but somehow separated by Mum's death. As though Mum provided them with the means of communication. Although he is thin and has been working out, his nipples are distinctly visible, puckered against the cotton of his T-shirt.

'Dad, did you want to say something?'

'No, not really. I just came up to see if you were all right. Phones at three in the morning are unsettling.'

'It was just my crack dealer.'

'Oh fine. Perhaps we can get a family discount. I'll go. You're working tomorrow.'

He stands up a little stiffly, his head only inches from the roof, and then he bends down to kiss her.

'Mum's nightie?'

'Yes. Do you mind?'

'Not it all. Lucy, it was good of you to come for a walk.'

'It was a privilege, as Ms Jiggly Tits so movingly demonstrated. She has already told all her friends about you. You're like a living god to us girlies. We revere you.'

'Oh shit, you can be quite annoying when you try.'

'Funny, that's just what Ed told me only a few days ago.' He pauses, half out of the door.

'You know what Iago said, "I am not what I am." '

'Meaning?'

'I'm not sure what he meant.'

'OK, well, if I don't see you in the morning, I'll give you a ring during the day.'

'Night night, darling.'

I am not what I am.

She wonders how much of him she contains. Perhaps it is from him that she gets the sense that there is another life that she could be leading. Is that what he means? I am not what I am. As she falls asleep she remembers what God said: *I am that I am.*

7

THE CHILDREN SEE the house – this jerry-built late-Victorian villa, enervated by a century and a half of dirty rain – as a shrine. But I – David thinks – have lost any affection I ever had for it. Every day it looks to him more obviously what it is, a box made of bricks, cheaply finished to a plan by a speculative builder so that every house in Inverdale Terrace is similar, although gentrification has given them little flourishes of planting and fruit swags, arrow-headed railings, and large door knockers. Door furniture. Brass, he notices, is being replaced by a sort of brushed aluminium. Multi-layered plants, blue conifers, anodised letterboxes, gravel, slate, pebbles and uplighting decorate an increasing number of the houses in the terrace. He often finds himself thinking about the absurdities and the delusions which govern most lives, what someone called the 'whole inventory of human disgrace'. When we were a family, here at No. 9 Inverdale Terrace, we were by no means exempt from delusion: family delusion, money delusion, sex delusion. And he, in particular, the anchor of Global Television's Sunrise Report for twelve years, was as much prey to delusion as the rest of them. The whole rickety business conducted from a few warehouses near the M25 was a fraud; his position as senior anchor was a fraud. He knew it at the time, but now he regards it with shame. His apparent omniscience, the ramped-up glamour and intensity, the special reports, the reliance on show-business PR, his occasional forays into the field – like a viceroy during the Raj – the cynical nods towards community, the shallow acknowledgement of culture and science, the grovelling subservience to rock stars (until they went into rehab), the trivialisation of politics – eagerly encouraged by spin doctors – the endlessly repeated and meaningless piety about global warming: *Get up the fucking polar bear on the fucking ice-floe shot*, and conservation: *Get that Greenpeace gob-on-a-stick into the studio*, and the fascination with celebrity: how many frightened, drug-addled, alcoholic, bitter, pompous and ludicrous 'celebrities' had he interviewed in his life? God knows. Setting off every morning at 4 a.m. from Inverdale Terrace with his driver, Ted; reading the papers that Ted had collected for him at King's Cross; checking, in the last few years, the running order on his Blackberry; phoning his thoughts through on his second Blackberry, speeding through the still-dark, empty streets; making notes, ordering the world to his image and understanding, all in forty minutes. Then he would be in make-up, his suit brought to him with a selection of his famous ties – he was elected Tie-Wearer of the Year three times – attended by little producers coming to see him in streams, holding scripts and revised running orders, like leaf-cutting ants. Seamlessly, effortlessly, he could listen to some raddled journalist analysing Saddam's latest manoeuvre while listening to the gallery with one ear and catching up with the football scores on autocue, so that he was ready for his famous banter with Jonno Jameson, sports correspondent. His one, undeniable, talent was to keep everything together with urbanity; the contributor and the eager-to-please freelancers and the desperate-to-please academics were held in a silken web; without thinking consciously he knew exactly when to stop someone who was rambling or losing his train of thought or repeating himself, but he did it with a lightness of touch, a quip, a little compliment that left everyone feeling good. Feeling good was important. It came in two categories, feeling good because of light, cheerful elements in the news, and feeling good when some ghastly child murder had taken place because you were confirmed in your strangely pleasurable notion that the world was a shit-hole. The theory, which had Global in its grip, was that you kept the viewers hooked by announcing the exciting, unmissable story coming next, so that nothing tedious, serious or original should permit the idiot viewer to switch channel before the shark attack, soccer transfer or the celebrity scandal. Poisonous snakes and man-eating crocodiles were also effective in this cause, and were kept in reserve for quiet news days.

When the second Iraq war started, a professor, in a live interview from Oxford, tried to warn of the coming cultural and patriotic reaction that a foreign invasion would inevitably invite, but the gallery kept up a barrage in David's ear, because the Professor was bald, spoke too fast, and used too many long words; the viewers would switch channel in droves. But what the Prof, whose baldness, anarchic eyebrows and dark, troubled eyes conveyed something of the seer, was saying was absolutely true, that a people is its culture and cannot be persuaded in a short space of time to abandon its ancient prejudices. The producers wanted David to discuss victory, a triumph of good over evil. They regarded this fuddy-duddy as out of touch with the popular mood, which they, of course, could measure.

'Thank you, Professor, that was most interesting, but I am afraid that's all we have time for this morning.'

I sold myself. At the villa in Rome, Richard Burton once spoke to him about the Gnostic heresy: we are all potentially divine, but trapped in a material world. Burton seemed to subscribe to this view, and David quickly realised that he did, too. Elizabeth's children were visiting and they gazed at Burton with sunstruck Californian indifference. Even then, 1966, at the height of his fame, Burton could see personal ruin ahead. He told David that he should have been a quiet Oxford don rather than an actor. Adam managed to find David a small job on the film and he spent a lot of time watching Burton at work: one of his jobs was to make sure his drink supplies were kept stocked. The sets were absurd, with elements of the psychedelic: weighty medieval compasses and protractors and globes and bubbling phials of liquid were scattered about. There were huge leather-bound tomes in cuneiform and Greek and Hebrew and Latin, as if in a lawyer's office in an unspecified historical time. Behind these was a skeleton which Burton could address to add poignancy to a line about mortality. There were plenty of these. The phials were actively steaming, with multicoloured liquids bubbling away. The liquids had the same garish qualities as the lights in Sabrina, which spurred on the dancers and illuminated the five go-go dancers in gold bikinis suspended above them in cages. They danced as though they were thrashing corn or lassoing a mustang or pulling on a hawser. Even on that kitsch set at Dinocittà, he saw what a great actor can do. And he thought that Burton had some of the divine quality of the Gnostic heresy, because great acting – and probably high culture – strives for divinity.

He is prone to these high-rent thoughts these days, as if a life of second-rate preoccupations needs some redress while there is time. And that is what he was trying to tell Lucy. Now, sitting here in the family house, vacated by the family, he sees Burton happily and orotundly explaining the Gnostic heresy, glancing at Elizabeth with her astonishingly pale breasts and her cool, flawless face, as if to remind himself that this woman is his reward for possessing – drunk or sober – the divine spark. The trouble is, he doesn't look completely happy about the deal.

One night Adam's Fiat was stolen. The grips at the studio were able to locate it and have it returned, the tank full of petrol. There was cheek-tweaking and knowing gestures to indicate that they all were men of the world. David was entranced: Rome was a kind of epiphany, the happiest he has ever been. It was as if he had never been shown the earth and its possibilities before. He, too, would be a professional actor and live in a vivid, charged world. All these years later he remembers the warm stones of terraces, the hours at the Piscina Olimpica, and sex in the pensione with Jenni in the lingering heat of the afternoon so that their skins made a comical – but to him ineffably sweet – sound, like water on the side of a swimming pool, like the Piscina Olimpica.

His mobile phone rings.

'Hello, you won't remember me. I'm the woman with the dog, on the Heath.'

'Sylvie, owner of Wolfie.'

'You remembered. That's amazing. So, so amazing. I'm flattered.'

'What can I do for you?'

'I wondered, and I know this is a bit of a cheek, if you could speak to our book club.'

'I haven't written a book. Not since the Afghanistan one five years ago.'

'To be honest, you could just chat away and we would ask questions. You've had such a fascinating life.'

'Probably less fascinating than it sounds. When would you want to do it?'

'We have a meeting next Friday. It would be such a surprise for the others: CELEBRITY GUEST, TA RA!'

'I'll have to get back to you.'

'It usually starts at about seven with some nibbles and a drink and then the chat. A reading or a question-and-answer, whatever you prefer, for about an hour, and then we go on to the Rasa. But you wouldn't have to do that, obviously. I know you are busy.'

'Sounds like fun. I'll ring you back when I've consulted.'

He finds it difficult to give a straight answer to this kind of request and always takes refuge in the promise to call back, the suggestion of consultation with his non-existent staff, so that he can say no politely. He won't talk to Cy, his speaking agent, about this one.

Ms Jiggly Tits. He feels a slight stirring in the blood. Since Nancy died, he has been free to do what he likes, but he has not contemplated a sex life. Perhaps he should see what she really wants from him: his instinct tells him that she is not too firmly attached to reality. He's met a few crazy women in his life. And crazy men, but with men you don't have to deal with the sex business. It's a strange thing, the gulf in expectation that separates men and women. A woman friend of Nancy, whose husband had died, joined an expensive dating agency and found that the first two men she met were disturbingly close to being insane, one desperate for sex and for money and the second with a grudge against women, which led him to sneer at her and insult her after a few drinks. He wonders if there isn't a low-level battle going on, a battle of values. At Global they liked to say that the BBC had feminised itself: the inference was that it had become preoccupied with family and divorce and neglect, and encouraged an unpleasant whine about men: men start wars, men are ruled by pride, men always want to be complimented for routine acts, men can only carry out one task at a time, men are chronically insensitive to the higher feelings of women. What he hears on the street is a rising volume of accusation and lies, men and women running each other down or lying about where they are, what they are doing and why they are late. Mobiles have revealed a new level of deceit and delusion: he often hears, now that he is a *Fussgänger*, young women, loudly needy, talking chirpily about drinking binges and men – the despised men they also can't do without. He feels a certain sympathy; perhaps they are obliged to perform like this in public: they must have an assertive persona and they are prepared to advertise it, in the face of indifference. Sometimes he wonders who they are calling: maybe other desperate people who have created a fantasy of a happy, upbeat life of sexual and social fulfilment.

He pulls on his running shorts. His legs are still good, although the knee joints seem to have become pronounced and knobbly, like the head of a shillelagh, which is made with a natural joint in a straight piece of wood, maybe hazel. (You learn all kinds of things when you are a cub reporter.) He puts on his new tracksuit, blue with two white stripes down the legs, conscious that Lucy said it is a style favoured by Romanians. But then he has nothing against Romanians. He seldom uses the neglected Jaguar;

he runs to the gym, which is about half a mile away in an industrial building that reminds him of Global. It's subsidised by the local council. Once he belonged to an expensive gym staffed by smiling young men and women in polo-shirts, decorated with the logo of a palm tree. Through plate glass he could see a room full of elaborate equipment, designed to tweak and titivate every cranny of the subsiding body. There were machines that allowed women to exercise their inner thighs, presumably for greater sexual heft. The members all appeared to belong to that strangely joyless community of international finance. After the first two weeks he never went there again.

This place, where disadvantaged youths are employed, often with disastrous results, suits his mood and his circumstances as a man reduced yet in some ways resting more easily on the earth's crust. The pavements are wet and encumbered. The earth beneath is compacted by millennia of use. He trots on happily, adding his weight to the process, weaving between the wage slaves near the tube station, and then on through the market, which offers knock-off DVDs, spices, nuts, designer jeans at suspiciously low prices, unfamiliar brands of trainers, razors and individual tubes of toothpaste. Shawled Somali women with small watchful children are shopping cautiously. He remembers doing a story on the humiliation suffered by asylum seekers who had to shop with vouchers rather than money. Oh God, all the stories, all the causes, all the synthetic outrage. At Global, outrage was never quite genuine, but easily assumed.

When Lucy asked whether we have a self, he could have said no, only postures. Gorillas being killed for bush meat, one of his most famous stories, produced more emails than his story of child soldiers conscripted after their parents had had their arms cut off with pangas. A town full of the mutilated; young women with stumps instead of hands and feet, trying to find food or stir millet porridge. It was the worst thing he had ever seen, a suggestion of what might be buried in the human heart. Television has no time for the problem of evil. Sometimes he felt like a Jew who had to live in a world not of his making, and yet he was complicit and that was in part because of his eagerness to be at the heart of things. Although the heart of things, as it turned out, is a subjective concept.

Soon after Nancy was diagnosed, he was summoned to a meeting. It was suggested to him that he have a makeover: for a few weeks he had his hair teased upwards at the front so that he looked startled rather than youthful and *branché*, the intended effect. One day he asked Marie in make-up to go back to the old style and she said, 'I didn't want to say anything, but I didn't like it, David, it wasn't you. You looked like you had your finger in the socket or something.'

She was saying that he looked ridiculous. He decided that day, using the excuse of Nancy's illness, to hand in his notice, and six months later, less than a year before Nancy died, Ted drove him home for the last time. His choked farewell words, as he stopped outside No. 9, were, 'They don't make 'em like you no more, governor.'

Cor blimey, strike a light, Ted, me old china, you're as good as gold, ain'tcher?

Ted had to take the bus home, as Global had given David the Jaguar. He saw then, as he had really always known, that twenty-four-hour television news is a greedy business, anxious, unreliable, prey to cultish beliefs and blinded by self-importance, which it mistakes for public service.

*

He's breathing evenly when he arrives at the gym.

'Hello, Dave, concession, innit?'

'That's me,' he says. 'I like the ring, Ash.'

Ashley has a new ring in his eyebrow: David is not being ironic. His eye is attuned to street fashion, he thinks. After all, fashion is what you adopt when you don't know what you are, as Quentin Crisp said. And who knows what they are? Not me.

'Thanks, mate. Here we go.'

The concessionary rate is less than the price of a cappuccino. Since he and Ted were parted, he has travelled free on buses and the underground, too. His mother was always complaining about the cost of things and the need to save and he finds himself hearing her words and honouring her memory by taking all the freebies available to him. As he starts on the rowing machine, he has an aberrant thought: I am where I belong in this simple democracy – T.E. Lawrence, joining the Air Force. He decides after ten minutes, perhaps over-oxygenated, that he will see Sylvie. At the book club he will be able to assess the human and sexual possibilities in safety. When he's in full flow, his mind seems to free itself and alight where it wants to.

Now, as he has done so often since Nancy died, he thinks of Jenni. Back in England, he and Jenni continued their relationship. He had an acting agent, thanks to Burton, and had his first small acting job before going back to Oxford. But his sex life had taken on a different quality. What had been joyous and innocent became in England furtive: Jenni had a boyfriend she had forgotten to mention in Rome and he felt a retrospective gloom, as though the innocence and happiness of Rome had been a deliberate deception. He found himself going over those few weeks in minute detail, to see what he had missed or, worse, in what ways he was deceived. Their lovemaking, he felt, had become sullied: something rotten had entered it. He couldn't put it out of his mind and he also felt he was in competition with the unknown Garry, an assistant director working at Pinewood on some soon-to-be-forgotten epic, involving togas. Jenni was freelancing on commercials, so there were opportunities to continue their now furtive lovemaking. One weekend, desperate to re-create the happiness of Rome, he asked her to come down to Chichester where he was rehearsing, to spend a few nights on his uncle's boat, moored out in the harbour. The plan was to sleep on the boat and use the dinghy, with Seagull engine, to go to beaches and pubs round about. She could only get away for one night so they set off early on a Friday. And in the boat, an old teak – or perhaps mahogany – sloop, he felt impelled to discuss honestly the subject that was on his mind.

'Jenni, I know you don't want to talk about Garry, but why didn't you tell me early on?'

'I didn't want to spoil it.'

They are lying on the deck, drinking Mateus Rosé, and eating beans and sausages warmed up in the galley on the little stove, which is mounted on a gimbal.

'You didn't want to spoil it? When was the right moment to spoil it?'

'I wasn't thinking ahead. I just got deeper and deeper in and put off telling you.'

'And now you and this Garry are back together?'

She doesn't answer directly.

'Why are you always trying to analyse everything? Here I am.'

'I didn't realise it was my fault. Sorry.'

It's doomed. Once that note of injured self-righteousness

enters a relationship, it's all over. Around them other boats are just beginning to tug on the moorings as the tide turns; soon they are all swinging round, with their bows upriver and their dinghies streaming out behind. He knows nothing about boats. People who understand boats – or horses – are in possession of arcane knowledge which warms and comforts them: *my boat, my horse* – they confer a kind of hieratic status. His uncle is an ex-naval man who was at Normandy and Okinawa, a generous man who in small ways expresses his kinship with the sea. The sea and ships and this boat – this creaking creation of wood and brass and rope – are his spiritual world.

Jenni wants to go to the pub. Understandably she doesn't want to be subjected to an inquisition. She is a free spirit. She says the Mateus is piss, nothing like Frascati.

'Can't you just enjoy this for a bit?'

'I am enjoying it, but I would like to go to the pub.'

'OK, but it closes in an hour.'

He is not an expert with the Seagull motor or the dinghy, which has no lights for the return journey, but they launch off. The water is running strongly now, out towards the open sea, and the engine seems pathetically underpowered, but they make it to the jetty outside the Walrus and the Carpenter by heading way upstream, and he and Jenni enter the heavily scented fog of the pub. The air contains particles of human life in suspension, something Jenni apparently craves after being closeted with him.

On the way home, drunk, he sinks the dinghy by standing up too quickly when they strike a buoy and the propeller becomes caught up in a line. In a moment the dinghy has gone. Jenni goes under. The water is icy. He swims after her and finds her arm, and pulls her to the surface. She clamps her arms around his neck.

'I can't swim,' she says.

In her embrace he is sinking.

'Let go, for Chrissakes. Let go. I'll hold you up.'

But she won't let go. He tries to push her off. She's panic-stricken, and holds more tightly. Now they are both panicking. They go under and he kicks hard to get them to the surface. He hits her in the face, something he has read in a manual: knock the other person unconscious when that person has his or her arms around your neck, preventing you from saving his or her life. But it's not that easy to knock him/her unconscious when that person has his/her arms around your neck like a boxer in a clinch. He takes a deep breath and they sink. Eventually she lets go.

He moves from the rowing machine to the cross-trainer. He has never told Nancy or anybody else the truth about how Jenni died. He simply told the police that she was drunk and fell out of the dinghy when it hit something and was swept away in the dark. It turned out that it was a spring tide, which added credence to his story. He managed to seize a mooring and climb on to the deck of another boat. Jenni's bruised body was found on a sandbank at the mouth of Chichester Harbour, near Selsey, and his youth and his foolish hopes of divinity through acting were over. He told his agent he was not suited to acting. He had been shown the wonders of the earth in Rome and he had overreached himself. When he had finished university he started in Fleet Street on the paper where his father had been a sub for thirty-five years. He told nobody in the office that Burton had offered to help him with his acting career and found him an agent. He was already making a small reputation for himself as an actor.

Since Nancy died, he has found himself thinking of the moment when he took a deep breath, sank down into the freezing torrent, prised Jenni's arms from his neck and gratefully let her float away. He has no memories of her face, but he can remember the force that the certainty of death gave her. Her boyfriend Garry, described, to David's surprise, as her fiancé at the inquest, gave evidence – 'I last saw Miss Cole at three-thirty. I thought she was going away on a location shoot' – and then he sat very quietly, perhaps humiliated, too. Her parents did not speak to him, for which David was grateful. These days bereaved families issue statements, proclaiming that the victim was caring and life-enhancing. In those days, death was a reproach to all concerned.

Garry went on to direct some episodes of *Z Cars* and *Dixon of Dock Green*. On the few occasions when David saw his credits on screen, he felt the sea water closing and Jenni's insistent arms around his neck.

8

ED FINDS THAT he is summoned by Robin. Robin
observes old-fashioned protocols. He sends messages
through his Mandy, handwritten with his antique pen. He
has leather-bound folders for his correspondence, so that
he signs letters presented to him by Mandy as if he is an
ambassador signing a treaty. He favours small Wedgwood
coffee cups, decorated with those awful washed-out blue
flowers. The legal life has given him a regard for the
quaintly florid and the hand-tooled. Ed wonders how he
and his father could possibly have been friends, but he
knows they go way back to National Service. One of Robin's
men shot a Greek in Cyprus, and it was covered up. But
Dad has sworn him to silence.

Alice is away at a wedding in Scotland until Monday.
She is chief bridesmaid. The office seems to have been
drained without her vibrant presence; motes of legal dust
hang in the air, still, undisturbed, Dickensian. Ed hasn't
been to see his favourite client, Mr Fineman, and his avid
Eastern European assistant. Instead he sent Alice to prepare
the brief on the grounds that it would be good practice for
her, and of course provide him with an opportunity to closet
himself with her, their knees touching, in the conference
room, and to take an outing to Middle Temple to see the

barrister. Only once in the past week has he been able to meet her in Stoke Newington; he was very nervous, not fully reconciled to his new entitlement, at least not before he had shared a bottle of Rickety Bridge with her. She was so eager she didn't undress fully and this sexual directness excites him, but also causes him to speculate unhealthily about how someone so young gained this degree of expertise. She has absolutely no inhibition, and urged him to come on her breasts after she had come twice. She held her smallish breasts together invitingly, something like a sundae, and watched his cock curiously from her vantage point a few inches away. The knowledge of her cheerful abandon makes her neat appearance in the office deliberately provocative. Now that she is in Scotland he can see more clearly, and the prospect is disturbing. But he has told himself that his sexual prowess is being enhanced, and this will in turn help in the baby-making department. In psychology it's called transference, he thinks. Not that there is anything wrong with his sperm count, of course.

Robin says that he wants an update on the Fineman affair. He is concerned that they should be going to the High Court with something so frivolous. He is sitting in his swivel chair behind the vast desk; as he leans back to pronounce, the bottom buttons of his Turnbull & Asser shirt are subjected to pressure.

Ed reassures him that it is never going to court. The Council will buckle.

'Are you spending too much time on it?'

'Alice is handling the detail. It's good experience.'

'I've never believed in using trainees just as slaves. Delegation, while not always easy, is important.'

'I agree.'

'How's she doing?'

'She's doing well. Fineman is a tricky devil, slightly crazy, but he likes her.'

'Can he pay if it all goes tits up?'

'He's already paid into escrow.'

'Well done. How's Rosalie?'

'Rosalie? Oh she's good.'

'Lovely girl.'

'Thank you.'

'Look after her.'

'I will.'

'Oh Ed, I'm thinking of asking her to decorate and equip the flat I have bought. She has such amazing taste. Do you think she would do it? I'll pay her, of course.'

'I'm sure she would. Perhaps you should ask her yourself. She wouldn't want me to be the messenger.'

'If you think it's a good idea, I will.'

Ed looks at his watch, as if to suggest a uxorious intimacy with Rosalie's every movement. 'She'll be home by now.'

'Just one thing before you go, Ed: Alice seems rather keen on you. Don't let it get out of hand, will you? Office relationships are not a good idea.'

'There's no suggestion of that, I hope, but it is true that we do get on well.'

'Sitting where I am, metaphorically, one gets a sense of how things are and I think she may be a little too keen. I've put her on the child-support case, if that's OK with you. Colin is on holiday.'

'Absolutely fine.'

'Good. How's your father?'

'He's slightly worrying. He wears elephant-hair bracelets and spends hours in the gym.'

'He's not ill? He looked, frankly, gaunt when I saw him last.'

He says 'gaunt' with a certain distaste, as though a man at ease with the world should be plump and sleek. Like him, in fact.

'He's fine, I think. Although he denies it, Dad is missing Mum.'

'I am sure he is. We all are.'

Is Robin missing his wife, who defected with a large chunk of his money, which is the reason he has had to sell the house? Now Robin wants to be closeted with Rosalie, looking at fabric swatches and paint samples and even going on outings to select taps and soap holders and large showerheads. Robin wants to infiltrate his life and, by making him a partner, he has made his first incursion. Perhaps he has heard some of the baby-making rumours. Perhaps he thinks he could do better.

Back in his office – he now has one of his own – Ed accesses the Fineman papers. Fineman now wants to go to the European Court, encouraged by Alice. This way lies madness and bankruptcy. After a while he walks out to the square, shaded by untidy plane trees, and buys a sandwich. He rings Alice, but her phone is on message and he doesn't want to leave a message about Robin's hints. He wants to talk to her, to assure himself that the risks he has been taking are worth something. He wants her to say that she loves him. Without that, the fevered sex and the casual lying are harmful to his soul, to his true self, which is consequently in jeopardy. *I am selling myself for the careless Alice.*

Other people, carefree people, are grouped on the grass. They eat sandwiches and wraps and bags of crisps and they laugh with their colleagues and friends, sometimes friends on the end of phones. These friends are hilarious. Squirrels and pigeons wait for handouts. A tramp, a little beacon of

Dickensian despair and grime in this upbeat, besuited crowd, is drinking strong cider from a prone position on a bench. He is partly covered by a once-pink duvet. God knows what his sputum contains: he coughs with the consumptive resonances of the workhouse, so that around him there is a distinct cordon sanitaire.

Plane trees are always dropping something or other – surplus twigs, bits of bark and rough Christmas-bauble seeds – and in addition the leaves are now beginning to loosen their hold and fall in melancholy spirals to the ground, although it is still hot and sunny. Ed feels autumnal himself. He has only had sex with Alice twice, but he has been sexually active at home, half believing that there must be some biological imperative at work. He and Rosalie don't discuss cycles in detail any longer, yet they both know that this is her most fertile time and they must get on with it. When they are making love, he is aware that they have a consciousness about the act, which is quite different from the insane lust that seizes him when he is with Alice. The truth is there is something grim about sex with Rosalie, lovely as she is naked on the bed, with those long dancer's legs, firmly muscled, and the slim hips, which he loves. Even now, deep in his human essences, he knows that Rosalie is his ideal woman. Their sex is dutiful but he feels obliged to be even-handed and feigns the same intensity. He sometimes thinks of Alice's legs parting, and this, he knows, is the worst kind of betrayal.

'Golly gosh, Ed, what's got into you?'

'I'm a big swinging dick. I'm empowered. I'm a stud.'

'I've already come twice.'

'Only twice? Have some ambition, woman. Think twins, think triplets. Whole tribes. Oh my God.'

*   *   *

His phone rings. It's Alice.

'Hello, big boy, how's tricks?'

'I rang you.'

'I know. Look, I'm ringing you back. I was in the middle of a Strip the Willow practice. We bridesmaids are supposed to lead the Scottish dancing tomorrow.'

'Are you having fun?'

'It's a laugh. Men in skirts. What do you think?'

'I don't think they wear undergarments.'

'Let's hope not. I'll keep you informed. Did you ring for a specific reason, Mr Fineman, for example, or for a chit-chat?'

'I just wanted to see how you are. I miss you.'

'That's so sweet.'

But she doesn't say she is missing him.

'One thing, Alice, Robin called me in. He wants you to move to the child-support case. He hinted in passing that he thought we were a little too close.'

'Oh did he?'

'Yes.'

'And what did you say?'

'I said we got on very well, but there's nothing going on.'

'Oh.'

'What? What should I have said? Yes, we're fucking like rats but it's entirely professional?'

'It's funny, isn't it, with these old-smoothie blokes. He tries it on and gets nowhere, and now he's sniffing about. It's sad. If you are ringing to bale out, feel free.'

'Good God, no. I'm not. I just thought I should tell you.'

'Thanks anyway. See you Monday. I've got to go and do the Gay Gordons.'

'All of them?'

'Och aye, as we say up here. The whole regiment. Bye-bye.'

'Bye.'

When the phone goes dead he looks at it reproachfully for a moment as if it's concealing something from him. He feels abandoned and a little unease seeps into his stomach. She is having fun, giving him barely a thought, and he is torturing himself both with his treachery and the question of what Scotsmen wear under their kilts. He can see her doing a reel, skipping about, face slightly flushed, enjoying the attention of these solid bankers, barristers and lairds. He sees a rugby scrum of admirers, with big calf muscles and thick, sandy hair, courting her. Their faces are perhaps a little fleshy and pale in this picture, but you can't have everything. There's something clannish and heavy-shouldered about them as they do the Gay Gordons. He has never seen a Gay Gordon, but he believes he knows exactly how it works, everybody hopping and twirling and eyeing the likeliest partner, and becoming a little moist on the charcuterie cheeks. There's a determinedly conservative cast to upper-crust Scots, with their love of roast meat and their distrust of central heating and their use of the word 'aye'. Worst of all is their unsubstantiated belief that they are superior to everyone south of the border.

Under his duvet the tramp is beginning to shout. He's a Scot! He's fed up: Ed can almost see, floating in the air, the stream of *cunts, fucks, bastards* he utters, followed by inchoate threats to all who have done him wrong. Nobody takes any notice. Nobody suggests he go and take a one-way trip to a bench in Princes Street Gardens or deep-fry himself a Mars Bar and stick it up his arse. Instead they turn away to exchange those infuriatingly dismissive little English smiles, and carry on with their conversations.

On the way back to work he passes a shop selling old maps and prints, and then he sees a boy and a girl standing outside a small office building which houses a stockbroker; they are carrying signs reading: *This company supports experiments with live animals.* Their posters reveal dogs and apes wired to diabolical machinery. Both of them are wearing camouflage jackets.

The boy is speaking.

'It was like in the Depression that the rich people sold all their shares, the J.D. Rockefellers and them, so that they could buy them back cheap. They made millions. It was like a huge scam.'

The girl nods.

'Yeah, I heard that, that's like so fucking typical, isn't it?'

Three more of their colleagues turn up with pictures of dogs and monkeys wired up. They start shouting, 'Stop animal experiments.'

Two workmen in boots watch, amused: 'Fuckwits.'

Ed is inclined to agree, but he says nothing. After all he is a lawyer, a partner no less, and an adulterer. But suddenly he finds he has cheered up. It's only been a lunch break, but he has seen a rich panorama. As for Alice, maybe it will be a good thing if she falls in love with a Pict in hairy clothes, so that he can get on with the business of baby-making and wealth creation.

When he gets home, relatively early, Rosalie, too, is in a good mood. Robin has phoned to ask her round to see his new flat tomorrow. He's said his budget is over one hundred thousand pounds. She will get fifteen per cent. Also, she thinks – actually, she knows – that she is pregnant.

Like the French, the English now believe that a good meal is the only way to celebrate all significant occasions in life's journey. He suggests a restaurant.

'What are the signs?' he asks, without wishing to sound sceptical.

'I'm overdue, and my nipples feel funny,' she says.

The state of the nipples is the clincher. The minute examination of her physical changes is intimately tied to her mental state, which is mercurial. The question is, which comes first?

Later at the restaurant she says no to champagne, her face severe, because of her condition. Just as he's finishing off a glass of Pol Roger, she says, 'Oh no,' very quietly.

'What?'

'It's started.'

For a moment he thinks she is in labour.

'My period.'

She's crying now, just a few delicate drops. He feels irritated, which is the wrong response, and unsettling.

'Let's go home, darling. I'll explain that you're not well.'

'I'm perfectly OK.'

'You know what I mean.'

'Crazy? Mentally unstable?'

'Darling. No, no. Not at all. I just mean I would make an excuse.'

'Make an excuse for your wife who is so loopy that she cries when she can't have a baby. What a weak, silly fool. She must be excused. And of course you must never look bad in public.'

She stands up; he's not sure whether she is leaving or going to the Ladies'. With relief he sees that she is heading that way. One day he walked in there by mistake and saw two young women kissing deeply. It was an erotic image, which lingered. One of them winked at him as they passed to their table. He sits alone and uneasy. Eventually Rosalie returns, her face now composed, even philosophical. A sort of fatalistic serenity has seized her, so that she looks as if she is just an anonymous worshipper in a religious procession, although, of course, she is alone. She often needs to concentrate on a role to make sense of her life. When that is fixed, she is comforted. This is the artiste's life, necessarily tragic.

'Sorry,' she says. 'Sorry, darling, I was unfair.'

'We're in this together, Rosie.'

'Are we?'

'You know we are.'

He holds her two hands over the small vase of anemones in the middle of the table. Her hands are very cold although the restaurant is warm, throbbing with human life.

'Are you all right?'

She moves her lips to form a small kiss, and nods. The kiss is the sort of impersonal blessing a holy person might convey on the laity. Why is he thinking in these religious terms these days? None of the family, except for Uncle Guy, is religious; he writes long, quasi-mystical letters from the bush. He left England soon after Dad became a television face, possibly unable to bear the thought that his younger brother had become undeservedly famous. In those days, apparently, television was regarded with awe, the viewers treasuring the gifts of enlightenment it brought.

Meanwhile, Rosalie is suffering in silence, chewing unconvincingly on a premature artichoke, done in the Italian style on a grill and accompanied by some broad beans, all full of goodness; twenty minutes ago, when she ordered, Rosalie was thinking trace elements. Now she accepts a glass of champagne, its celebratory function ignored in favour of its tranquillising properties. They order the rest of the bottle. By the time they leave the restaurant, Rosalie has lost some of her severity and most of her dancer's poise, and her feet seem to be making unusually clumsy contact with the pavement outside the Wolseley. In truth they are both drunk.

She forgets the rituals, which involve creams and rigorous hair brushing, and slides into bed fully dressed. Ed finds himself worrying that the life will be crushed out of her favourite dress, the gravity-defying flower print (perhaps fuchsias), which contains a suggestion of Never Never Land, and he slips it off her. Her hair is spread over the pillows.

He goes down to the kitchen and opens a beer, although he knows he will pay a price. Rosalie has already begun to think about the possibility of in vitro fertilisation although Mr Smythson had said it would happen naturally. Lucy told him. Lucy is a good listener and encourages other people to be indiscreet by her apparent interest. He turns on the television and watches tennis from New York, where of course it is still late afternoon. A very tall Slovak called Daniela Hantuchova is killing the ball with elegant disdain. She's probably an economic migrant, like Mr Fineman's assistant, but on a much higher economic plane.

This little house, a hen coop really, was supposed to be the family home, a refuge, a haven for a small but plucky family, which would expand and prosper. The reality is that he is lying, idly lustful, on an Ikea sofa, watching Daniela Hantuchova, while his wife, reproachful even in sleep, lies in the marital bed, unhappy that she is being denied a child because of his inadequacy where it counts. And his mistress – if two sexual encounters really qualify – is stripping the willow in some draughty old pile in the Highlands. Her mind is on kilts; the lardy faces are closing.

He has another beer and then two paracetamols.

He wonders about the deal he has made with life. Is he a lawyer in his essences? Is he a family man whose only wish is to produce children and nurture them for twenty-five years and make sure they go to good schools and learn to ski and play the fucking oboe and get into Oxford? There's something faintly fanatical about Rosalie and her determination to have children. He can already picture himself in the clinic again, passing his sperm sample through the hatch, and, he thinks – although of course he is drunk – that maybe he could make a run for it with Alice. But then he's not sure Alice sees him as anything more than a diversion.

And now he wishes Mum were still here with her sensibly ordered universe, which accompanied her wherever she went. He knows that life is not other than the one we live, but he wishes it were.

9

SOMETIMES YOU LOOK at the place you live in and think happily about its possibilities: a new kitchen, all granite and squeaky-clean implements and ovens that never get dirty and subdued lighting, which demonstrates your command of stylish living and material goods, although you treat such things in an ironic fashion. And at other times you look at the place and think, This rat-trap should be condemned, with its ingrained dirt and a stove that looks like something that's fallen out of an old tractor. Everything in Lucy's kitchen is – and always has been – heavily greased like a Channel swimmer. A pigeon sits on the window ledge, watching her knowingly as she makes coffee. This pigeon is obese because Lucy leaves bits of bread and sometimes rice or pasta for it. It no longer flies anywhere; it has no incentive to forage. She thinks it is probably diabetic and depressed, although it gives every impression of contentment. The only time it stirs itself is when another pigeon tries to make a landing on the ledge: then it uses its impressive bulk to intimidate. Lucy opens the window a fraction and pushes out some muesli. The bird pecks at it without standing up; soon it will be like a battery hen, with splayed, useless legs.

Viewed from a neutral standpoint, Ed's, for instance, her

relationship with Josh undoubtedly has comic aspects. But for her it is living proof of her lack of clearly defined principles. When Mum was still here Lucy could measure herself against her mother's unbending standards, which included housekeeping and tidiness. Rejecting them was in itself reassuring. Now that Mum has gone she has very arbitrary standards, and of course arbitrary standards are not standards at all. On the one hand she's happy to be free of the guilt her mother could invoke without trying – she had no need to try – and, on the other, she feels guilty that she is not living up to her mother's expectations. It's a muddle, a moral shambles.

Mum died neatly and uncomplaining, although deeply distressed at the unimaginable prospect of never seeing her family again. A few days before she died she whispered, in the voice the drugs had made thin and at the same time rasping, 'Look after Dad. He needs it, even though he won't show it.'

Was this true, or a self-serving idea that Dad's detachment sprang from a kind of hidden need? On the face of it, he needed Mum less than she would have liked. But what your parents really think is forever a mystery. In the secret mesh of their lives, in the intricacies of their history, which included the production of two children, they must have suffered small wounds and developed instinctive understanding, like those climbing plants she learned about in biology which intuitively know how to find support. Did they have affairs? She doesn't know. Were they sexually at ease? She doesn't know. Sometimes she got the impression that Mum was impressed by Dad's celebrity; although she said, 'Oh, he just reads off the autocue,' she knew that there was far more to it than that. He had a charm and an authority that reassured people. And some of his special reports made a huge difference to the public perception. One was his story of an Iraqi girl who had lost her whole family of fourteen in a bombing raid and was sitting with her mother's body when the camera found her. Dad does not often speak about the horrors he has reported, but he said to her, 'Look, anyone with a cameraman who found that girl could have done the story. It wasn't me that made it a tragedy. I wasn't writing a novel.' Now, in his lean, ascetic reincarnation, he seems to be happy to be leaving the public consciousness.

The problem with Josh, she thinks, is that he has a very ungenerous soul. When you become intimate with another, when your bodies are doing irrational and strange things, your lips devouring, your tongues entwining and so on, you are actually giving that person not only access to your body, but to your soul. But sex for Josh is a form of recreation devised solely for his benefit: it has no deeper meaning than ping-pong. Its only aim is to gratify him. He is the hero of their sexual encounters, he's the narrator of his own epic. When he came round to the house and demanded to be let in and more or less obliged her to have sex, because she didn't want Dad intervening if there was a row, she felt demeaned. She wanted to say he was using her, but she was sensitive to the soap-opera banality of the phrase. In the morning, as soon as she heard Dad go to the gym, she woke Josh, sleeping noisily, and kicked him out despite his protests.

'You're in love with your father. It's sad,' he said in that pompous and complacent way of his.

'Oh just fuck off. This is it. The end.'

'You wanted sex last night.'

'I didn't, actually. I only allowed it because I didn't want to scream rape and wake Dad.'

Now she is without a man again. In logic, women don't require a man in order to exist, but in practice, as all women know, there are powerful old-world currents involved, which are difficult to swim against. A lot of this turbulence is created by women themselves. They will listen to men lecturing them, they will accept men's relentless self-promotion or men's explaining things they already understand, and they will in some minor ways submit; they do it because they don't want to be alone. It is a perennial belief that women without men are incomplete. Like so much else that is widely believed, it is untrue. It is a time of transition. Rationality – she thinks of those doctor bombers at the airport – is no longer winning. Ethics are unclear. History no longer has a purpose. Public service is discredited. Instead, gestures – supermarket credos, slogans and infantilism – are everywhere. A man who wants to have a proper relationship should understand these things: he should open his soul to you and want to enter yours. Of course you can't use this kind of highfalutin language in a time of simplification, but you would recognise a generous spirit when you found one, that's for sure. With Josh she found an empty vessel, although he is good-looking and, for someone who drinks so much beer, in good shape. She has formed a separate relationship with his cock, and she may miss that. It's like the relationship you might have with a simple-minded Labrador or a seal. Also, she and Josh made a good-looking couple; arriving at dinners or parties together, she was aware that they made a strong impression. At first she enjoyed it but soon she realised he was always talking a little too insistently, underbriefed and half-informed, and she was embarrassed and tried to intervene to save him from himself. When it became clear to Josh that she thought he was a 'dipstick', she tried emollience: 'No, not at all. I just thought maybe you were going on too long. They were all too drunk or stupid to keep up.'

'Brilliant. And when you were banging on about fucking Roman coins, they were like totally entranced? I don't think so.'

At Grimaldi she has applied herself determinedly to the cataloguing of the early Christian Roman coins for the sale, and was complimented by the head of antiquities and classical artefacts, Rachel Owen Jones, who is a ferociously serious person with wild, twisty Celtic hair, that would have ornamented a warrior queen, although she herself is extremely composed, with the sort of fluting voice and over-enunciated vowels which experts seem to acquire. Experts and serious musicians.

The pigeon is settling itself down, as if it deserves a good rest, plumping up its feathers and cooing happily. Perhaps it wants to show its approval of the conservation-grade muesli. Outside a few unregulated trees are shedding their leaves. If the garden below were hers, she would regulate the trees. These town gardens need form and structure. You don't want a cat's lavatory with self-seeded trees for a garden.

The coins of Constantine the Great demonstrate his political and religious paths, Rachel says. You can see the exact year he adopted the chi-rho, the shepherd's-crook version of the cross, as he understood the political importance of instituting Christianity in the empire. He sent his old mum Helena to Jerusalem, and she came back with the True Cross. She was herself what we would now call a Serb or a Croat, and an innkeeper's daughter, a woman with a past. She ordered the demolition of the Temple of Venus, which stood on the site of the crucifixion, and she ordered the building of the Church of the Holy Sepulchre. Modern research shows that the Holy Sepulchre is in fact built on the true site of the crucifixion. Constantine forbade crucifixion and replaced it with leisurely hanging. You can trace lines in history: nothing comes from nothing, says Rachel, but of course she says it in Latin: *ex nihilo nihil fit*.

Ed rings.

'Josh is upset. He says you are being unfair.'

'Josh is upset? Oh dear. Why have you been appointed his spokesman? Although, to come to think of it, it's better than talking to him myself.'

'He says he loves you.'

'What's that supposed to mean?'

'This is as far as I can go, Luce, without putting my finger down my throat. I'll tell him you said piss off.'

'Good. Succinct.'

'What are you up to?'

'I'm having an exciting evening at home communing with my pigeon and thinking about Helena, mother of Constantine. I've been writing catalogue descriptions of early Christian Roman coins.'

'Different strokes for different folks. Do you want me to bring round some takeaway?'

'Where's the lovely Rosalie?'

'Why do you always say "the lovely Rosalie" like that? As it happens the lovely Rosalie is giving a dance class – don't laugh – to Congolese orphans. Or perhaps they are Zambian.'

'Just what they need, tutus in the jungle. Come round. I'll lay the table.'

'Right. I'll be about forty minutes and I'll bring some chicken tikka and strong drink.'

'Great, let's get smashed.'

She suddenly feels elated, as if the pigeon and Helena have been holding her back. She tidies up and lays the table and even runs down the road to the underground to catch the flower-seller, a deranged but harmless woman who chain-smokes in a wooden hut. She is restlessly confined in this small cell of gaudy flowers and plastic buckets; Lucy has the sense that she is tethered there, like a dog in a kennel. She buys a mixed bunch, all that's left, carnations, gerberas and chincherinchees all miscegenating happily; when she gets home again she throws out the carnations and loosens the bunch and sticks it artlessly in a jug, where it looks good: *We English with our petty snobberies, which extend even to flowers*.

Ed's late. But then he's always late, always distracted by something. Eventually he buzzes from below.

'Hello, it's me.'

'Hey, it's the legal hotshot. Come on up.'

She can hear his progress as he comes up the two flights.

'Sorry, sorry, I had to speak to one of my clients. I couldn't get him off the phone. His wife has withdrawn all the money from their savings account and gone, and he thinks this may be a bad sign.'

'I'm no expert, but it sounds like it.'

'It does, doesn't it? Now to important matters. This chicken may need heating.'

'I've already fired up the oven.'

She loves him. He's come because he wants to talk to her. His eyes are dark. They seem darker than she remembers them. How is this? He has changed out of his office suit and wears jeans and large trainers, but his Jermyn Street shirt, with knotted-silk cufflinks, diminishes the intended effect. As he leans forward to unpack the fragrant chicken tikka, she sees that his hair is thinning a little at the crown. His features, a slightly less defined version of Dad's, are beginning to bunch under the forces that life is exerting. Soon the kitchen fills with a dense aroma. Domestic aromas are usually missing from this kitchen. Instead it has the aroma of apathy, which is perhaps more a psychological notion than something real. Ed opens a bottle of good wine: *good wine* is one of his recent lawyerly affectations.

'How's Rosie?' she asks.

'She's getting a little desperate.'

'No signs yet?'

'No, not a thing.'

'I'm sure it will happen. I just know it.'

'Mum used to say that sort of thing, but usually it was just a kind of comforting thing.'

'I'm sure it will. I'm not just saying it.'

'That's a relief.'

'No, I mean it.'

'The trouble is the whole thing begins to take over your life. Shagging becomes something totally different.'

'Too much information.'

'Sorry, but I mean that it's just that Rosie's becoming preoccupied.'

'Why are children the be-all and end-all?'

'It's not just about children. We can't have a normal conversation any more. Everything we say seems to have another meaning. I find myself becoming completely fucking stilted.'

'You'll get over this. You know what Mum would have said.'

'It all comes out in the wash?'

'Yes.'

'I miss her wit and wisdom.'

'So do I. But it upsets me that Dad seems so, I don't know, sort of . . .'

'Detached?'

'Yes, deliberately detached.'

It seems unfair that she and Ed should still have a strong sense of loss while Dad has little or none. What she and Ed want is in some way to cling on to her, even as her presence fades and is replaced by phrases and incidents remembered for no good reason. And maybe we are worried because it suggests that our lives are just a kind of flare in the dark. She looks closely at Ed, who is noisily propelling the wine round his mouth to make absolutely sure that it is up to standard while sitting sideways on an armchair, his legs hanging over one side.

'What's bugging you, Ed?'

'What do you mean?'

'You didn't come just for my company, brilliant though I am.'

'Nothing. I'm fine.'

'Oh dear. I know you.'

'Rosie's out and I just thought I would call in.'

'What is it?'

'Do you really want to know?'

'Yes.'

'This business with Rosie and the sperm count and so on is getting me down.'

'And?'

'And now my new best mate Robin is beginning to get up my nose, too.'

'In what way?'

'He sort of thinks he's got me where he wants me because I've taken the shilling. He's in love with Rosie. He's asked her to help decorate his bachelor flat, which he calls a pad. And he's interfering with my assistant.'

'The perky one with the short skirts?'

'What are you saying?'

'*Moi*? Nothing. I'm like just asking.'

'You more or less accused me of banging her.'

'Are you?'

'Oh Jesus. Of course I'm not.'

'You are, you devil. You are. Admit it: you'll feel better.'

'Please, Lucy. What happened was, OK, we had a one-night stand. It was a mistake, nothing; I was a little overexcited by being made a partner. You had one.'

'What?'

'You told me you had a one-nighter.'

'Ed, there's a big difference. I'm not married. Does this bimbo say she loves you?'

'She doesn't even like me, I don't think.'

'Ah, now I see.'

'What do you see?'

He pours himself another glass.

'I see why you came round. You want me to give you a Mum-style blessing for your folly.'

'I know you won't tell anybody, but do you swear?'

'Of course. Who am I going to tell? Rosalie, Dad?'

'And I haven't come for your blessing, by the way.'

'It's called transference. You're trying to replace Mum with me.'

'Bollocks. Don't overestimate my affection for you. I'm seriously thinking of looking for another job.'

'Already? Oh shit, the chicken's burning.'

She gets it out of the oven and spoons it on to plates. It's only lightly charred. Ed drinks a little too deeply.

'Ed, maybe you should give it another few months, seeing Robin is Dad's pal.'

'I won't do anything silly. I'll just put out feelers.'

She sinks on to the stained carpet and sits holding his

leg against her cheek. Like Mum, she thinks, I am in thrall to some very unfashionable instincts, for instance, unthinking love, even hero worship, for my older brother.

'Ed, do you think Josh is a wanker?'

'I don't have any empirical evidence of his personal habits, but as a metaphor, wanker may be a little too kind. Forget him.'

'Oh good, all settled then. The adulterous brother and his spinster sister.'

'They're lining up for you, pumpkin. You are almost certainly one of the most attractive young women in early Christian coinage, I'm sure.'

'You're such a shit. You unburden yourself on me, and then you let me have it.'

'You know that's not true. I trust you and – listen, because I may never say it again – I love you not just as a little sister but as a truly lovely human soul.'

'Oh – my – God, is this what marital infidelity has done to your brain?'

'I told you to listen, now it's too late. You're annoying me.'

She sees that he is deeply shaken by his one-night stand – usually a few more than one in her experience – and he needs to demonstrate to somebody that he has a capacity for loyalty, that he is really a decent person. Perhaps, as much as anything, he needs to hear himself say it. She looks up at him. It's a strangely unfamiliar view, like looking from ground level at the enormous statue of Constantine on the Capitoline, from where the great emperor's nostrils are cavernous. Constantine had once lived in York but she found this difficult to believe when she first read about him: York sounded too damp to have been part of the Roman Empire.

'You've got hairs in your nose.'

'Everyone has. Now you really are turning into Mum.'

'Oscar Wilde?'

'Is that the one about every woman's tragedy . . . et cetera?'

He defers to her in matters of culture.

'Yep. That's the one, *The Importance of Being Earnest*.'

'I thought so.'

'Of course you did.'

'I hate Oscar Wilde.'

'Why?'

'It's just that he is not half as funny as people think he is. It's all camp bitchery.'

'Are you homophobic?'

'Of course I'm not homophobic. I like individual gays or dislike them in exactly the same way I like or dislike individual straight people. And by the way, you are not homophobic just because you don't warm to the idea of putting your cock up another man's bum.'

'I don't think they do that any more.'

Their conversation goes on in erratic leaps as they eat. She thinks that a transcript would make very little sense, but what a transcript could not reveal is the human texture, which they both crave. She knows that her hotshot brother, in his very clean trainers, has come for just this, the meaningless provocations, the loaded exchanges, the sense that they are of one flesh with a shared understanding.

When he leaves, rising quickly in response to Rosalie's phone call, Lucy feels that she has been revived. She thinks of those desert ticks that lie in the dust and can be dormant for years, disguised as pebbles, until a mammal breathes on them. Ed's revived her. But she feels a little unease.

Naturally she's on his side, with blind loyalty, but she can't help fearing what will happen to him and to Rosalie. The lovely Rosalie. When her mother died, she realised with surprise that the world is not at all stable. She remembers a line – *the strange disappointment which overcasts every human youth* – which is sobering: the bloom of youth fades too soon. She found it in a package of spiritual-transcendental nonsense from her father's brother Guy, sent from the back of beyond, part of a campaign to woo Dad away from excessive worldliness. Or success.

10

DAVID IS RUNNING on the Life Force treadmill.

He remembers that, before she turned to Pilates, Nancy used to say that her mantras helped her to think calmly. In Sanskrit, she said, 'mantra' simply meant an aid to thinking, what the newspapers these days call a brain workout. David finds running an aid to thinking, although the value of his thoughts is unclear. After her affair, he found himself unable to see Nancy clearly. Now he feels he can inhabit her mind, as if he's moved into a vacated house. She was desperately lonely while he was travelling to the Congo and Israel and Washington; she was young and needed some respite from the children. A former boyfriend provided it. When the Dutch au pair, Marjamiek, told him on her last day before going back to Aalsmeer that Nancy had been seeing a friend of theirs, he deliberately cauterised his feelings for the sake of the children. It took a determined effort of the will never to bring the subject up, never to confront Nancy. He couldn't anyway take the high ground, although by comparison his occasional encounters in different countries with an assistant producer from NBC were casual misdemeanours, and when she said she wanted him to come and live in the US, he told her he wouldn't ever see her again. Although he and Nancy were friendly and even affectionate, the only way he could maintain his silence was to avoid exposing his soul to her, the person he had loved. He sometimes thought he should have had it out with her, but he remembered too vividly his own parents' desperate, choked rows, caused — he understood much later — by his father's adultery, rows which had blighted his childhood, and he felt that he could not inflict that on his innocent children in turn. More than anything, he wanted to avoid the sordid banality of the recriminations; he remembered his mother shouting in the middle of the night, 'If you don't get rid of your fancy woman, you'll see the back of me.' He wasn't sure what she was saying, but he suspected it meant he would soon be an orphan.

After a year or more he found that the pain of Nancy's affair had passed, but the detachment had become a habit of mind. Perhaps typically, he believed his willed blindness had given him some inner strength. He thought of Burton, who believed in the possibility of divine qualities on earth. He had a fear of bringing vengefulness or even contempt into his relationship with Nancy. He became a poor lover, but he believed it was because sex and love were too closely allied in his mind.

The reading group has suggested that he read for ten minutes from his book on Afghanistan under the Taliban — *To Afghanistan in a Burkha* — and then talk about his career. He hasn't been to a book club for at least four years and wonders what Sylvie and her pals want from him. As he runs, he feels a familiar nervousness. In all his years as newsman, every new assignment, every day in the studio started with a little nervousness. Politicians with their conceits and evasions made him pleasantly nervous: he couldn't wait to drive a hole through their strategies for coping with an interview. In his last five years, they were all coached to say good morning and to appear utterly reasonable in the face of provocation. But he usually knew what message they were trying to deliver and what they were trying to hide. Under Blair they had become aware that staying on message, any message, was the way to get promotion; Dr Johnson talked about *the unnumbered suppliants crowding Preferment's Gate*. He doesn't know what Sylvie and her book group are hiding. Book clubs, he thinks, are cover for the myriad longings and disappointments of female life. Women have a far stronger sense than men of what life might have been.

He's running very easily as he passes the 5-km mark. From where the weightlifters are flexing or walking about, yawing as if they have just stepped ashore, he knows that he must look a little ridiculous, perhaps even obsessive, but still he finds satisfaction in his fitness and the lightness of his tread as though he alone may escape life's gravitational pull. Actually, he doesn't want to divide his life into phases, for example, the years of promise, the years of success, the years of reflection, the years of decline. As he zips along, like a dragonfly over a river, he sees that the important phases of his life correspond not to his age or his success, but to a personal barometer of his moral worth. How pious that would sound if he ever articulated it! He smiles as he runs: in the privacy of your own consciousness you can say and think whatever you want to. When he left Rome, Jenni attached to him with the sensuous, slightly sinister insistence of a python, he was in a froth of youthful hubris. He, like his new friend Richard Burton, could avoid many of life's constraints. The little people, the small-minded, the unambitious, made the coils that held them back.

And I believed it.

His feet are barely touching the rolling track of the treadmill. His own life force is strong. Ashley told him that these machines cost nine thousand pounds each, a fantastic amount of money when you think you could run around the streets for nothing. Many people do: girls with bottles of water and headsets and a grim determination; men of all the physical types that you could imagine. Only children never run, perhaps not yet feeling the existential pressures. Many of them are anyway far too fat to break into a trot.

It's not that easy to stay upright as you approach maximum speed while pressing the LCD arrows. He finishes every run with a minute at full speed, 16.5 km per hour. His footfall is not so light now; his feet pound the rolling track. He is breathing heavily, gulping, as he finally slows. After Jenni was buried he returned to Oxford only long enough to pack his things and say goodbye to his tutor and some friends. He was given compassionate leave, and went back six months later, chastened, but more determined. He hardly left his rooms for two years. Adam had left by then: he was two years ahead because he avoided National Service on medical grounds.

He does some light exercise on the cross-trainer; it's firming his chest although his nipples remain obdurately puckered. Some of his friends have become monumental, with slabs of flesh on their chests. Their faces have assumed an imposing density, with floes of flesh jostling and competing. He aspires to be light and lean.

Ashley is inducting a woman into the mysteries of the machines. She has a helmet of bleached hair and is as rounded as a seal. Now he explains to her how the cross-trainer works: quick start, programmes, levels of achievement, heart rate, et cetera.

But she is not listening; she is intent on telling him about her domestic arrangements.

'Then he fucking come home and pulls the fucking blinds down what I only paid for with me allowance. And then he pissed, can yer believe it, right on the fitted carpet, 'e's that drunk. Fuck me, 'e'sananimal.'

Ashley continues, 'And when you is settin' the programme you like enter your weight here,' and she says, 'And then in the fuckin' morning he only says I'm a slapper and where's me bacon an'eggs.'

'Now you start this one. Press here, like this, and I'll be back in five minutes to see how you're gettin' on.'

'Talkin' of slappers, 'is daughter, she's what I call a right slapper. She brung some bloke round at four in the morning, old enough to be her dad 'e was, they was at it like fuckin' rabbits, screamin' and shoutin' and movin' the fuckin' furniture about. It's a fuckin' madhouse. That's why I joined the gym, to get some fuckin' peace.'

Ashley pushes the button and sets the machine in motion. His smile has a glazed quality now. David winks at him as he turns away but the woman, alert to insult, spots him.

'What you winkin' at, you cunt?'

'Sorry, nothing, I've got blepharitis. I can't help it.'

'You're that cunt off of the telly, ain'tcher?'

'That's me.'

'Well you can fuck off an' all.'

As he jogs home he feels enriched by these encounters. While he was waiting in blank corridors to interview maniacs and tyrants, he had neglected to notice what was going on in his own parish. This crazy rant is how some Londoners have always spoken. Although Dickens gave them the sentimental treatment, he was aware of the underlying desperation and fear: he felt it himself. This is the authentic voice – one of many – of the people, this welling of grievance, obscenity and self-pity. England's golden age of politeness and deference and honesty was brief and probably mythical. At Global they prepared stories on the problem of lawlessness and out-of-control teenagers and mindless crimes of violence and schoolgirl pregnancy with relish, but they never suggested that in large swathes of the country this was perfectly acceptable, even traditional. In his experience, depraved behaviour is often the norm. One of his stories from Iraq was about the growing culture of pornography. He was the first to make the connection between the soldiers who thought pornography was harmless fun and the humiliation of Iraqis in the jails. These soldiers were pissing themselves laughing at the pictures of towel-heads pretending to give each other blow jobs; the soldiers were sending their hilarious holiday snaps to their pals, as you might send a picture of a bridegroom handcuffed, trouserless, to a lamp post in Prague on a stag night. At Global, stories were always rated first and foremost as a form of entertainment. Torture was understood to be voyeurism and so usually found its way to the top of the running order if there were good pictures to go with it.

He jogs up through Kentish Town. When he speaks to Sylvie and her friends he won't tell them the truth about his experiences. They want to hear about the glamour and the excitement, the world leaders he has met. What they don't want is an account of the endless waiting, the compromises, the hordes of desperate people in dusty hopeless places, the faked seriousness, the manipulation of figures . . .

The streets are anticipating winter: they already have a defensive look – they crouch. The bricks of the Victorian houses are streaked with mineral salts; the trees have lost their vitality. But he feels renewed, as though he is ecstatically in tune with the seasons and the place. He wonders if he isn't going mad. If he is, he doesn't mind. Ed has a theory that he is missing Nancy more than he realises, so Lucy says. In fact the feeling he has is one of relief, as though now that she's gone he can love her memory without reserve, as once he loved her. All those resentments he felt when he heard that she had once taken the small children with her to her lover's house have been dissolved. He feels free. Nancy spun little myths around the family, and he didn't try to resist them, but now he is released from his contract. You don't understand the notion of necessary fictions when you are young, but it is one most people embrace fervently when they know they are dying.

Sylvie lives in a flat in a tall Victorian Gothic house on the upslope of Highgate Hill. Near it is an enormous, apparently deserted, Catholic church. The Catholics don't have good church architecture. As he rings the bell, a large, pockmarked brass dinner plate, he hears the dog Wolfie barking.

'David? Come in, come in, first floor, I'll meet you on the landing.'

The door lock snaps open and he pushes his way into the hall, which has a floor of brown and green tiles, an ecclesiastical look. It doesn't suggest intimacy of feeling. The dog bounds down the stairs ahead of Sylvie, who is waiting above, wearing a long olive-green skirt, with a border of red flowers, and a thin cotton jumper. Her hair is frothing wildly on her shoulders. Her breasts are under a stricter regime than when he met her on the Heath. The dog stops barking and wags its tail. He pats it on its head, which feels greasy and rough.

'Oh, look at you, right here,' Sylvie says.

'Yes, I am here. Thanks for asking me.'

'Oh pur-lease. Come up. We're all present. It's the best turnout we've ever had. May I?'

She kisses him on both cheeks. She smells delightfully of fruits and something more mysterious, perhaps the essences of health-giving plants: that cataract of hair must require a lot of nurturing. He follows behind her up the faded carpet. Her fluent hips are at his eye level and the procession suggests a certain calculation. She flings open the door and he sees ten or twelve people standing to meet him as if at a surprise party.

Holding his arm lightly, Sylvie says, 'Dedah – dedah – David Cross,' and he shakes hands all round.

There seem to be only two men. He knows that these book clubs are usually made up either of married people or singles, with hardly any crossover. And he guesses that these are singles. He knows, too, how they see him: a representative of a charmed world, of a life lived out under lights, a man of wide acquaintance, who has sat down with presidents and dictators and crossed borders in trucks loaded chaotically with gunmen, and who has seen huge events from the evacuation of Saigon to the inauguration of Nelson Mandela. It's true, but from these experiences, what simple wisdom can he squeeze? Not much, except perhaps the understanding that people everywhere are in thrall to delusion. And also that the balance has changed: huge industrial empires and well-equipped armies can be challenged by small groups of people who have fallen in love with the absolute. But these ladies – they are coming into focus now – and the two men, want to hear his tales without necessarily requiring him to place them in a philosophical context.

Sylvie pours him some red wine, which he sips. He is her catch and she is going to stick pretty close. She guides him with one of her long hands. Her hands, he sees, are always active; they accompany what she says with complementary gestures. Also, her hands are quite rough, probably from dog management. Quite soon he has some names and some occupations. One woman works for the BBC in costume design and he sees that her clothes have a romantic leaning: a large silk flower is attached to her bosom and her orange hooped earrings are dramatic. Another says she is a lifelong admirer of his work, and also Sylvie's oldest friend. She is a garden designer; he wonders if he should ask her to take a look at No.9 Inverdale Terrace before he sells. They seem to be about forty, or perhaps a little younger.

One of the men, who in profile has a strangely elongated face like the figures in an Egyptian painting, and a small goatee (which makes his face look even longer), shakes his hand.

'They don't make them like you any more,' he says, echoing Ted, David's driver. He seems to be suggesting that in this respect they have something in common. He is, he says, a life coach. His name is Glynn. David resists the temptation to ask what life coaching entails, because he suspects the answer will be very long, and will concern life choices and positive vibes and tips on how to cope with bereavement. Snacks are passed around. The vogue for elegant and exotic canapés has not yet reached this part of town: the snacks are rough-hewn. There is a large bowl of hummus with some celery sticks to use as cutlery, rolls of salami pierced by cocktail sticks, some prunes wrapped in bacon, smallish smoked-salmon triangles and plenty of nuts.

'There's more in the kitchen. We all made something, except the blokes, of course,' says Sylvie.

'How often do you meet?'

'Oh, about once a month. It's difficult with half-term and so on for some of us. But I don't have children.'

Sylvie gives him this last information as if to indicate that she, like him, is a free spirit.

'Only the dog,' she adds. 'I'll just make sure everybody has something to drink and we'll start.'

He is seated in a deep armchair, so that he has to look up to those on the wildly assorted seats. He reads an episode from his autobiography, about how he and a cameraman with a very small camera were smuggled from Pakistan into Afghanistan wearing burkhas:

We had chosen a relatively quiet crossing point at a village called Anyoor Ada, but even at this hour the road was busy and there were trucks passing with Taliban in their black turbans everywhere. In fact, black turbans are not their uniform, but commonly worn with the traditional dress that the Taliban favour.

As our truck crossed the border, I looked at Rick, crouching demurely in his burkha, and I thought this is going to be a very undignified way to die. The burkhas were itchy and the visibility from within limited, but I could see Taliban everywhere, searching buses, pulling young men out of cars. I heard a gunshot and saw a man dressed in a turban and a *chupa*, a loose coat, crawling on the ground, blood pouring from under his turban. If we had had any illusions about how dangerous this crossing was, we quickly lost them. After some heart-stopping moments we were waved through and our contacts took us on what seemed like an interminable drive to a house enclosed by a mud-walled courtyard, a *sura*, where we slept the night uneasily under goatskin blankets. The problem, we discovered, was that many small biting insects already lived uninvited in the skins.

I wondered, as we were roused before dawn, if I was really up to this. Rick, like all cameramen, was certain that in some mysterious way he would be protected by his camera, which he had been cleaning in the night by candlelight. That night, I didn't share his confidence. We set off as the dawn rose over the mountains, which were at first hazy and delicately coloured, quickly to turn to a uniform harsh brown, and I remembered that in 1873 the British had come this way and encountered people dressed in the same costume. In the end the small British garrison that was left behind was massacred, months after the British proclaimed that they had conquered the lawless south. This is not a country, I thought, which plays by, or cares for, our rules.

A few days later when we filmed women whipped for some minor infringement of the law or executed for adultery, kneeling in the penalty area of the National Football Stadium in Kabul, I was sick inside my burkha. I wondered then why we were becoming involved. The idea that we could bring order and Western values to this place was absurd. Even the phrase, 'Western values', was ridiculous. And the smell of vomit was choking me. I felt that possibly there was something symbolic about this, but I couldn't quite articulate what it was.

He finds that as he recalls the three wretched women being forced to kneel while a Taliban fanatic reads the sentence

147

and the women are shot in the head with a pistol, one by one, watched by a large crowd in the stands, that he cannot go on for a few moments. Sylvie watches him anxiously, until he composes himself. If we come out of this alive, he remembers thinking, we will have an astonishingly powerful piece of video. He explains to the book club, who are appalled by the detail, almost panic-stricken, that he and the cameraman stood high in the stands to film and late that night by the light of a kerosene lamp he recorded his famous piece to camera, which began, 'Today I have seen what no man should see . . .' It was immediately taken across the border to Quetta and sent by satellite to Global.

'People said that we changed the world's attitude to the Taliban. I have to tell you that Rick Matthews, my cameraman, died two years later in the Sudan, when a mine blew up the vehicle he was travelling in. I miss him still.'

He is aware of how easily he is able to pause and look at them for dramatic effect.

'Any questions?'

Glynn, the life coach, speaks.

'Would you say that it is true that you are a kind of voyeur when it comes to executions? You describe three such occasions in the book, as I recall.'

'That's a seriously dumb question, Glynn. David has reported from all over the world on all sorts of things,' says Sylvie.

'Yuh, but isn't this book a little negative? A little doomy? There's lots of good things going on in the world if you know where to look, but somehow the positive vibe always gets neglected. It's all yobbos and youth crime and benefit fraud and so on.'

But the mood is against Glynn.

'It's OK, Sylvie. I'll answer, if I can. In forty years of

news, first as a print journalist and then as a television correspondent, it is absolutely true that things changed. Now, twenty-four-hour news is obsessed with holding the audience. Where I finished my career, at Global, they perfected the technique of holding the audience, so that sensation, shark attacks, celebrity scandal, child kidnap and so on – *coming next* – were used to hold the viewers over the break. The old idea of informing and educating the public – so the argument ran – was OK when you had the audience tied to one or two channels, but now commercial survival depended on keeping your audience. Those who wanted serious information, they said, knew where to find it in newspapers or on the Internet. As for the executions, I see them as the ultimate expression of man's inhumanity to man. Somehow the problem of evil never goes away. It's like a subclinical virus, ready to break out when the conditions are right.'

How fluently he can still justify and explain. There's nothing intellectual about it, merely a kind of mimesis. For all those years he has assimilated the weasel words, the easy hypocrisies. He doesn't tell them what was in his heart: the reality of Afghanistan incorporates the smell of mutton fat, the twisted mulberry trees in the *suras*, the perfume of melons so evocative that the Mogul Emperor Babur wept whenever he was brought one, because it reminded him of his beloved Kabul – the looming mountains, the parched riverbeds, the 14,000-ft passes. He doesn't say that Kabul has been the crossroads of trade for a thousand years; the caravans from China, Turkestan, Samarkand, Firzan and India had come this way over countless passes and rivers and owed nothing to the West. Afghan folklore incorporates the Old Testament, and Issa – Christ – is remembered as a nice bloke. Pity he didn't have a brother willing to avenge the crucifixion. In the markets of Kabul, there were melons, peaches, apricots, pears, quinces and almonds, and eleven languages commonly spoken – Arabic, Pashto, Persian, Hindi and Turki just for starters. What did they want from us? Nothing.

Glynn persists.

'I just think the news should be more positive. It should reflect the good and the positive in human nature.'

David looks at his long, crafty face. Really this Glynn is presenting himself as a man in step with the buzzy, upbeat zeitgeist, the heir of Norman Vincent Peale, the positive thinker. David guesses that he is the only one here who has heard of Peale. It's people like Glynn, the over-simplifiers, who open the door to fundamentalists. He doesn't say it.

'I am sure we would all, in theory, like good news. But as you know the journalistic maxim is that dog bites man is not news, but man bites dog is news. You never hear about the rules a politician didn't break. In some societies so-called positive news is all that is allowed, and in the end that just means unmediated praise for the ruling party. I remember about fifteen years ago watching an endless broadcast on Kenyan TV of President Moi greeting a delegation of Bulgarian agricultural experts. It was, frankly, arse-numbingly boring, as they tried to translate the sheep-meat production plan from Bulgarian to Swahili. The one good thing about satellite and twenty-four-hour news is that almost no corner of the world can shut it out. Dictators hate it.'

The questions come fast. The women are interested in his personal life, how he was able to reconcile travel and family. They want to relate his life to their own experience; they want to know how his children and his partner coped while he was away. He doesn't, of course, tell them that Nancy coped by having a two-year affair with an old boyfriend. Instead he says that, as in all marriages, there were strains, but they worked their way through them; the hardest thing for him was to hear that the children were having problems at school when he was thousands of miles away, unable to help.

The human temperature in the room is rising. He finds this warmth, the nearly-young women, Sylvie's proprietorship, the desire for some common understanding, unexpectedly uplifting. None of the women asks him directly about his wife but he senses that the unspoken question concerns his plans.

One woman asks him how he manages to stay so thin.

He says, 'Since my wife died, I have found I don't cook much, and I try to resist invitations. Most of my friends and my daughter think I am too thin. Yes, one daughter, twenty-six, and a son who is thirty-two. He's a lawyer. Obviously he looked at my life and decided he had better get a proper job.'

It's not true. Even now Ed is struggling with the idea that he is a lawyer, or that 'lawyer' is his defining principle. Perhaps the partnership, even the cut-price partnership Robin has given him, will soothe him. Money so often has this effect. It also convinces its beneficiaries that they have acquired wealth for some good reason, some special knowledge. That is why successful businessmen speak that crazy spiritual-practical language: they have understood the springs of society; they have understood the unwritten, that is to say the real, laws of human behaviour.

After an hour or so, Sylvie declares that it is dinner time. Most of them set off through the resounding hallway in the direction of the Rasa, although both men have dropped out. The air outside is cool. Sylvie is still concerned about the dog's tragic disappointment at being left in the flat.

'Will you come with me afterwards to take Wolfie for a short walk?'

'OK.'

'Oh, great.'

She squeezes his arm for emphasis.

'You were great, by the way, awesome.'

'Just the usual banalities, I am afraid.'

'I wouldn't exactly say so. You were brilliant.'

The restaurant is empty, but one long table is laid for them and the owner greets them warmly. Sylvie introduces David. There's an air of suppressed panic in this place, as though the furtive waiters from some backwater in Kerala are expecting the Revenue and Customs or the Border Agency to launch a raid at any minute.

It's only ten o'clock when Sylvie and he go back to collect the dog; it shows no lingering bitterness as it bounds out of the front door and in the direction of the woods, which are deep and dark.

11

ROSALIE HAS ADOPTED a resigned look. Her face, her dancer's face, the features slightly taut from excessive exercise, is now composed. Her hair is severely pulled back, which contributes to the tautness of her features. Ed thinks of those widows he once saw in an Andalusian cemetery, placing small bunches of flowers in a wall of tombs. The look says, I have been foolish and naive and now I must accept what God has dealt me. There is a logical problem, of course: IVF can bring about the miracle of birth but so far there is no cure for death. He finds Rosalie reordering her clothes closet, as if she has to decide what clothes are appropriate for her reduced rank as a childless person. Her philosophic demeanour is more painful to him than any row they have ever had. He feels deeply sorry for her; he knows that his compassion is suffused with guilt, because he has been banging Alice. Only twice, of course. At the same time he feels a little anger: Rosalie is far too ready to strike a pose. He's sure they will have a baby by one means or another, but already she has gone into tragic mode. He wonders if the ballet isn't in some way to blame: it's all so damn melodramatic. He's late for work because he wanted Rosalie to reassure him that he could go, but her permission — 'Yes, yes, you go. I'll be fine, I'm sure' —

was spoken with such dismal stoicism that he felt he had to make her some tea; fresh mint is her favourite, very refreshing in Morocco, but slightly nauseating on an autumn morning in England, and then he suggested that they make an IVF appointment with Mr Smythson and get on with it and she looked at him with pity.

'Look, Rosie, we can either roll over and accept this, or we can do what thousands of people do, and go for IVF.'

'It's funny, isn't it, that just a few days ago you were saying don't worry, I just know we are going to have a baby, and I believed you. Now it's apparently time to face facts.'

'That's so fucking unfair. You are miserable and I just don't want you to suffer. Everybody has to face facts some time; unfortunately that's not your strong point.'

'Don't worry about me. You know, Ed, more and more you become aggressive when you can't handle something. I suggest you just toddle off to your little firm, and I'll stay here tidying the house. That's all I'm good for, apparently.'

'You were teaching Congolese Pygmies en pointe and pirouette on Tuesday, while I hung about waiting to pick you up.'

'With your sister. Eating curry.'

'Oh, so that's a crime now? Eating curry with your sister is a crime. I didn't know.'

'I was only teaching these refugees, who are not Pygmies, by the way, but AIDS orphans, because I am so lonely.'

'Rosie, darling, can we talk tonight?'

'In other words, can I go now and get away from this whining bore? Yes, you may. Go.'

'Please, Rosie, don't let's go down this road. We are in it together.'

'Oh good. I'll see you whenever.'

'I may be a little late, but I'll ring.'

'Absolutely fine.'

'I've got to go now. It's expected that as a partner, et cetera . . .'

'As a partner, et cetera, in a clapped-out law firm owned by your dad's best chum. Carry on.'

'Oh Christ, see you at about eight. And as for my dad's best chum, you seem happy enough to go looking for bog-roll holders at John Lewis with him.'

'Don't hurry.'

'Love you,' he calls, rather unconvincingly, as he opens the front door.

He's angry, but he knows that the anger will quickly dissipate leaving him guilty and depressed. When he finally arrives at the office he finds that Alice is not there. Gloria says that Alice failed to show up for work and left no message. Her phone is dead. But Mr Fineman has rung six times, saying that he has been waiting for her since eight-thirty. He says they're under siege.

'I'll go and see him. Call him and tell him I'm on my way. And get me a cab, quick as you like. Where's Robin?'

'He's not coming in today. He's gone to Geneva.'

'Was he carrying a brown bag?'

'Oh dear, we mustn't speak ill of our beloved leader for life.'

'No, naughty me. I'll wash my mouth out with soap.'

As he tells the cabbie the address, he wonders if there is some sinister connection between Robin's unscheduled flight to Geneva and Alice's non-appearance. He tries her home number now but it, too, goes straight to message.

'Hi, Alice. It's me. Just off to see Mr Fineman. He's

anxious. Hope all is well with you. Give me a call when you can.'

Mr Fineman and his assistant are both in a poor state of mind. Olla's face has become flat and confused. Fineman is angry and vengeful. It turns out that the Council has been adopting very heavy-handed tactics, showering them with writs, hand-delivered by bulky men in leather jackets. This visit may well have reminded Olla of the bad old days her parents told her about. Alice was supposed to have sent them a withering legal reply, threatening action in every court in the land and beyond.

'Don't worry, it's all bluff. This is a very minor matter.'

'It can be very minor to you, my boy, but to me it's life and death. Or worse.'

'You vant tea?' Olla asks. 'Vee have Vagon Veals.'

She's smiling rather too determinedly in what he sees is a state of panic.

'Where is Alice? This is not professional. Most unprofessional.'

'I would love a Wagon Wheel. I'm very sorry, Mr Fineman, Alice had to go to Geneva. Unexpectedly. She said that I should apologise to you profusely, but I was late into the office and did not get the message in time. No sugar, thank you. Just tell me what's been happening and I will deal with it.'

'What's been happening? What hasn't been happening?'

In truth it's all pretty small stuff, the sort of bluster and fancy words that public bodies use, even when they are saving the environment. He reads the letters: they are nonsense, pretending to have legal force.

'These are not writs. These are just hot air.'

He is soon able to calm Mr Fineman, whose appetite for the legal battle, recently so keen, has diminished. It is a good thing. He can't really win this case for Mr Fineman, although he may be able to get some compensation on the grounds that he wasn't given the statutory notice. Olla is back on bar-hostess form, now that she sees that the big lawyer has restored some calm to her anguished old boss, who is prone to ancient anxieties. He had earlier sent her to the locksmith to buy a huge, industrial-strength bolt for the door. She skips off to the dingy kitchen behind a plastic curtain and soon she is humming, delightfully, a ditty from her native Carpathians. When she comes back, the little milk teeth and the thin, lively mouth are in full working order again: she produces sympathetic facial gestures as the legal facts are discussed, as if she is not Mr Fineman's assistant at all, but Marcel Marceau's. The effect is strangely erotic.

Mr Fineman, the subsiding volcano, is now subdued. He sinks back, almost crouching, into the swivel chair, a chair of a type no longer often seen, and then suddenly he leans forward, his heavy brow now knotted so that there is a solid groove horizontally across his forehead, like a windbreak planted to shield his eye sockets.

'My boy, I think the time has come we should settle.'

'Perhaps we should. I can probably get compensation for loss of revenue when I demonstrate that they did not serve the notice in due time.'

'How much are we talking?'

'Oh a few thousand. Maybe ten?'

'And legal costs?'

'And costs.'

'Lawyers win every way round.'

But he says this in a no-flies-on-me, I'm-a-man-of-the-world way: I know how things really work. It's a delusion of many small operators like Fineman that they believe themselves part of a bigger, wised-up business world. But it's clear that the threat of writs and distraint of goods has rattled him.

'Leave this with me. If anybody comes to see you, just tell them to refer everything to me. You have my card.'

'I will. Certainly. Olla, you hear that? This matter is in the hands of our lawyers.'

'I goddit,' she says. 'In the lawyer hand. More tea, Mr Edvard? Another Vagon Veal?'

He needs her female proximity, so he says yes please. She stands very close as she proffers another biscuit and he imagines he can feel a nervous heat from her. He doesn't tell her and her rather rumpled old boss that he will just call the Council's solicitor, saying that he has persuaded his client not to go to the local newspaper about the victimisation of a small business, and that he has also, with reluctance, agreed to accept a modest settlement as compensation for the fact that the Council did not observe due process and he has lost income. All settled, he leaves the two of them in their den, decorated from floor to ceiling with spectacle frames and certificates of Mr Fineman's competence. Mr Fineman has an attractive quality, and also a vulnerability, which appeal to him, and the feverish Olla is – he thinks – sending him messages of an unmistakable nature. He thinks of asking her out for a drink after work, but checks himself: a terrible anarchy has already entered his life.

Back in the office he shuts himself away and tries Alice's number again, but she is still not answering. Perhaps the bull-calf Scots have kidnapped her or she's decided a life of eightsome reels and good plain food is just what she needs. But instead of welcoming the possibility that she has jumped ship – and who would blame her? – Ed finds himself desperately anxious to speak to her. *I am becoming obsessive. I am poised on the edge of disaster.* If Alice were in love with him, ready to do anything to keep him, it would be easier to ditch her, with high-minded assurances and his self-esteem intact. If only she were threatening to kill herself, for example. But the evident fact that she doesn't really care for him that much is causing him existential pain. He looks out of the window of his new office: two floors below are people going about their ordinary business happily. He looks directly down on to an antique-map shop. Robin buys these maps, which demonstrate his familiarity with the antique world. Next to this is an organic café called Manic Organic. The owners are far from manic, in fact so calm as to be somnambulistic. Until today, despite the fact that the building's rubbish bins are directly below, he has found this view of London delightful and the knowledge that it is all his, inspiriting. Now his mood has changed: he's in a hutch with a sliver of London to gaze at, past the service entrance of their three-storey building, a building that Robin owns and leases to the partnership. Also, he sees that the people passing below are unbearable – wage slaves, drones, cretins, all doing meaningless jobs. Maybe there's something wrong with us as a family, if we are still a family, sneering at honest endeavour and believing ourselves to have some artistic claim on the world.

His next task today is no great shakes: to call some time-serving lawyer in the Council office and make a deal. You only have to warn them about Health and Safety or the local paper and they forget the law. As Bismarck said, if you like law and sausages, you don't want to see how they are made. The law garlands itself with principle, but in practice it is a shabby business. He picks up the phone.

It's a good sign that he is put straight through to Kevin Peggley, head of the legal department.

'Hello, Ed. You'll be ringing about your bonkers client, Mr Fineman, I imagine?'

'Kevin, Kevin, what sort of way is that to talk about a refugee from the Nazis, eighty-six years old, long a pillar of the local community, and a fine optician?'

'Let's not piss about. We didn't serve the notice correctly, he's become nervous and you advised him to settle, am I right?'

'More or less. But you forgot one point: men with big shoulders came to frighten him, presumably because he is old.'

'OK, we'll wave the penalties, we'll reduce his rates because of ongoing disruption and we'll call it a day.'

'I don't think that will do, Kevin. He's lost nearly half his income for ten months. His accountant has supplied me with the figures – I am looking at them as we speak – and he's down nearly forty thousand in turnover. People don't, apparently, want to be run over just for a new pair of specs these days.'

'You're hilarious. How much are you looking for?'

'Fifteen grand.'

'Don't be ridiculous. We'll go to ten if you promise me . . .'

'If I promise not to go to the local rag to tell them how your goons hounded a man whose parents died in a concentration camp, and how a mother and baby were just a millisecond away from death by a twelve-wheeler outside Mr Fineman's premises. It says on here on the affidavit, which I have in front of me, that the woman's name is Ms Dondhi, which sounds Indian, and she is having counselling, it also says here. That's such a shame. We must share her pain. Just send me a note confirming the details of our conversation. I have been taking notes, by the way.'

'All right,' he says wearily.

'And we'll want our costs.'

'Within our strict guidelines, of course.'

'Of course. Thanks, Kevin.'

He rings through to reception and asks to speak to Robin in Geneva, but he's in conference with some new clients, of Russian origin, and can't be disturbed.

'If you speak to our supreme leader, will you tell him that the Fineman case has settled. Any word from Alice?'

'None. Vanished off the face of the earth.'

He sits staring out of the window. His mother died two years ago and his soul has swooned slowly. My soul was neatly boxed and bound and now it's swooning; it's gone rackety; it's longing for warm beds, for warm, full-blooded life. Lucy believes that their souls – secular, of course – departed with Mum. She and Dad have quite a flexible idea of the soul. For Rosalie dance is the hidden voice of the soul; when she says this, she's quoting Martha Graham. Here I am sitting in this doghouse, wanting to fuck Alice, wanting to fuck Olla the Romanian sexpot, wanting . . . Wanting what? A child? Flight? The soul is not the sort of thing you can discuss with Brent Council but it's certainly the sort of thing you could discuss with Mr Fineman, who, despite today's tactical compromise, is essentially engaged in a struggle with the forces of darkness. He smiles as he thinks of Mr Fineman, a man of high, but crackers, principle, a man who understands instinctively that anyone set over you is bound to develop dangerous tendencies. He still writes to Prague and Vienna regularly, attempting to find details of how his parents died in 1944.

When the heavy men from the Council arrived with their bits of meaningless paper, he was taken back sixty-five years and more to the time the Czech police came for his parents and their appointment with Terezin. He was in hiding with an aunt across the river.

'It's just Brent Council, Mr Fineman.'

'That's how it starts. Look at Hitler in 1933. *Ein harmloser Dummkopf*, they said.'

Historical precedent looms very large in Mr Fineman's life.

He calls Rosalie and leaves a conciliatory message: *I love you, darling. Please keep calm and we will see the experts.*

He is conscious that he is speaking in the strangulated fashion you employ when trying to be sincere and natural to a message service. At least she's not at home arranging the closets. Her childlessness is now biblical to her: the barren woman in a stony land. And, despite his more than adequate sperm count and his energetic commitment to the task, he is also diminished. It's the connection between fucking and children that needs looking at. Production of children is clearly not, as the Church suggests, the sole purpose of marriage. Feeling guilty about having difficulties conceiving is a hangover of the religious disapproval of the barren woman. After all, what have he and Rosalie done wrong? Even in the strictly technical, the plumbing, sense he is a hundred per cent confident they have done nothing wrong. The time for IVF is upon them. But also, he must free himself from the shackles of this little place with its excruciatingly limited horizons and its banality. It's weighing heavily on him: it's not human to lack a sense of humour. We are, after all, the only animals that laugh and smile. In this place, from Robin downwards, humour is the retelling of jokes heard at parties or jokes that have appeared on the Internet. Invariably his colleagues tell them badly. They are unaware of what somebody called the cleansing baptism of irony. This person, someone like Kant or Kierkegaard, said – approximately – that anyone who has no ear for irony lacks what is indispensable to being human. *Introduction to Philosophy 1* is fading into obscurity. He must look the passage up. But he is cheered by these musings: they give him the hope that he is not yet enslaved.

Mum never understood irony: it seemed to her a silly artifice and wholly unnecessary. Yet in her own way she was the most human of us. Even when she was dying, she made lists of minor tasks, which she entrusted to him and to Lucy. But the great irony – that none of this would matter after she was dead – escaped her. When your mother dies, you feel it particularly strongly because you and she were for a while one flesh. He misses her every day and he knows that Lucy does, too. When he thinks about childbirth, he sees a sacred mystery, that you can create new life in this strangely primitive and messy fashion. He and Rosalie don't seem to be able to create new life as easily as people on the tundra and the savannah and the rainforest do, routinely.

He rings Mr Fineman. Olla answers.

'Hello, Olla. It's Edward Cross.'

'Mr Edvard, how are you?'

'I'm fine. And you?'

'I quite a bit happy.'

'Good. Can I speak to Mr Fineman?'

'Sure, I put through.'

'Fineman.'

'Mr Fineman, I've had a preliminary talk with the

Council. In principle they have accepted that they were derelict in serving the notice. It's just a question of getting the agreement signed and sealed. It will take about a week, but you can relax.'

'I'm relaxing.'

'It was good to see you.'

'Something bothering you?'

'No, why?'

'Are you unhappy?'

'No, just the usual stuff.'

'You don't sound too good.'

Mr Fineman has told him his family spoke German in Prague: other lives, almost always a surprise. He feels deep sympathy – not unconnected to his own problems – for Mr Fineman and the teetering Olla in their rundown little parlour, adorned with spectacle frames, certificates and pictures of women who contrive to look beautiful despite being four-eyed, and the scent of sprays intended to disguise the creeping mushroom-flavoured invasion of their doomed building, now stranded on a traffic island. Maybe Mr Fineman is hoping to ditch his elderly wife in favour of this trembling beauty with the milk teeth. Stranger things have happened. Her skin has a faint sheen, a suggestion of goat's milk. Alice's skin is very white, with the tiny indelible pencil lines of veins on her inner thighs. Which he's never going to see again. He tries calling her. It's that heavy time in the afternoon when the urge to work is dulled. She doesn't answer. She's still in the Highlands or the Trossachs; the geography of Scotland is something of a mystery to him, apart from Edinburgh, where he was in a student production of *The Real Inspector Hound* at the Festival. He played Birdboot. Dad wanted to be a professional actor: Rome was his high point. It's strange how older people seem to feel a greater intensity about what happened to them forty or fifty years ago than things in the present. What's happening to them now seems to be short on meaning, thinned out. It's as if in retrospect they recognise certain key moments in their lives on which the whole thing has turned. Robin would call this a tipping point. You don't necessarily know it at the time, but Ed has the feeling that here, in this narrow little office, in front of the half-dozen leather-bound books in the dark cabinets, which he has never opened, he may be at a tipping point.

12

'LANGUAGE IS BEING debased. That's not a good thing.'

'Give us an example,' Lucy demands.

' "Head up your arse". Once English people used to say, "He has his head in the clouds." Now they say, "He's got his head up his arse." '

'Languages are always changing. And by the way, "head up your arse" is not the same thing as "head in the clouds".'

Nick ignores her nit-picking.

'Yes, language is changing but that doesn't mean you should limit yourself to a few portmanteau words. Or approximations. Most people seem to think "picaresque" means "picturesque" in French, but it has a very specific meaning relating to literature. But if you don't know what the word means, especially if you think you do, it is just another useful word down the toilet. Soon you will be saying things like, "Ooh, like that's so fun." Soon every halfwit from Hawaii to the Scilly Isles will be using the same half-baked phrases. I am being boring?'

'Not too bad, so far. But you are probably going to go on to texting and email next, and how they are dragging the language down.'

'I'm not, actually.'

She watches him as he talks; talking is something he evidently likes a lot. He has a long, very straight nose, flanked by cheeks that slope away rather urgently, so that he appears to be very alert, almost raptor-like. This alert, sniffing-the-wind look reminds her of pictures of Native Americans, before they became obese and bipolar. He may be gay, although he's not at all camp. When he interviewed her on the phone for the *Evening News* a few days ago, he suggested they meet to look at the finished magazine piece.

They are now in the coffee bar he suggested. He loves coffee and claims to know all the best places in London, although she suspects he must once have had to knock off a feature for the 'What's Hot and What's Not' section in the Friday colour magazine *People and Places*. They have this section open in front of them. The café is in a blank street behind a theatre which opens on to Shaftesbury Avenue and it has – he says – a unique blend of beans from Turin, which he calls 'Torino'. He recommends something called a *bicerin*.

'There are three versions, *pur e fiôr* – coffee with milk, *pur e barba* – coffee with chocolate, and *un pô'd tut* – a bit of everything.'

'You are truly one of the worst know-alls I have ever met.'

'You should get out more. Which one do you want? If you asked me, I would be a devil and have the third, a little of everything.'

He orders in Italian, but the waitress is from Gdansk, so he has to point at the menu. The photograph of Lucy, busy sorting early Christian Roman coins, appears above the caption: *Golden Girl Gives Lustre to Golden Hoard*.

'If we are talking language, what about this headline?'

'Ah subs, subs. A law unto themselves. They live in a

parallel universe because they are never allowed out of the office. Troglodytes, poor cunts.'

For a moment he seems genuinely moved by their fate.

'Actually,' she says, 'it sounds like "Golden Girl Gives Blow Job".'

'O – my – Go-od. Now I am shocked. Oh – my – Go-od.'

'I don't speak like that, if that's supposed to be me.'

'It isn't. Tell me, did you like the bit where I said, "Lucy Cross, daughter of television icon David Cross, definitely belongs in London's smallest minority, young women with brains and beauty. She is in at number 6"?'

'It wasn't news to me, of course.'

'Which part, the brains or the beauty?'

'Neither.'

'Look, let's be honest, the whole series is a load of crap, but because I liked you, I promoted you from number 14.'

'Lucy says, "I love the early coins. They breathe, they whisper, they break down the barriers of history." Did I really say that?'

'You did. But a little more prosaically.'

'Thanks. I know about you, by the way.'

'What do you mean?'

'I rang somebody in your office. No, don't ask. She said the editor thinks you are talented but erratic.'

'That's about right. Have you got a boyfriend?'

His questing features incline towards her.

'No. As it happens I gave him the push a few days ago.'

'So you are on the rebound.'

'Am I? I might be. I hadn't really thought about it like that.'

Lucy thinks that if they are talking like people in a

British comedy – brittle and ironic – that's OK with her: it's undemanding and even restful, a familiar gambit.

She glances at the magazine. In the picture she does look almost beautiful. She can see something of her mother, too, in the way her eyes appear to have slightly more white beneath the iris than other people's. As a result, her mother sometimes looked startled without cause. And her smile is similar to her mother's, with the appearance of spontaneity, although the photographer made her laugh by telling her a joke. He was a rumpled, bald fellow called Arnold, wearing a grimy Belstaff jacket.

'What's pink and tastes of ginger?'

'Dunno. What is pink and tastes of ginger?'

'Fred Astaire's willy.'

She laughed because the joke was so venerable and he told it with such lack of verve.

'Works every time,' he said, although she imagined that she might be the only under-thirty in London to get it, and that was only because her mother loved Fred Astaire movies.

'Why did you chuck him?'

'He is very good-looking, but it's deceptive. He's a twerp. It took me a while to see past the looks.'

'Twerp. Nice antiquarian word. You haven't asked me if I have a girlfriend.'

'I didn't ask, but thanks anyway.'

'Are you pleased?'

'That you can't find a girlfriend?'

'You know what I mean.'

'I'll pass on that one. But can I ask a supplementary? If you didn't know who my dad was, would you have asked me to be in the series?'

'Frankly, no. The editor's assistant knew who you were. But the truth is the editor is under pressure from the management to deliver celebrities, even daughters of celebrities, so she lays it on us, the Oompa-Loompas.'

'I wouldn't have had you down for an Oompa-Loompa. Look, Nick, it's been great, but I have to go now, back to the fourth century — that's the three hundreds to you journos — in old Byzantium. The coins are whispering to me. In fact they are screaming, "Get back to work." '

'OK, bye.'

'Thanks for the *caffè con tutto.*'

'Can we meet again?'

'You have my mobile number.'

Back in her corner with the coins in front of her on green baize and a pile of reference books to the side, she finds that the coins are indeed breathing. When she took this job, to write up the catalogues, she had no idea that ancient coins and pottery and pieces of vellum could interest her. But now she sees, perhaps a little too late, that she has a keen interest in imagining what the world was like when these things were made. Perhaps she could have been an academic. She wonders who handled the coins and how the coins survived: she is familiar with every face that appears on them, a sort of family album of the Constantines at play, which involved incest and murder. Her favourite is Julian the Apostate, who reinstated the old Roman gods for a while.

These coins, all gold, are new on the market. She has met the man from Derbyshire who found them with a metal detector; he sees great wealth coming his way, and he could be right. Up until he found the gold, his best find had been a Swiss Army penknife. Her good mood, she knows, is partly to do with Nick, perhaps also a result of drinking very strong coffee with chocolate. Everybody in old Torino must be buzzing. Her friend Yvette at the

News said that Nick is only given minor pieces, but everyone can see that he's a natural journalist. He's curious. As her father says, journalists will read the small print on a cornflakes packet when they have nothing else to read. Journalists cobble together meaning from whatever is at hand, a chimera. It's not real meaning, built to last. Her mention in 'What's Hot' at number 6, because Nick fancies her, is a perfect example of a journalistic rendezvous: pretty girl, daughter of once-famous TV person, posh semi-academic job – all compacted to make sense. She understands better than most that, while what appears in the media is not absolutely true or real, it acquires a reality of its own. Her father once told her, quoting somebody or other, that diplomats lie to journalists and then believe what the journalists have written. Now she almost believes that she has brains and beauty.

She wonders what it would be like to have sex with Nick. It's impossible to tell by appearances. Men are always speculating about women in bed; it's as if they have a masculine obligation to keep tabs on women's sexual potential, in some wider and disinterested pursuit of knowledge. They are apparently unaware that women do the same, although – broadly speaking – women are more interested in the emotional aspect of sex than men are. Not all of them, though. She looks at Helena, mother of Constantine, commemorated on a coin of Constantine II. She was a slapper. On this coin, Helena has become an icon, the subject of a Christian cult. Her hair is elaborately coiffed and she wears a diadem. But she was once, some scholars claim, a prostitute – 'a sex worker', as they kept saying at the prostitute-murder trial – and her elevation in the Roman Empire was a triumph of sexual politics. Coins and medals tell you a lot about politics. When her son first adopts the chi-rho, his coins still have an image of Venus on them: he's working both sides of the street. By sending Helena, his old mum, to Jerusalem to bring back the True Cross, he is trying to ally himself and his empire with what he sees as the future. And in this way Helena goes from sex worker to Christian saint. The edited version of her ascent is recorded on the coins.

Maybe I am turning into a blue stocking. I will be one of those daft old parties with snaggly, crazy hair, who wears thick dark tights in all weathers. But then she remembers that she looks pretty good in the magazine and the magazine places her at number 6 in the brains-plus-beauty stakes. Who is she to argue with London's leading evening newspaper?

Noel, who is a trainee in fine-art evaluation, comes in to see her. He often drops by in his broadly spaced pinstripe, in what he imagines is a casual fashion. His ambition is to conduct auctions one day, effortlessly debonair. But he doesn't have the kind of confidence that Lucy finds attractive: he is ingratiating and awkward. Today's ruse is to say that he has some tickets for a gig next day at the O2: 'Gold dust. Absolute and total gold dust. Four hundred big ones each on eBay. Some mate of mine knows the promoter. Want to come?' She doesn't but at the same time she doesn't want to be cruel: he was very kind to her when she was low and he even took her to Sotheby's Café down the road for a lobster club sandwich. The combination of *lobster* and *sandwich* is a masterpiece of nuanced snobbery, a signifier, if ever there was one.

'Oh no, can't do it, Noel. This catalogue is way behind.'
'Too bad. By the way, I saw your picture in the *News*.'
'Did I look OK?'
'You looked great.'

'It's all in the lighting.'

'I thought it was exactly you. I liked your dress.'

'Noel, you're a sweetie-pie. Thank you. Now I have to finish off the Derbyshire Hoard, or I'm dog-meat. Sorry, really, really, really sorry; another time.'

He leaves awkwardly, unable to close the conversation in the way that assertive men do, with a hint of threat or a self-congratulatory pay-off, which trumps all that has gone before. He was at boarding school in some damp part of the country. It's odd that this habit of boarding school lingers on. All her London friends at university were far more worldly and socialised than the boarding-school boys and girls, who substituted slogans for conversation, as if forms of words, learned from that odd assortment of monks, spinster teachers and boys who never grew up, were more important than feeling or emotional truth. In a world loudly preoccupied with self, this third column of the stilted, polite English person – over-represented in British comedy – is still turned out by these remote schools. Noel has that sort of slightly chubby, formless face, neither good-looking nor unpleasant, just somehow neutral, which won't age well: this sort of face lapses into anonymity. She can't help thinking that it is very different from the planed, sculpted version of a face sported by Nick. It's true that we all have a kind of sexual ideal, which explains why people often marry someone who looks like their first love. Dad doesn't go for women like Sylvie, owner of the wandering, hirsute dog, women with a kind of outdated, breathy girlishness. At least she hopes he doesn't. Just as she settles down with the coins again, her mobile rings. She sees, with a lurch of anxiety, that it is Josh.

'Yes?'

'Is that the best you can do?'

He is slurred. The words are unstable.

'More than. What do you want? I'm working.'

'I saw the piece about you in the *News*.'

'Oh, good. And?'

'And I just think they missed a trick.'

'What would that be?'

'They didn't mention what a fucking cunt you are.'

'Goodbye, Josh. I think possibly you should see a doctor.'

She clicks off her phone. She feels as though she has been kicked, but at least she has no nagging regrets about Josh. How could he have such violent resentment towards her, when he treated her with a kind of contempt and insensitivity which crossed all the familiar existential barriers between men and women? His only ambition, his motive force, seems to be to cause women to fall for him. He rings again almost immediately: she declines the call. Now he texts: *Who ladyboy u r having coffee with?*

She calls Ed.

'He's in a meeting,' says the receptionist. 'Who shall I say wanted to speak to Mr Cross?'

'His sister, Lucy Cross. It's urgent.'

'Of course, Miss Cross. I don't anticipate that he will be long.'

She is right. Within seconds Ed is on.

'Hi, Ed, thanks for this. Sorry to bother you.'

'What's the problem?'

He's perhaps a little brusque, but this is no time to quibble.

'Your friend Josh is harassing me. He just rang me at work and called me a fucking cunt, and now it seems he's been following me.'

'Jesus, did you see him?'

'No, but he must have followed me from Grimaldi, because he saw I was having coffee with someone.'

'Who?'

'Who? Now I can't have coffee?'

'Lucy, just give me the facts.'

'It was somebody from the *News*, who wrote a feature in yesterday's paper. Nick Grimczek.'

'I saw it. You look great, by the way.'

'Thanks.'

'Can you talk to him?'

'I'll try. It may be a bit early to threaten him with an injunction. Keep a record of his calls and texts. Was he drunk?'

'He may have been. He was slurring.'

'I'll deal with it, but don't speak to him, particularly don't reason with him or shout at him. Just ignore him.'

'Thanks, Ed. And how are you?'

'I'm a lawyer. Bye now. Leave it to me.'

On television, people often stare at the phone after a dramatic conversation. She finds she is looking at the phone as though his human warmth is still somehow lingering in the receiver. But she feels calmer now, although not calm enough to concentrate on the power-hungry and murderous Constantine, who had his son killed when he was found dallying with his wife Flavia. Flavia was parboiled when she took her bath. She wonders what set Josh off: he probably saw her moment of fame as a personal slight. Now she looks back on their brief relationship and its violent ruptures and she thinks that maybe she always knew he was unbalanced.

She tells Rachel that she has to go over to the British Museum to check some sources. Rachel waves distractedly in the direction of Bloomsbury as if she is egging on a sheepdog and says, 'Go, go,' without looking up. When she is concentrating, which is very often, her Celtic eyebrows meet darkly. Some in Grimaldi call her Offa's Dyke, but Lucy guesses she is uninterested in sex. She leaves by the back door, looking carefully to see if Josh is loitering. But out here in the street, a street of expensive art and fragranced men in pale, old-fashioned raincoats and Church's shoes, men who have enough time and money to perform this art-themed, self-regarding *paseo* with confidence, she feels the reassuring familiarity and ease with London. She walks past St George's, Hanover Square, one of the most beautiful churches in London. Near by very thin people often exit from Vogue House, like a delicate forest-antelope emerging from a glade. The sudden change as you cross Regent Street into Soho is always a surprise. She knows the name of every north–south street, the way some people know railway stations. She goes out of her way to calm herself, taking Brewer Street, past the Japanese Supermarket, the hardware store, the health-food place and Randall & Aubin, once famous for its Toulouse sausages, now an oyster bar. Dad loves Soho: he thinks it is the remnant of a lost city, with its small-scale enterprise, crafts, film-production houses, publishers and restaurants, all wrapped in an urban classlessness. He says that, when he lived here for six or eight months as a cub reporter, he knew everybody: it was a village. Where he sees old, sausage-eating London, peopled by friendly prozzies – 'Lookin' for a good time, darlin'?' – and Chianti bottles with candles in their necks lighting dark cellar restaurants, she sees clubs and sushi bars and niche fashion. What we both like is that it is a real and human place in a vast city. Authentic.

She cuts up Frith Street and on through Soho Square, where there is a sense of stillness, pigeons foraging calmly on the dead, dead soil, and two of those thin, thin junkie girls in tight jeans which emphasise their flat, flat, spatchcocked buttocks, walking aimlessly and one man with that detached feral look rocking slowly in a breeze directed only at him. They are all silent, but there are times of the day when these people burst into emotional raucous laughter or violent abuse, with the suddenness of budgerigars. At other times – this is one – they are weighed down with the understanding of their true position, as people who have a morbid relationship with oblivion.

Now she's trotting across Charing Cross Road, up through Coptic Street, where Ed works, maybe talking even now to Josh, and on into the vast forecourt that leads to the museum. She has no real need to be here; as she pauses on the broad steps up to the portico, she hears a strange pounding, a city clamouring, but she thinks it is maybe from within. She goes quickly up to the room which holds the statuette said to be of Helena: there is no resemblance to the image on the coins, although the period is right. Actually, it's not too important: she's only writing up the catalogue, adding a little sonorousness to the description of the images on the coins, but she thinks, as she stares at this Helena, that she does look like the picture of her on the ceiling of Constantine's palace in Trier. In that image she is surrounded by a luminous nimbus, a little personal halo of sanctity, a bit like Dan Dare's space helmet in the vintage comics they auctioned. Big business. Ed used to collect comics and also *Star Wars* figures, and the attic in Camden is full of these, which, he still claims, will one day be priceless. Here in the museum she regains some calm, although she's still shaken by Josh's explosion of hatred. She feels a loss of innocence. At twenty-six, she sees that innocence is not about sex but about a state of not knowing: and life, it turns out, is a process of wising you up.

She goes to see the frescos from Lullingstone, some of the most moving things in the museum, early British Christians praying – *orans* – with their arms outstretched like *The Angel of the North*; they are the deceased praying for their friends on earth. Evangelicals are fond of this posture: perhaps they believe they are already in heaven. These people have none of the imperial confidence of Constantine and his *familia*: they look more traditionally humble, with low self-esteem. They are the forebears of Anglicans; it can only be jam tomorrow with these folks.

When she leaves the museum the sky is violently disturbed by grey clouds rushing at different levels in opposite directions, passing each other distractedly like commuters on a busy platform. London clouds, like the skin of trout, have subtle variations of light in them, which they pick up as they pass overhead, as though escaping gases and stray reflections reach them.

She decides to go to Camden rather than to her flat; the last thing she wants is to find Josh waiting for her. He still has a key. She rings Ed to see if he has spoken to Josh, but his phone is on message. She rings his office and speaks to the receptionist, who of course now sees her as an obsessive, and she says that he has had to go to Geneva unexpectedly. She rings Dad, but he's not answering either and now she wishes that Mum were alive, always available, keen for a chat that would restate first principles in an irritating but reassuring fashion. She took endless pleasure in any account of her children's lives and the domestic detail was a kind of litany that needed diligent recital.

Lucy lets herself into the house, which is acquiring a bachelor aroma, of embrocation and fruit on the turn and the staleness of air which has not been sufficiently stirred. Although the cats are missing, their presence remains. She wishes she had brought some flowers as an antidote. Mum loved simple arrangements of tulips and daffodils and – only in season – garden roses. She tidies up a bit: it's probably a feminine thing, an atavistic reaction, but it's also in honour of her mother. She sits in the armchair where her mother used to read, and suddenly she finds that she is weeping, despite having brains and beauty. Then she gets up and makes some coffee, nothing fancy from Turin – *Torino* – just some Nescafé. She wipes her face with the scrap of kitchen towel left on the roller.

She hears a noise at the front door: an animal is scratching and whimpering. She looks out of the window and sees Ms Jiggly Tits. She walks into the hall. She can't remember her name. She opens the door.

'Oh, hello, Lucy. Is your dad in?'

The dog's nose is already in. Some way behind, its owner is fighting a losing battle to keep it from taking possession.

'You remember her, don't you? From the Heath?'

'Yes, I do, Wolfie, come in, bring Wolfie.'

With a rush Wolfie tows her owner into the hall.

'I'm really sorry, I can't remember your name.'

As Lucy says it, she realises that this is a serious gaffe: she has remembered the dog's name, but not its owner's.

'Sylvie.'

'Oh, of course. I am terrible with names.'

'I saw your picture in the paper. You looked lovely.'

'Thanks.'

In the hand that is not restraining the dog, which for the moment is galloping on the spot, unable to gain traction on the French-oak floorboards Mum had put down, Sylvie holds a parcel, wrapped in soft tissue paper of pistachio hue. It has a little card attached in a pink envelope, with elaborate script.

'Your dad came and spoke to our book club – maybe he told you? – and we always give the speaker a gift. Not that we always have a speaker. And this is it. Will you give it to him?'

'Of course. If he's coming home. He's a bit of a dirty stop-out these days.'

This is not true, but she wants to check, for a moment, the emotional energy rushing from Sylvie and her dog, a spring tide of enthusiasm and eagerness, which is threatening to inundate the place.

'I had better be going,' Sylvie says unconvincingly.

'No, no, come in.'

She leads the way down to the basement and the kitchen.

'Shall I put the gift here, on the table?'

'I am sure that would be fine.'

'It's nothing special, just a token. It's the thought that counts, don't you think? David, your dad obviously, was absolutely amazing.'

'Yes. He's surprisingly lucid still, isn't he?'

'He had us eating out of his hand.'

'What about a drink?'

'I would love something.' She fans her face briefly with her hand. 'It's hotter than you realise. Do you have any white wine?'

'Probably. I'll have a look.'

'And perhaps Wolfie could have some water? To be honest

her coat is a little thick for this weather. Normally I can't have her stripped until June.'

'Sure. She can have my old Peter Rabbit bowl. I hardly ever use it, as you can imagine.'

Lucy fills the bowl and then finds a bottle of Chardonnay, already open, in the fridge. After its loud drink, the dog subsides, its moist needy eyes firmly on Sylvie. As she pours the Chardonnay – cold, straw-coloured – she wonders if Sylvie has dressed up for this encounter with her father. She is wearing a sort of peasant blouse out of *The Bartered Bride*, which allows her breasts considerable free range. Below that she has a long skirt, possibly Anatolian, with threads of light sewn into it, and her hair is falling artlessly and abundantly below her shoulders. Long and abundant hair, Rapunzel hair, is traditionally the mark of the free spirit.

'What did Dad talk about?'

'Oh, he was just brilliant. The thing that I found most moving was his trip to Afghanistan. The poor women being shot and lashed in the Football Stadium; I wonder how seeing something like that affects you in the long term. I should have asked.'

'He never spoke to us about his feelings in that way. I don't think he wanted us to be frightened when he was out of the country. But I know my mother was always terrified that she would get the dreaded phone call. His favourite cameraman was killed in the Sudan, but we had to read that in the paper. So he kept fairly quiet.'

'I can imagine. What do you do, Lucy?'

Lucy explains that at the moment she works on catalogues for Grimaldi, the auctioneer, and that she is very busy with a new catalogue right now, but Sylvie misses any hint contained in the information.

'And what do you do?'

'I work, at the moment, in an organic café in Highgate, but I am really an artist. Unfortunately, I can't sell enough of my paintings to live on.'

The world seems to be filled with people who see personal salvation in an artistic or literary career: life is a project of self-development. Her favourite saying of Camus is *Life is not to be built up but burned up*. Although of course Camus had a pretty good career himself saying this sort of thing.

'What kind of painting do you do?'

At this point the dog growls and Lucy hears the key turning in the lock. She goes to the front door.

'Hello, Dad. Your friend Sylvie is in the kitchen.'

'Hello, sweetheart. How nice to find you here.' He kisses her. 'Sylvie?'

'With dog. Come down. We've started on the Chardonnay. Sylvie was telling me that she works in an organic café but is a painter at heart.'

As they enter the kitchen, Sylvie is calming the dog, which is suspicious of intruders. Sylvie stands up, Venus from the waves, and extends both hands like a charismatic offering a blessing.

'Hello, David. Forgive me. I just came to drop in a gift from the book club, and Lucy dragged me in.'

'Oh, hello. How are you, Sylvie? I enjoyed the book club . . .'

As her father speaks the dog wags its low-slung tail. It knows him, Lucy thinks.

'Dad, I have to go home to finish some work.'

'OK, sweetie. You're welcome to stay the night, as you know.'

'Another time. Bye, Sylvie.'

'Oh, bye.'

As she leaves by the front door, Lucy hears laughter from below, her father's slightly mechanical but professionally charming laugh, and Sylvie's excited giggle, almost a yap.

13

IT HAPPENS IN films but almost never in real life: when David wakes he reaches across the bed and finds she has gone and he has no idea when she left. He looks at his watch. It is seven-thirty. The space next to him where she lay is fragranced, but the warmth obviously departed some time ago. The thought that she may have crept out disturbs him. Perhaps she was embarrassed and feared that he might say something dismissive, or perhaps she was feeling guilty and couldn't wait to get home to the security and familiarity of her own bed. He has had that feeling himself. He gets up and looks in the mirror, which Nancy had fixed behind the bathroom door. He realises, perhaps for the first time, that he wants to get out of here because of Nancy, because of her presence. His breasts are slightly puckered, despite all his running and rowing. His efforts to cross the Atlantic single-handed. I am not exempt from delusion. Far from it. He wonders if she noticed his obdurate nipples and the threads of grey on his chest. He tries to recall the number of separations he has had from women in the night, in places like Damascus and Ho Chi Minh City and Johannesburg, but none is as charged as this separation. He wonders how Nancy felt when she had to leave her lover in the night to get back to the children.

All he feels now for her is sympathy; the little coal in his heart that he kept fanning for so long is suddenly cold. In the popular wisdom you cannot live without loving. Perhaps it would have been possible, but when Jenni drowned – when he drowned her – he limited the range of his heart deliberately. He had overreached himself, like Faustus and Burton, and he wanted, in some way, to atone by becoming a regular Joe. For a long time he told himself that he had made sensible decisions, but he knows that he lost something along the way, what his brother would probably think of as the possibility of transcendence. Mutely, he has always carried with him a sense of failure. It seems almost crazy: in anybody's estimation he has had an astonishing life, even achieved some acclaim without looking for it – finding without seeking – and yet he can't shake this sense of disappointment in the personal realm, where we live.

He goes to the kitchen to make coffee. He has a scoop that measures precisely and neatly the amount of coffee he should put in the Pavoni, but he can't find it and tries to use a teaspoon unsuccessfully, so that half the coffee spills. More and more, small actions cause him difficulties. As he struggles with the coffee, he thinks that his life, like his father's, will end in aimless pottering. His father was forever making repeat trips to his storeroom or the garden shed or the kitchen, trips that started with promise and ended in confusion. As he looks around in the dull Camden morning light that finds its way via the damp bricks into the basement, he sees what Lucy has been hinting at, the grimed surfaces, the broken hinge causing one of the cupboard doors to limp, a missing light bulb; he realises that she has been too tactful to tell him directly that he is neglecting the place. Everyone has always had undeserved respect for my feelings. He knows she feels unease not so much because of the neglect, but because she sees the state of the house as evidence of his detachment. Nancy said that houses always need attention and he hadn't realised that it was literally true. The place is crumbling in front of him. I've been in this murk too long. It's better for everyone if I get away.

He takes the coffee back to the bedroom. The sheets are stained. There are different kinds of stain, invested with significance, sometimes of happiness, sometimes of guilt. These are evidence of something ecstatic. It's as if he had never had sex before. He remembers how it was: before you have done it you only have a vague notion of what it's like, but immediately afterwards you cannot imagine how you lived your life without it. He drinks his coffee. For forty years he has relied on coffee in the morning to produce a little murmur of optimism. Now he feels keyed up by his decision to go, and he will take the memory of this night as a benediction, a charm. Fucking. A word of Germanic origin, which sounds mechanical, but hides an infinite variety of delicate meaning. In families, ancient taboos survive. The older generation – he is the sole survivor in this family – is not expected to show any direct interest in fucking, although it is permitted some ironic references, e.g., *Dead birds never fall out of the nest*. Older women sometimes make ironic reference to the need for a toy boy, but they are forbidden to abandon the code and say what they really mean, that they want to enjoy the rite of fucking, which somehow will confirm their relevance.

As he drinks his coffee, he feels blessed as though he has inoculated himself against bitterness by this unexpected sexual encounter.

He remembers what Lucy said: 'Sylvie tells me she is working in an organic café, but is really a painter.' It was a warning that a fruitcake and her dog had come to camp.

'How are you, Sylvie? I enjoyed the book club . . .'

'Oh, it was such a pleasure for us. A privilege. I just came by to drop off a little token. Actually, it is literally a token, from our local bookshop. A token of our appreciation. I was taking the dog for a walk anyway.'

Her hair, as he looks at it now, seems too abundant, like that guitarist's from Queen, almost a periwig. She seems to be sheltering under there, as one might under a magnificent tree, just for the sense of occasion.

'You shouldn't have.'

'I wanted to.'

She gives out a short, unmotivated giggle, and as she does so there is a significant movement under her blouse, which, despite himself, catches his eye.

'Anyway, I was taking Wolfie for a walk. As I said. Did I? Yes.'

'You didn't walk all the way from Highgate?'

'It's not that far.'

Maybe she is suggesting that they are close neighbours who inhabit the same territory, share some turf. The dog, however, lies pretty still, as if tired, although lugubriously watchful. David has a picture of Sylvie roaming north London with Wolfie; she is a seeker after something, one of the many people who believe that it's all out there to be discovered, if only you can acquire the knack.

'I'd better go now,' she says, but with an equivocal note.

'I was just going to make some tea. I prefer tea. But seeing the Chardonnay's open, how about a drink?'

'Well, all right. Just a small glass of wine. I love this kitchen, by the way.'

'It's a bit shabby. I see that when people come.'

'It's got character. It's you.'

It's nothing to do with him; it reflects Nancy's firm views on how things should be. He could tell Sylvie that for thirty-seven years he lived within Nancy's domestic universe, bound by the greater force of her quotidian convictions, but he doesn't want to exchange this kind of intimacy although he can already feel the warmth of the other kind reaching him. He wonders, as she tells him about her difficulties selling her pictures – she's experimented with acrylics recently – what it would be like to have sex with her. He can imagine that there would anyway be consequences. She has an overwhelming femininity, a feminine neediness, which he knows would spell trouble. And also, he fears the humiliation of taking his clothes off and trying to cope with this abundance. Even though he has been working out, he knows that there is really no turning back for the human body, just degrees of decline.

'Won't you have a drink?' she asks. 'I feel a tad like an alkie drinking alone.'

'OK, I will.'

'Maybe one evening I could cook for you.'

'That would be nice.'

'What sort of thing do you like? I'm almost vegetarian. Just a bit of fish or chicken occasionally.'

'Oh, I eat more or less anything.'

'I don't think your daughter likes me,' she says skittishly. 'How old is she?'

'She's twenty-six. In fact I think she does like you. Anyway, she hardly knows you.'

'She probably thinks I am after you.'

'I very much doubt it.'

God, I sound so stilted. He finishes his glass of wine. His phone rings. It's Rosalie.

'Sorry, forgive me, I must answer this.'

He walks to the stairs outside the kitchen. Rosalie is in tears. She wants to come round to talk about something, and he feels his spirits sinking.

'OK, come as soon as you can.'

'Sylvie, I'm afraid there is a bit of a crisis; you'll have to go now. I'm so sorry. But I'd like to take you up on your offer of a meal some time.'

'I understand. I hope it's not serious.'

'I hope not. It's a family thing.'

'Come, Wolfie, come, girl.'

She turns to the dog, her plain best friend, the way schoolgirls do when they have been snubbed.

'I'm sorry I intruded like this.'

'Don't be silly. It was absolutely great, but something has come up. It's bizarre – I can be here for days without a visitor.'

'I don't believe that. But whatever.'

He hugs her to make up, and feels the urgency of her breasts against him. The dog, gung-ho, is straining at the leash. She kisses him on the cheek and her lips are full, quite leathery, and scented with Chardonnay. She takes a handkerchief and wipes the lipstick from his cheek, which he thinks is deliberately intimate.

He tidies up a bit, now that he is fully conscious that the place is deteriorating under his stewardship. Rosalie's taste is for the decorative and pastoral. He puts the wine in the fridge and keeps one glass out. In a way he is elated by these intrusions, three young women wanting his attention, because he feels that he is slipping unnoticed out of the world. Simon said over the steamed dumplings a few weeks ago that we are fading like frescos in unvisited churches. Simon likes Italian churches, and has a hit list of triptychs and frescos he must see before he dies. And this is an urge that David notices among his friends, the urge to store up abstract images and experiences, as though they will be handy on the other side. Why? Thirteen hundred years ago the Venerable Bede wrote, in that heart-stopping image, that a life is similar to a sparrow flying into a hall where the thanes and earls are feasting on a winter's night. The sparrow flies briefly through the light warmth and out into the cold again, almost in a flash, Bede wrote, but we are utterly ignorant of what went before and what follows. From winter going into winter again. Simon is frightened of death but he doesn't say that to his friends. Nor does he repeat Wittgenstein's remark, now often heard, that death is not an event in life.

Half an hour or more goes by as he waits for Rosalie. The doorbell finally rings weakly – even the doorbell sounds as though it is on borrowed time. He is apprehensive.

She stands in the doorway for a moment, pale, her tea dress – all the rage, he has heard – striking a note of innocence. Her dress is similar to the one his mother is wearing, standing next to his naval-lieutenant father. Her russet hair is tied back, not with full balletic severity, but with some wisps hanging down over her face, although there is nothing dishevelled about her.

'Rosalie. Come in, come in.'

'Thanks, David. Thank you.'

She hugs him and begins to sob, so that he can feel the tremors passing from her highly tuned self into his, as if he is the seasoned, resonating body of a violin. Her sobs choke themselves and he leads her down to the kitchen. He feels hopelessly ill-equipped to deal with her distress, and he feels deeply dispirited, because he knows that Ed is at the bottom of it.

'Would you like a drink or some tea? Or something?'

'I would love some tea.'

He offers her the chair from which he watches television – he and Nancy rarely strayed from this basement – and he fusses with the tea. Rosalie sits elegantly slumped. He thinks of ballerinas between exercises, always nursing their overworked legs. He hopes she doesn't detect the more earthbound legacy of Wolfie and Sylvie, dog hair and banal opinions. Rosalie comes from an altogether different class of womanhood and wouldn't be seen dead communing with a dog. Luckily there is a lemon, just about OK, for her tea, and he slices that as neatly as he can, discarding the green-mottled bits.

He hands her the tea. The Tate Modern cups are grubby. He says gently in the voice he used in Bosnia and Rwanda and, even further back in time, in Nicaragua, 'Would you like to tell me about it now?'

'David, I am so sorry, but I have nobody else to speak to.'

He leans forward.

'Is it to do with Ed?'

Her eyes, which contain a few blood trails of distress, look up at him. She nods.

'Did you know?'

'Know what, Rosie? I have no idea what you're talking about.'

'Ed has been screwing some trainee from his office.'

'Oh Jesus, are you sure?'

'She told me.'

'When?'

'This morning.'

'She came to see you to tell you that she was having an affair with your husband?'

'Actually, she came to see me to tell me that she has been fired by Robin, for having an affair with my husband.'

'Robin.'

It's not a question, but she answers it anyway.

'Yes, Robin. He's got a crush on her and is always sending her little notes and presents, she said. And cute little emails.'

'Has this been going on for a while? Ed, I mean?'

'Not long. A few weeks, probably. But this girl, Alice, feels she's been unfairly treated.'

And wants to share the misery around generously, David guesses.

'Does she say she loves him or anything like that?'

'To be honest, I don't think she gives a monkey's fuck about him. She's just very young and up for a good time.'

He's never heard her say anything that crass before.

'Have you spoken to Ed? He may have another take on it.'

'I haven't spoken to him. He's in Geneva. But also, as you know, we have been having fertility problems, and I just couldn't face this now. That's why I came to you.'

Now she draws her knees up and sits sideways in the old chair as if demonstrating her flexibility, which is impressive.

'Rosie, what can I do?'

'You're his father.'

'Do you want me to talk to him?'

'Perhaps you could tell him that Robin has hinted to you that something has been going on.'

'Wouldn't Robin say something to him? He's going to have to explain why this girl was fired.'

'Alice.'

'Why this Alice has gone.'

'He may, but I think he's got Ed where he wants him now.'

'Let's have a drink.'

She nods. Her nod seems to say that she has lost her hold on small details, and he opens a bottle of Newton Unfiltered from the Napa Valley. She stares in his direction; her stare is directed not at him, but beyond to the great imponderable.

'Rosie,' he says, as the cork comes fatly out, 'I think that what we need here, particularly what you need, is to consider the consequences of doing anything too hastily.' (He can't really be sure, of course, because nobody knows another's mind.) 'I know Ed loves you, even worships you. If it is true what this Alice says – if it's true – it may be that Ed is under terrible strain.'

As he drinks from his glass of the unfiltered Chardonnay he wonders irrelevantly why it hasn't been filtered.

'That's why I came. I'm terrified that if I confront him he'll say he loves her or something.'

'Rosie, nobody, and I mean nobody, could imagine him loving anybody but you.'

In a way he's speaking more for himself than for his errant, slightly chubby son. She's weeping again, and now her face is hidden on her knees, so that he only sees the convulsions in the undulation and bobbing of her hair. He puts his hand on her shoulder, as one would with a child sobbing, and she looks up at him and rests her hand on his for a moment. He thinks that every movement she makes is borrowed from some ballet, as if ballet provides her whole emotional universe.

She looks up at him, her face very pale, misery draining the colour away in that mysterious fashion; her sobs have become sporadic tremors.

'I'm so sorry, David. I have never really suffered in my whole life and I have no experience to draw on to deal with it. You just think it's for other people. The idea that Ed could have been screwing this girl is unbearable. The worst is that we have been trying to have a child. Trying too hard, I am sure.'

'Rosie, can I tell you something which I have never told anyone?'

She looks at him, her attention caught even though she is in terrific pain.

'A couple of years after Lucy was born and I was away a lot for the BBC and then ITV, I found out that Nancy had been having an affair for two years. I was completely devastated. I know how you feel. It's horrible and it seems like an attack on your inner self, a complete and utter humiliation, but worse because it's a negation of your self and all the possibilities of life.' (He finds himself warming to his theme.) 'But I decided with Nancy never to mention it because of the children. I had anyway had a few flings, although of course I didn't think they were important. They didn't affect the children, for a start. And she never knew that I knew, although there were times when I was tempted to tell her. But the reason I am telling you this is because I think if you love Ed, you will forgive him and get over it. As I did.'

Although I never got over it entirely and never forgave Nancy entirely.

'Is it really possible to forget?'

'Probably not completely.'

But he can't say that it is not possible until you find

someone else, when the rites of love usually obliterate the other. And he would probably have left Nancy, except that, from the moment Jenni drowned, he believed he had forfeited his rights to second chances.

'I can't see how I can get over it. I feel as though I have been torn apart. Do you really think it's possible?'

'I really do.'

'Can I have another glass of whatever it is?'

'Of course.'

He pours and she drinks half the glass in one.

'Maybe if I have a baby, that will help.'

'I'm sure it will. It's one of the things that everyone tells you, but of course you can't really take it in until it happens, that once you have a child everything changes.'

In his experience, there's also often a transfer of moral capital to the mother. Sometimes this has deep effects, the shifting of cargo in a storm, which can capsize the ship.

'Do you have any music?'

'I bought *Das Lied von der Erde* after we were at Covent Garden.'

'Could you play it?'

He puts the CD in the little-used player and presses the button, which is not like buttons were, but more like a sixpence that has been run over on a train line. As a boy, he and his friend placed coins on the line, mostly coppers, because sixpence was his entire weekly pocket money. It was illegal to deface the coin of the realm. *The coin of the realm* is one of those sonorous phrases that people enjoyed and believed. His mother once said you must never approach royalty and he never has. Nor has he run with scissors.

Now, as Rosalie struggles to come to terms with the fact that she has been for ever diminished, that she has been granted no exemption from life's humiliations and reverses, he feels heavy and burdened himself. He wonders how Ed could have put so much at risk. You never dip your pen in the company's ink: that's another old saying.

'My feelings are so confused,' Rosalie says. 'I literally cannot think.'

Das Lied von der Erde, which seemed so soulful at Covent Garden, now has a suicidal gloom to it, a very poor choice. Rosalie responds to the sixth movement, 'The Farewell', in a very direct way. Her eyes are moist; the liquid resting on their surfaces catches the light from the large, clumsy spots. These spots have been here ever since he was photographed at home for the *Sunday Times Magazine* in 1973; then they were the height of chic, like the quarry tiles.

Rosalie is in thrall to her feelings, but feelings are not reliable in this situation: *Feelings are stars which guide us only in the brightest daylight*. He can't remember who said it.

Her eyes seem to be looking for the music or what it represents, to see if she can somehow set a true course for her turbulent, chaotic feelings.

'You have to accept that there is no quick fix. Gradually things will settle.'

'Do you think so?'

'I do. Absolutely.'

He doesn't, but he can't say this. Nor can he say that for the bystander there is a kind of fascination in these domestic dramas that the protagonists can never appreciate. He has seen enough marriages fail and he has heard enough bitter denunciations and listened to enough wildly one-sided accounts to know that, however hard you try, it is impossible to take someone else's problems as seriously as they would like you to. And this is always true of jealousy, that is both consuming and demeaning, and even as you are being consumed, you are aware that you are demeaning yourself and even as you are demeaning yourself, you know that you are going too far and that people are bound to back away. But when someone tells you their troubles, you see with perfect lucidity the banality of the situation.

He pours Rosalie another hefty drink, which she downs before he has poured one for himself. *Das Lied von der Erde* is reaching its tragic climax. It's excruciating. Rosalie is still gazing upwards – perhaps she sees Darcey Bussell – and moving her body minutely, as if she's remembering every step and every hand gesture.

'I'm as drunk as a monkey,' she suddenly says. 'Pissed as a fucking fart.'

'Do you want some water?' he says foolishly.

'No thanks. Just another splash of the old unfiltered what's-its-name.'

Now she stands up and begins to dance, although the kitchen doesn't offer much room and the low ceiling seems too cramped for one so astonishingly graceful. He watches, both entranced and uncomfortable, as she follows the music, although in a necessarily limited way.

'Will you dance with me, David?'

He imagines himself trying to pirouette around the kitchen and smiles, sitting back determinedly.

'I can't dance.'

'You can. Of course you can.'

She takes his hand and, when he stands up, she places one of her arms on his shoulder and the other around his waist. Soon there isn't a paper between them and her body, unnaturally pliant and fluent, seems to have flowed over the rough and imperfect contours of his.

'You never really forgave Nancy, did you?'

'No.'

'It was all bollocks then?'

'More or less.'

She laughs close to his ear.

'Were you trying to make me feel better?'

'I was.'

'That's so sweet.'

She places a light kiss, so light it is like the passing of a moth, on his cheek.

'Let's go and do it.'

For a moment he wonders what she means.

'You're my son's wife.'

Even as he says it, he knows he sounds biblical, his voice echoing in a wadi in Sinai.

'That's the whole point. I'll have done something far worse than him.'

He sees the logic in a way.

'And me?'

'It will be our secret. It will have to be, don't you think?'

He drinks coffee in this rumpled, ambivalent bed, which has taken on its morning demeanour. He feels himself unexpectedly set free, although he can't understand exactly how this has happened. He tucks a towel round his waist and walks down to the kitchen, aware that he is an absurd figure. Underneath the towel, his cock and scrotum although weary, are still recognisably the original male attachments, which once on a filthy beach in Ostia he imagined with youthful hubris to have heroic qualities. What an arse. Last night – he wants to remember the precise details, in just the same way and for the same reasons that Simon wants to see every fresco in Tuscany –

he remembered Jenni. But it was Jenni before she floated away into the dark water. The strange thing is that he didn't see her terrified rictus and he believes that he never will again.

He knows that he must go away, for Rosalie's sake, for Ed's and for his own. But rather than feeling guilty, he feels absurdly happy, almost ecstatic.

14

WHEN ED ARRIVES back from Geneva, he realises that something of that city has got to him. He pictures the lambent lake with the huge water spout, the circling mountains lightly topped with snow, the clean streets, the yachts moored almost in town, the old city, which gives the citizens an interesting and risk-free glimpse of what life in Bohemia could be, and he sees the road to Mont Blanc and Chamonix as a highway to escape from Fennell, Dunston and Bickerstaff. Yesterday, while lunching in Le Grand Quai on schnitzel and rosti – done with a light, modern take – he was offered a job by Laurent Foubert, of Zwingli, Robinson, Foubert et Cie, to start next month. He has told Laurent that his experience of international trusts is limited, but Laurent says that he has enjoyed working with him over the last six months, and believes that he has what it takes; he suggests that Fennell, Dunston and Bickertstaff is going nowhere, way off the pace. He also says that Ed's French is easily improved with daily saturation classes. The salary he is proposing is startling. He and Rosalie can make a new life, and the baby – he's sure the Swiss know all there is to know about IVF – will be skiing parallel by the age of three. He will disentangle himself from Alice, if she hasn't already done it herself.

He will also escape from his old dad, whose large presence, scented with decay, still breathes on him. And he will leave London, which is far too complex and ironic and racked a place for family life.

In Geneva, in the spirit of Calvin, the citizens believe in the redemptive power of activity: 'What? Would you have the Lord find me idle when He comes?' said Calvin, who was a trained lawyer, and this could be the city's mission statement. Dad's idea of redemption is the search for something beyond this world, as if life is other than the one we lead, a notion he picked up from Richard Burton, although in Rome he was probably dropping acid, as they used to say back then.

Ed envisages a multilingual, snowy, and prosperous life. Laurent races huskies, which he says is a fantastic sport, very elemental, absolutely vital as an escape for the modern man. Ed knows nobody in Camden who races huskies. He has asked Laurent for a week to consult with his family.

He goes straight to the office from the airport. Nervously he calls Rosalie but she is not answering. At least her phone is now on. The office looks benighted and Gloria, in front of the rather tacky plastic-brass sign glued to the dull-coloured hessian on the wall, is in her own way an affront to his new vision of life among the Euro elite who sail billowing yachts and race teams of howling huskies.

'Morning, Mr Cross. How was Geneva?'

'Fine, thanks. All well here?'

'Hunky-dory, thank you.'

From his office he buzzes Alice, but he finds her phone extension is giving a curiously insistent tone as if designed to encourage mental illness.

He calls through to Gloria.

'Gloria, where's Alice today?'

'Not sure, Mr Cross.'

'Not sure? What do you mean?'

'I'm not sure where she is.'

'Why not?'

'I can't say why. We was just informed by Mandy on Wednesday that she would be leaving the firm with immediate effect.'

'Did she ever come back from her trip to Scotland?'

'She just come in for an hour or so to see Robin.'

'Is he here today?'

'No, he's in Southampton at the conference on family law.'

'Oh yes, he did tell me. OK, thanks, Gloria.'

'No problem, Mr Cross. Got to take a call. It's gone mental here all morning.'

He tries to call Alice but her mobile phone number is discontinued. Before he speaks to Rosalie – thank God she didn't answer – he must speak to Alice to find out why she's not here. He feels beleaguered. He can't speak to Robin, he can't find Alice, and now he certainly can't speak to Rosalie until he knows what's going on. His phone rings, and he sees, with a sinking heart, that it is Rosalie.

'Hello, darling, just got in a few moments ago. I'm knackered,' he says, the hint of self-pity to indicate that international jet setting is not all it's cracked up to be.

'How was Geneva, sweetie?'

Her tone immediately dispels his foreboding.

'It was great. Tiring, but great. Rosie, I've got to tell you, I have been offered a huge job there and I think we should go.'

'Geneva? Good God. Can we discuss it?'

'Of course, I've asked for a week to talk it through with you. I'll be finished here about six and then let's go out to dinner. Will you book somewhere?'

'OK.'

'How are you doing?'

'I'm fine. I think I may be pregnant.'

'Jesus, that's wonderful. How do you know?'

'Nothing too scientific. I just have a feeling. A certainty, actually.'

'Oh, OK. Will you take a Boots test?'

He recognises that self-romanticising tendency, the confidence of a connection to higher spiritual truths.

'Yes, I will take a test in a few days. But trust me, I am pregnant.'

'God, I hope so. Rosie, I love you more than I can tell you.'

He feels such a rush of affection – it's only partly relief – that he is on the verge of tears.

'I love you, too.'

'Rosie, I am so sorry I have behaved so badly. All I can say is the pressure was getting to me. Whatever happens, we will see this baby business through.'

'I know we will, darling.'

'See you at six-thirty, seven. Love you.'

Now he feels released. He wants to call Robin immediately to tell him that he's resigning, but he decides that it is premature. His little office with its mean aspect will soon be replaced by a view of Lake Geneva – Lac Léman as the natives – we natives – call it. Down below, near the bins he sees a tramp pissing, as if to endorse his decision to embrace emigration. Mind you, emigration no longer has the same connotations of permanence: we are all citizens of the world; there is absolutely no reason why anyone should be confined to one country. Although he is prepared to accept that Romanian gypsies and Congolese militias should probably stay where they belong. He wonders if they have a ballet in Geneva. He Googles it: Ballet du Grand Théâtre de Genève. Isadora Duncan and Nijinsky both performed there. Since its inception it has explored the stylistic plurality of the dance of the twentieth century. Also, *les jeunes* are offered the opportunity to discover the lyrical arts and choreography, by means of diverse activities. Goodness! If Rosalie is indeed pregnant, there will be no end of possibilities – *activités diverses* – for a mother and daughter with balletic inclinations. Huskies, yachting, ballet. He also realises, with relief, that he can now cut his ties with Alice, and never try to speak to her. After all, she has made it very obvious that she doesn't want to see him. Where, a few minutes ago, he was desperate to find out why she had left, now he thinks it best to accept with dignity and reticence her sudden departure and to prepare himself for his own. He calls Mr Fineman, who is delighted to hear from a big shot. The way he sees it, the little man has won: he believes he has achieved a major legal victory, which will give freedom to thousands; he sees himself as the Clarence Darrow of the North Circular Road.

'Mr Cross, thank you. I have sent you a small gift.'

'That's very kind. Let's meet soon.'

'Have you had the gift?'

'No, but I have just got back from Geneva.'

'I dropped it off yesterday. I came on the number 19.'

'Thank you. I will ask our receptionist.'

'Goodbye. Olla sends her thanks also.'

He feels touched by Mr Fineman. He doubts that in

Geneva he will be dealing with the little people, if there are any, but he will miss him.

'Gloria, have you got a package for me from Mr Fineman?'

'Oh yes, sorry, it arrived yesterday.'

'Can you bring it in?'

'It's still gone mental here. Can it wait a few minutes?'

'No, it can't. I'll come and get it.'

He strides truculently to the reception. Gloria has the parcel ready for him; without looking directly at him, she employs her very mobile face to indicate just how tied up she is with nuisance callers, such as clients. Back in his office he discovers that he has been given an enormous box of shortbread decorated with a tartan cover. He opens it and helps himself. The shortbread comes in five sizes and shapes. He tries to imagine why Mr Fineman would see this as an appropriate present after the famous legal victory. Then he finds a note: *You made _short_ work of them, Kind regards, Julius Fineman.*

He has another biscuit, and calls his sister.

'Can you keep a secret?' he asks.

'I am the only one in the family who can.'

'You remember I said I wanted to get away from Robin Fennell?'

'Yes.'

'Well, I have been offered a huge job in Geneva.'

'Geneva? Isn't that the city of the living dead?'

'What do you mean? Have you ever been there?'

'No, but it is famously dull. Banks sponsor art, everyone wears a suit, even in bed, and they make Swiss jokes.'

He wants to tell her about husky racing but he guesses he may sound foolish.

'Don't be ridiculous. That is so typical. It's one hour

from Chamonix, the streets are clean and it's one of the most sophisticated places in Europe.'

'Oh dear. Have we cracked?'

'Jesus, you are annoying. You're supposed to say wonderful, congratulations.'

'Congratulations. Wonderful. Have you told Rosie?'

'Of course.'

'And?'

'And she's very keen to hear all about it. How's Dad, by the way?'

'I think he's carrying on with a fancy woman.'

'Are you sure?'

'Well, she came round to the house the other night and made herself right at home. Her dog settled in, too. In no time at all they shovelled me out of the door.'

'Who is she?'

'Her name's Sylvie. She's a fruitcake with a dog. We met her on the Heath.'

'What do you mean, "We met her on the Heath"?'

'Dad and I were walking and her dog got lost and we found it. Or it found us. I think it is trained to get lost and find single men.'

'What's she look like?'

'Massive talking knockers, loads of wavy hair, very enthusiastic. Speaks like a weather-girl.'

'Sounds perfect. Maybe it's not such a bad thing. Has it occurred to you that he's lonely? It's just possible he's missing Mum.'

'He could be. He rang me this morning to say he is going to see his brother.'

'For how long?'

'I don't know. A few months at least. Uncle Guy is not well. Frans emailed Dad.'

'I'm not sure Uncle Guy has ever been well. Anyway, how are you? And how's Nick the boyfriend?'

'Possible boyfriend. He's on probation, but he's great, so far. I'm seeing him tonight.'

'Good luck.'

'What's that supposed to mean? That I need luck to pull?'

'No, no. Just a general sort of blessing from your older bruv. Let me know how it goes.'

'It's funny with married people that they are always interested in other people's sex lives. How's yours, by the way?'

'Believe me, I'm not interested in your sex life at all. And if that is a sly reference to Alice, that's over. So over, as you would say. Goodbye.'

If only she knew the whole truth. He wonders if Dad really is carrying on with this woman. In logic it's absurd to expect your father to behave in a decorous way. And it's absurd to think that there is an appropriate period of mourning but, despite his own lunatic recklessness, he hopes that his father is not in some way dishonouring his mother's memory by jumping into bed with a woman he met on Hampstead Heath, someone blinded by his celebrity and probably just a little desperate. It's not actually dishonouring her memory; it's an attack on their childhood, which should be seen for ever through rose-tinted spectacles. What I have done is far worse. As he thinks about it, his cheeks become warm. Maybe there's a hierarchy of betrayal, and maybe you expect more of your parents, as if they, at least, should hold on to some principles.

And he thinks that this is undoubtedly the tipping point: he and Rosalie off to Geneva, where they will have a child, whether or not Rosalie is pregnant by the conventional method; Mum dead; Dad off to Africa and the old Cross family fragmented. Lucy will be free to pursue her own ends. She's the most intelligent of us all and also the one most distressed by Mum's death. But – he sees where the Tibetan Buddhists are coming from – you can discern a cycle going on here, and you can take comfort in that idea. Dad seems to understand this wheel of change better than Lucy. He's trying to step out of his role as paterfamilias.

Down below he sees another tramp, a woman: she's looking through the bins. He can't see her face, but there is something oddly predictable about her shape and bearing, as though tramps go to a school – *diverses activités pédagogiques* – to learn how to walk in this crabbed way and to carry their shoulders as though they are bearing a bundle on their backs. A fardel. Why do words you haven't heard for a million years pop into your mind? Fardel. Fred Vuliami at school read the word as 'fartel' causing wonderful hilarity among the twelve-year-olds. Even Mr Cheeseman laughed. Fred Vuliami died of a drug overdose at university and his parents split up, each believing that the other was to blame. Mum was always a forcefield of tranquillity because she had a very clear idea – maddening to him as a teenager – of how things should be. He sees that it is this steadiness which has gone from the life of the Cross family.

Down below the woman has found something to put into one of the many bags she has attached to a Tesco supermarket trolley, which is her chariot of fire. Now she's off, shuffling, busy, talking to herself, he imagines from the movements of her head, as she rounds the corner and he loses her from view. In his new, expansive, Helvetian mood, he recalls fondly one of Mum's most annoying saws: *all part of life's rich tapestry*. These tramps, one pissing, one foraging; Robin Fennell in his matching tie and pocket handkerchief; Dad in his cargo shorts and elephant-hair bracelets; Alice squeezing her breasts together to receive his sperm; Gloria with her mangled notions of gentility; me, Lucy – all of us – are part of this tapestry. In fact it's a skein of hopefulness and delusion, but somehow it always holds together, whatever the setbacks. Mr Fineman, with his victory for the little man, demonstrates how some modicum of ideals, however mad, keep the human enterprise on the tracks. And he sees suddenly, with blinding clarity, that the urge to produce children is the most noble ideal of all, and at the same time he is overcome by the profundity of his thoughts – he's really a lawyer-philosopher – and by his love for Rosalie, which he has so nearly put in jeopardy.

He's just about to call her again when Mandy calls him.

'I have Robin on the line from Southampton.'

'OK. Thanks.'

He waits. Mandy comes on the line again, and tells him Robin won't be a moment.

Finally he speaks.

'Eddie, sorry, I got caught up. Eddie, is that you?'

'Hello, Robin, yes, it's me. How is Southampton?'

'Interesting. Very interesting. I'll brief you when I see you. Now look, I wanted to speak to you privately but I have to stay on here overnight. I asked Alice to explain why she was back two days late from her trip to Scotland. I don't want to go over the details, but she claimed that I was harassing her because she'd been having a relationship with you. As you had already assured me that no such thing had taken place, I chose to see this as further evidence of a slightly hysterical nature and told her to pack her things and go immediately. I consider the whole matter closed. Do you follow me? There are both Rosalie and your father to consider here, and I think that girl is a loose cannon. I value you very highly, as you know.'

'Robin.'

'Don't say anything you might regret. Think about it before you speak.'

'I just wanted to say that . . .'

'Don't. Please listen to my advice, Ed, and say nothing.'

'All right.'

'Good. We need to cut this off at the pass. I'll see you on Friday.'

He wanted to tell Robin that he is off to Geneva, but he sees now that it would have been a mistake because nothing is fixed with Laurent. There seems to be a direct connection between his queasiness about Robin and his growing admiration for Laurent, like two buckets in a well attached to one rope. I have seen the future, and it's not here looking down at a bin while Robin explains why he has sacked Alice. He has another shortbread from the Fineman bequest. The real reason he got rid of Alice is sexual jealousy. Ed sees that he has been saved just in time from his own folly. He will force himself to wait a few days before he accepts Laurent's offer. In the meanwhile he emails to say how flattered he is to be asked, and to say that he has already consulted with his family, and he has every confidence that it will all work out. His antipathy to Robin is growing uncontrollably, like some awful cancer. He sees his mother in hospital in those final weeks: drugged, tired, serene at times, but giving glimpses of her horror at what is to come. One night he was sitting with her when she muttered in her sleep and moaned the names of her children over and over. In her turmoil she still hoped her children could exercise some magic or expend some of their youthful essences to bring her back from the abyss.

He would have given any organ or any limb. So he imagined. He is now desperately ashamed of himself: I am the one who has been dishonouring her memory, not Dad. Good luck to him with the fruitcake, if that's what he needs.

He spends the next couple of hours going through papers and dictating letters into his little machine. He wants a clean break when they go to the shores of Lac Léman, and he closes off the Fineman file in the way that Robin likes with a note that the fees are agreed and will be paid within thirty days. He also has to read through a divorce petition, drafted by Alice a week ago for his approval. And this is a penance, which he is happy to accept. These petitions are coded misery, and it is in code that lawyers work, turning every tragedy and every anxiety to fit an existing legal template. It's the myth of Procrustes, the stretcher, who killed travellers by cutting them or stretching them to fit his magic bed. Form D8, Form DBA, statement of arrangements for the children. In this case the arrangements for the children are proving difficult. The man has a new woman who doesn't want him to see his children more than strictly necessary. The wife is petitioning on the grounds of infidelity. It's not necessary, but she wants her feelings to be known. And in the background somewhere are three cowering children whose lives are going to be blighted for ever: they will be forced to spend weekends with their father's lover. They will have to watch their father with embarrassment and shame. The husband doesn't deny adultery, but he is contesting the level of maintenance. In Geneva Ed will be dealing with the rich, who are, understandably, always trying to protect their money from the taxman and from ex-wives by means of trusts. He has a copy of *Principles of European Trust Law* and he must start to read it. But even as he contemplates the move to Geneva and the higher class of misery he will be dealing in, he remembers Lucy's words, *It's famously boring*. The fact is his professional life is already boring, but he knows that by moving to Geneva he will be drawn deeper into the swamp. He puts a note on the papers: *Proceed*, with his signature, and puts them in his out-tray. He is, surprisingly, a good lawyer. Laurent has heard good reports of him.

And now, after his few hours of elation, he feels down again. At thirty-two, all those feelings he had, all those hopes he had, all those uncomplicated friendships he had, and the sense he had that anything was possible, have already been dissipated. The options are falling away, the horizon is lowering. Going to Geneva may sound like a wonderful move, but how do you come back from there? What are you qualified for, except the life of a highly paid, bilingual pander to a lot of rich crooks. And the rich, as Scott Fitzgerald discovered, are dull and repetitious. His mobile rings.

'Hello, Luce, I was just thinking that you are the most intelligent of us. Although there are only three of us left. What can I do for you?'

'Ed, sorry, I have to speak. There's a crisis.'

'What?'

'Josh, that friend of yours, has posted nude photos of me on the Internet. Except that it's not me. The head is me, but the body isn't.'

'Have you spoken to him?'

'No. Look, Ed, Google me – my name and "nude photos". It's like Carla Bruni. It's so unfair. I feel humiliated. What have I done to deserve this? He's the bastard.'

He opens Google and sure enough there is his sister, standing smiling, nude, and lying back on a sunbed, nude. Her pubic hair is trimmed in a Brazilian. It's clearly a crude Photoshop job.

'You're right, it's not you. Your tits aren't that big.'

'Oh thanks. Of course it's not me. What can we do?'

'You can request removal from Google. He could upload it again in minutes.'

'Can you speak to him, please? The pictures of me, my face I mean, I emailed him after a party five or six months ago.'

'I'll try.'

'Please, Ed, this is frightening me. You didn't speak to him last time, did you?'

'No, I didn't. I should have. Do you want to stay at our place tonight?'

'Maybe. It depends on Nick. I'm sorry to dump this on you.'

'I'll call him and get back to you.'

And now he feels weary, his upbeat mood, which was already fading, has gone, leaving no trace. Maybe I am bipolar. Today's theme seems to be the destructive effects of jealousy.

He calls Josh.

'Hello?'

'Josh, it's Edward Cross here.'

'Hey, Ed, how are you?'

He's drunk. He can hear pub noises.

'Josh, I am not calling you for a pleasant little chat. I want to make one thing clear to you. Leave my sister alone, don't harass her, don't post fake pictures of her on the net and don't ever again make any attempt whatsoever to contact her. I have put an emergency injunction in motion and I will only withdraw it if you promise me to remove these pictures. If you don't, you will be sued for your life, and if you break the terms of the injunction you will go to prison.'

'Wait. Hey, wait. It's nothing to do with me, man.'

'Oh isn't it? Well, how come the pictures you faked up are from photos Lucy emailed to you? And how come you followed her to a meeting with a journalist a week or so ago? And how come you called her a fucking cunt? You need help, but the only help I'm going to give you is a one-way trip to court. Do you promise me you won't harass her or contact her in any way at all?'

Ed can hear Josh gulping now, struggling with his breathing.

'I love her, Ed. I can't bear the idea that she's got someone else.'

'Just promise. You must promise or you're going to jail.'

'I promise.'

'Josh, let me make myself absolutely clear once more — you will wish you had never been born if you contact her ever again.'

When he puts his phone down, he looks at his sister's nude simulacrum, and he doesn't see life's rich tapestry. He sees something dark and malevolent. All those friendships and hopes scattered by the warm, foul breeze of what is called real life. In some way their mother had protected them from its stink.

15

LUCY WONDERS, AS Nick is shaving, whether she has slept with too many men. In theory there is no such thing: sleep with whoever you like. But in practice you are supposed to exercise restraint and judgement. We have come a long way since Jane Austen, but actually the underlying assumptions are more or less the same: you keep yourself, or some essence of yourself, for the right person. Nick is obviously a very thorough shower taker: she can hear him singing happily through the bathroom wall. It may have been a little hasty but it didn't have any of the illicit, slightly demeaning quality of a one-night stand. He comes out of the shower eventually and pauses in the doorway with a towel around his waist.

'What do you reckon?'

'To what?'

'To us.'

'In what way?'

'Have we got a future?'

'God, I hope so.'

'So do I. So do I.'

He sits on the bed, freshly sluiced and soap-scented. His few chest hairs are still moist. And his forward-pointing face finds hers, thrusting towards her eagerly. Their faces have a slightly bruised quality. Their skins are tender, in places chafed, and they have, she thinks, the kind of happy emptiness, the sense of emotional depletion, that sex can produce. It doesn't necessarily last, but at this moment the feeling that they have found a kind of understanding, a profound if inarticulate rapport, is very strong. They have explored the topography of each other's bodies, vigorously and frankly.

'Do you want breakfast? Yes?'

Their mouths are still attached, and there is childish pleasure in trying to talk in this conjoined condition.

'I'm starving,' he mumbles.

As they separate, a thin chain of saliva breaks from their mouths.

There's something complicit and romantic about sharing breakfast in a café after your first night of passion. It's a rite: the young lovers leave the bower to show themselves to the old, the married and the impotent. He, of course, has a favourite café near by where the pastries are almost as good as in Bologna. They order two almond croissants – *cornetti alle mandorle* as, of course, he can't resist saying – which contain a little nugget of sweet almond paste and are covered in slightly burnt almonds. They have expended their reserves in reckless exploration and they must be replenished. This exploration operates on two levels, she thinks, an instinctive, even prefigured, lovemaking, but also a sort of unbidden imperative to find out about the other person. (She doesn't rule out discovering the soul.) What does she know about Nick? She hasn't always been a good judge, but she thinks that she could love him and she is a little alarmed by the thought, because it makes her vulnerable. She thinks that he is clever and funny, and good-looking, certainly good-looking enough without being dangerously beautiful. He has another quality: although he is worldly and aware, he is also quite thoughtful and curious. So many men just want an opportunity to talk about themselves, but he asked her about the coins and Roman early Christianity, not obviously a first-date topic, and appeared genuinely interested. She told him that Constantine had seen a vision of the cross, the chi-rho, which he adopted before declaring, *In hoc signo vinces*: In this sign you will conquer. Nick said, 'My mission involves another cross, Lucia Cross.'

As he spoke she wondered if his whole family had this eager look. If there is a family. He probably has a complete and rich hinterland, very different from the Cross family, who are diminished and losing their purchase. She hasn't told him about Josh's latest atrocity.

'Can I say something before I rush off to the Daily Beast?'

'Yes. You will anyway.'

'You are the most fantastic person I have ever met. Last night was the highlight of my whole life.'

'Oh my God. Really, really?'

'I mean it. I'm saying this not just because I am trying to enslave you with my boyish charm, but because I am afraid you won't want to see me again, and I have to go to write a piece on pets. The big question on the feature editor's mind is, do people choose pets that look like them or is it that people begin to look like their pets? Really, I would like to spend the whole day hanging out with you. Can we meet again at seven?'

'Let's. I would love that.'

'Can we meet near my office?'

'Sure.'

'Good. I'll call as I leave.'

She holds his hand where it rests on the table. The

waitress, middle-aged, who knows him by name, gives her a thumbs-up from behind Nick's head and she takes this as an endorsement. She's one of the old-school waitresses Lucy likes, a little battered by life, with badly dyed dead hair, but also a heart of gold. Of course. They have mainly been driven out by slim, cheap Eastern Europeans.

He gets up and they kiss and he leaves. She is happy to sit here in the close, coffee-scented café. She calls her brother.

'We were expecting you,' he says, sounding a little petulant.

'Sorry. I went out with Nick.'

'And?'

'And I think he is going to be fine.'

'Oh, good. That's the main thing. Rosalie was looking forward to seeing you.'

'Please tell her sorry from me, or better still I'll call her and tell her myself. Did you talk to her about departing for Zurich?'

'Geneva. Yes, she's keen.'

'When will you go?'

She tries to sound unconcerned, casual.

'As soon as possible. Probably in about six weeks. We're going to try to let the house. Obviously we are not going to sell right away.'

'How is Rosie?'

'She's great. She thinks she is pregnant.'

'Wonderful. That's lovely.'

'Yuh. Maybe, but you know how it is with her, there's a certain imaginative dimension.'

'You're saying your wife is nuts. Everyone's nuts: Dad's got a New Age whacko, Josh is – clearly – a psycho, and now you are implying that Rosie is off her chump.'

'You sound happy. Good in bed, is he?'

'Oh dear. Married men. Did you speak to Josh?'

She wonders if Josh has been pushed off his list of concerns, shoved down the list by his emigration.

'Yes. I read him the Riot Act. I threatened him with a court order.'

'Can you do that? Really?'

'Yes, but it's not that simple. You would have to make a complaint to the police, and you can imagine how enthusiastically they would deal with it. Of course they would offer you counselling. But I can rustle up some paper to frighten him. He's promised to take down the pictures. By the way, when I was finished with him he was sobbing.'

'Literally?'

'Literally. Choking.'

'Good. You know when you go to Geneva and Dad goes to Africa to see Uncle Guy, I will be the only one left here?'

'The Cross family goes global.'

'The Cross family goes phut. Kaput.'

'Don't be silly. Geneva is only a couple of hours away.'

'It's a world away.'

'Ring Rosie and have a natter. She's at home.'

'A natter? What does that mean? Talking about nappies and Babygros?'

'That's the sort of thing.'

'Ed, before I speak to her, what's the situation with your little indiscretion?'

'It didn't happen. She's gone. Left the firm.'

'Are you upset?'

'Jesus, Lucy, let's not go there.'

'Any connection between her departure and yours?'

'None. To be honest, while I was in Geneva, Robin fired her for taking unauthorised days off.'

'How jolly convenient.'

'I always start off really pleased to hear from you and then . . .'

'And then I annoy you. I'm getting you back for never letting me play with your *Star Wars* things. Bye-bye.'

She orders another croissant and rings Rosie.

'Hello, Rosalie speaking.'

'Hi, Rosie. Sorry I didn't make it last night. You weren't really, really expecting me, were you?'

'Up to a point. I made up a bed. How are you, darling?'

'I'm fine. And how are you?'

Lucy tries to make this sound like the usual meaningless pleasantry.

'Fine. We're off to Geneva.'

'I know. Ed told me. That's absolutely amazing. Do they have dance? Silly question, they are bound to.'

'Yes, they do. Darcey Bussell once gave her *Swan Lake* there at the Ballet du Grand Théâtre.'

Lucy thinks that Darcey Bussell's endorsement may have swung it Ed's way.

'And there's skiing just up the road, Ed says.'

'Yes. Sham.'

'Sham?'

'Chamonix. Lucy, can I tell you something. Secret?'

'Of course.'

'I'm pregnant.'

'That's completely brilliant. When did you find out?'

'I haven't done a test yet, but I am. I am pregnant. I feel totally different. All sorts of things are going on in my body.'

'That's so lovely.'

Lucy hopes that Rosalie isn't deluding herself: she has always found Rosalie's belief that dance, particularly ballet, can produce some mystical experience charming. After all, why limit yourself to the rational? Rosalie was never a Zelda Fitzgerald, but she did put herself (and her feet) through a lot of cruel and unnatural punishment, without ever being taken on by a major company. When she met Ed, she was still living in hope of a career in dance. But in the last year or so, her search for self-fulfilment has found a new destination in the beatific condition of motherhood. God help Ed if she isn't pregnant.

'I'm sure you think I'm crackers, but I just know I'm pregnant. A woman knows. Do you believe me?'

She has a slightly flat, suburban accent, at odds with the lovely presence. But then, so does Darcey Bussell.

'Of course I believe you. Rosie, can we meet very soon?'

'Yes, let's. Come to dinner. By the way, Ed tells me you have a new boyfriend. You can bring him.'

'It may be a tad early to call him a boyfriend officially. But yes, I like him and he said – he was more or less completely sober at the time – he said that he was crazy about me.'

'Good start.'

'Absolutely.'

'I'm crazy about you, too, Lucy. You're the best sister-in-law a girl could have.'

'Rosie, Rosie, I'm touched.'

She is: she shares Dad's weakness for unexpected kindness and warmth. Mum saw it as a little suspect, emotional grandstanding: steadiness was her thing. Instead of heading for Grimaldi, Lucy lingers, thinking about this notion of kindness. Why do I respond to it? She and Rosalie don't really get on, yet this declaration, wherever it comes from, is moving. It seems, she has noticed, that there are people who detect in me qualities I don't really have. Dad once said something along these lines about himself, but he attributed it to the fact that people out there – the other side of the television screen – believe that television anchors are privy to all sorts of knowledge about the springs of life. They aren't, of course, permitted to tell the public everything they know. But Lucy thinks her own self, that elusive creature that we keep inside us (or perhaps that keeps us), is far from fully settled. Mum's qualities were somehow fully formed at birth. She annoyed Dad sometimes, but he seemed to need her certainties. Now, Lucy believes that Rosalie may really be pregnant; hormones are affecting her emotions to produce this unaccustomed warmth.

Five years ago Uncle Guy said on one of his two visits to England in forty years – he wasn't impressed – that every time he walked out into the Kalahari he saw *the heaventree of stars hung with humid nightblue fruit*. She's never forgotten it. He was wearing desert boots and rugby shorts in Piccadilly at the time. Not that she understood him fully, but Uncle Guy's views, freely expressed, seemed to suggest that the spiritual life is the only one worth living. And she sees now that Uncle Guy was right: life is not a sordid practical thing to be endured, but something that should transport you. And she knows, with a sort of intuition, that she will love Nick, if she doesn't already. Her own hormones are coursing, too. *The heaventree of stars hung with humid nightblue fruit*: how beautiful that is. She's smiling inanely. She feels that there has been a planetary shift. She smiles at the waitress as she leaves. They are complicit in a feminine-human understanding. She calls Rachel to tell her she will be going straight to the British Museum to finish up. Rachel is, as always, distracted, and barely listening.

She sets off for her flat to change her clothes. All big moments in life demand a change of clothes. Her mother was a demon for clean nighties and underwear and it's a habit she has inherited. Since her mother died, Lucy has realised that there are ritualistic aspects to her behaviour. She's in a way still placing offerings at the family shrine. She knows that Mum would have liked Nick.

She takes the underground; it's the time of stupefaction after all the people with a purpose have gone and only a few seats are inhabited by vacant, exhausted people. Free newspapers lie in drifts. There are cans and bottles, reminders of the night revellers. Two Chinese nurses are sleeping, and an African is rubbing his face as if he wishes to discover what lies beneath the surface; an earnestly consulting young man and a woman, probably Romanian – the shiny, striped tracksuits are the giveaway – are trying to fill in a form with a pencil, and a large, bald man in a yellow safety jacket is reading *Angling Times*. He could be dreaming of tench. There is also a family of tourists, perhaps wondering about the exact nature of this city with its innumerable secrets and compromises and illusions, and one of the illusions – widely accepted – is that Londoners know something – that this city has a kind of savvy and irony and tradition, not available (or wanted) anywhere else. The air in the carriage is dead, as though it has not seen the light, ever. It is photon-free. The air in a coal mine is probably similar. But the funny thing is, it's the neatly attired tourist family, ranging from blond to grey, most likely Danish, who look weird with their clean sneakers, pale jeans, anodyne sweatshirts, the wheeled luggage, the sensible, rolled, shortie umbrella in Mummie's hand, the guidebook poised in Vader's. They look like people from another planet. They are way too clean and nice for this manky rattletrap of a train. Way too naive for this city. Where they come from, people take away their cans of Red Bull – more likely lingonberry juice – and newspapers and generally do things in an orderly, rational manner.

When she gets home and opens the communal front door on to the hall, which houses a bicycle with one wheel, six plastic containers belonging to a tenant who left some time ago without paying his rent, a huge pile of junk mail and the rubbish of four flats in brown recycling boxes, the pervading aroma is poor: it includes cooking smells, a hint of sewage and air freshener.

But she is happy: she has Nick. She undresses quickly, leaving a carefree trail of clothes behind her. The bath runs slowly, making protesting noises which are replicated by howls and screeches way back into the walls somewhere. She takes off the remains of her make-up and gets into the water. She's singing. Water makes her sing.

'You sound happy.'

'Jesus, Josh. Get out.'

He has a pistol, which he sticks into his mouth.

'No, Josh, no.'

'I loved you.'

His voice is distorted by the stubby barrel, like someone talking with their mouth full. She is about to be showered with human bits and the bath water will turn pink, as in movies, where terrible things happen to women in water.

16

IF YOU SAW us from a distance, David thinks, you might not realise that we were brothers.

Guy is very tall, six foot four, but stooped, as though he has spent a lot of time in books or looking down at the ground. In truth he has done both. He wears rugby shorts of an antique design in a faded blue. His T-shirt is baggy, its tensile qualities long gone, and it is so worn that you can only just make out the logo of a canoeing company, with the Victoria Falls behind it. His shoes, worn with short grey nylon socks, are desert boots, which, he says, are called *velskoen*: they are made by craftsmen out of kudu hide. By the looks of them, that was some time ago. In television David was supplied with location wear, anoraks, hats, trekking trousers, even when he was delivering a report from the hotel grounds. Guy has no time for this kind of kit.

David is himself almost six feet tall, but in the past ten days he has been reminded that he grew up in the penumbra of his brother's great height. They are walking towards a jumble of immense rocks, piled by who knows what forces on top of each other. The rocks appear to be balancing precariously and improbably. At this distance, David sees that they have striations, ferrous red veins like those in a stick of Blackpool Rock. David has never seen a piece of this rock, but it's possible to have a familiarity with things you have never seen; unread books are an example. His brother has read many books, and closely, but he doesn't really like anything written since the end of the Great War and its immediate aftermath. He particularly loves Gerard Manley Hopkins.

From a distance they may not look alike, but close up they have a distinct family resemblance, a misleading nobleness in their biggish, strong faces – good for television – and their blue eyes. Guy's eyes are more or less closed against the sun, and the possibility of disappointment. He's had a lot of both in his life, so that now he has a wary look. This trip is a *tour d'horizon* for Guy, a chance to show his kid brother what has preoccupied and fascinated him for the past forty-five years, and a chance for David to put a very great distance, seven thousand miles, between himself, his son and his son's wife. Guy's son, Frans, has told David that his father hasn't got much time. As a consequence, David has assumed the unaccustomed role of respectful listener. Guy has said that he wants to end his days out here in the Kalahari and David wonders if this trip into the vast nothingness is a search for a place with the suitable spiritual qualities to receive him. The shimmering middle distance which stands between them and the rock cathedral – Guy calls it an *Inselberg*, an island mountain – is populated by the tiny figures of springbok. The heat causes their delicate bodies to come in and out of focus; their bodies have no solidity and can easily be seen, in just the way the Bushmen painted them, to be composed of something gaseous. This is a land, despite its dryness, of fluidity: landscapes curve and disappear; rocks turn out on closer inspection to be lizards or tortoises;

eagles and hawks glide in the heated air, appearing and disappearing as if they are flying through invisible smoke; whole ranges of mountains change from violet to black, and at sunset muted colours unexpectedly become vivid. At night the stars have a crystalline immediacy, which, it is easy to imagine, carries some message, like the rock paintings.

Guy is an expert on the rock paintings of the Southern Bushmen, and he has written two, self-published, booklets on their meaning. Academics, David knows, regard them as suspect, because they are far too subjective; Guy believes the paintings reflect the thought processes of the prehistorical world, when people had psychic abilities we have lost. He sees connections with the cave paintings of bison at Lascaux. But Guy says that academics are only interested in academic theory: they seldom get to the core of things. Guy, by contrast, with the help of Gerard Manley Hopkins, T.S. Eliot and Aldous Huxley, sees that at the core of everything lies spirituality; and he knows how to get there, although he hasn't finally arrived.

'Take the Bushman, for example. He's out here in this vast, apparently empty, landscape. At the very edges of it, he sees the white man and the cattle-owning tribes. These people have no understanding of the delicate beauty of the Bushman cosmos. They don't see that the Bushman in his own estimation – and mine, by the way – is part of this cosmos. He is both in and of nature. Do you follow me?'

He doesn't wait for an answer.

'The Bushman is our link to a time when none of us could separate himself from nature. When we walked around digging for grubs and gathering berries or snaring small animals. I call this the Bushman sacrament, what

Hopkins called the real presence. For Hopkins it was just as much in nature as in the traditional sacraments.'

David tries to interrupt.

'No, wait a minute, this is interesting.'

'I can't wait. There's a yellow snake just there.'

'Snake? Where?'

'Just there, there, right in front of us.'

'Shit. That's a Cape cobra. That's what killed Rusty. You bastard.'

The snake rears up as Guy attacks it with his stick. He hits it on its olive-yellow head, and the creature lies, writhing hopelessly, its head a pulp.

'Why did you kill it, Guy?'

'I hate cobras. One of these bastards killed my dog. I went everywhere with Rusty for twelve years.'

'What happened to the sacramental presence in nature?'

'Look, I hate fucking snakes, all right?'

David has tried to talk to his brother about his finances. Landlords, ex-wives – two of three are still alive – children, the taxman, all are after him. He needs medical care but he let his insurance lapse years ago, and his car is by now a hen coop in the town of Upington. He insisted on driving it all the way from Cape Town, about seven hundred miles, even though David offered to pay for a hire car. Some miles before Upington, in a place called, appropriately, *Allesverloren* – everything lost – the car stopped for ever. It was towed into Upington by a man with a pickup. He appeared to have Bushman blood himself – high cheekbones, little distinct twists of hair on his small head, and determinedly non-committal eyes, which had difficulty with short- to medium-range objects. He had two goats tethered in the back, looking calmly out, apparently suffering from déjà vu. Guy spoke to him in Afrikaans. When they got to Upington he asked David to give him some money to pay the man, whose name was Witbooi.

'I'll pay you back. But I think we should be generous. All his goats have died, except for these two.'

Witbooi took the money silently and folded it with a certain fastidiousness. The unimpressionable goats looked on without interest.

'Why don't we just leave the car here, Guy?'

'What's with you? Are you crazy? This is a fantastic car. I've been to the Kunene River in it.'

'It's fucked, Guy.'

'Look, my little brother, while you were trying to be an actor and then reading the news and so on, I was here, on the ground with real people. In the last more than forty years you would expect me to have picked up some knowledge of practical matters. This car is good for another ten years. It just needs a rebore.'

David sees that Guy has a fondness for the language of the common man: rebore, pistons, drive shaft, valves, the viscosity of oil. Strangely, for such a practical man, after the car had its first puncture a few miles from Cape Town, he managed to graze his knuckles badly on the wheel rim when the wrench slipped. David had already noted that he was using the wrong attachment, but said nothing. Then the jack folded and the hub was resting on the road, bent. All the way to Upington there had been an elliptical message coming from the rear wheel. The car was declared dead by a mechanic in Upington and they now have a hired four-wheel-drive Toyota Land Cruiser. Guy said that it was rubbish, the sort of flashy affair they rented to tourists. He seems, however, to have become quite attached to it since. Yesterday he declared it a fantastic vehicle. He is very promiscuous with his affections in the mechanical world. David thinks he can see why his wives left him.

They walk on, leaving the corpse of the snake, already under siege from lines of ants, *ball-biters*, according to his brother – 'Absolutely fucking lethal if you are wearing shorts. They go straight for the nuts.'

Opportunistic feeders – testicles one day, cobras the next.

The unlikely pile of rocks ahead is indeed an island mountain on the flat plain, probably 1,000 feet high. The afternoon sun is losing its harsh glare, so that shadows are appearing on the striated rocks, and David can now see that the slopes below – beyond the knots of springbok, which are moving away from their line of approach, ambling with the occasional anxious glance in their direction – are covered with what looks like a forest of menorahs. In 1966 he saw a menorah on the Arch of Titus in Rome, commemorating the objects in the booty brought to Rome after the sacking of Herod's temple in 70 AD. It struck him much later that this arch signalled a tragedy, both in the scattering of the Jewish people and in the looting and destruction of other people's sacred objects. In Afghanistan he saw what the Taliban had done to the Buddhas of Bamiyan. In all his years as a correspondent he had never seen anything that demonstrated so depressingly a contempt for the art, culture and hopes of transcendence of others. Doomed to disappointment these hopes may be, but this longing is in the fibres of human existence.

'Guy, what are those branchy plants on the hills?'

' "Towery city and branchy between towers; cuckoo-echoing, bell-swarmed, lark-charmed . . ." That is the quiver tree or *kokerboom*, once the material favoured by the !Kung Bushmen for making quivers. It is actually a succulent.'

As they trudge onwards, the mountain is beginning to take colour and now they can hear the harsh barking of baboons.

'This up ahead was to Bushmen what Chartres would have been to the locals in 1220. Just wait, you will be amazed, my lad.'

David sees that his brother lives very keenly in this world. It has come home to him in the last few days that, far from being here to save Guy from his foolishness and improvidence, he is here as a younger brother to pay his respects and learn something in the process. From Frans's email he knows something of his brother's financial and health problems, but not once on this trip has his brother mentioned his lack of money or his health.

He has, however, mentioned David's health.

'You're too thin. What happened? Cancer? Is that why you're here?'

'No. I came to see you. We're both getting on.'

'Nothing to do with Frans, I suppose?'

'No, he wrote saying we should get together.'

'Before it is too late?'

'Actually, that was in the back of my mind anyway.'

'Are you sure you're OK?'

'Guy, I'm absolutely fine.'

'Good. You walk a little slowly, if you don't mind me saying so.'

'Oh, sorry. I'll stride out.'

But after a few minutes he said, 'David, I just want to say I'm very sorry I couldn't come to Nancy's funeral.'

'That's OK.'

David had sent him a plane ticket, but he never used it. For the past week he has felt an obligation to stride out. Guy doesn't believe in using the hired four-wheel drive off-road at all. He prefers to leave it at remote farms and villages where he is known. He bestows generous tips, with David's money, on smallholders and people with no obvious activity. The recipients seem cowed and depressed. Not even the money cheers them up.

'David, what you are going to see here is one of the finest examples of Bushman rock painting that I know. Not many white people have seen this.'

The baboon protests are more frequent, but coming from a higher altitude in the mountain. David imagines a querulous rather than a nervous tone to their cries.

'This is a place that all the Bushman families – I actually prefer to call them camps – for hundreds of miles around visited once a year or more. They came from hell and gone. There's always water here. It soaks slowly down through the granite and sandstone of the *Inselberg*, comes out into a large underground basin, and flows through that into the sand. These families, by the way, are really groups of people who live together. They move around – less and less every year – and strangers join them. Sometimes they meet with other groups, and this place was one of their favourites. None of the Bushman camps I know remembers how to paint any longer. It's all gone. Gone, gone, all gone. It's a tragedy, because with it their ties to the spiritual world are going, too. And that, my bro, is terrible. A whole belief system, a complete explanation for sickness, health, fertility, hunting, the role of spirit animals has gone. And so is the urge to depict them. To me it's just helluva depressing. Nobody really cares, except for some bullshit-invented Bushman sayings you find in safari lodges by the bed, next to the goodnight chocolate.'

He attempts a mellifluous, persuasive voice.

' "This lodge honours the Kagalagadi family of !Kung

who lived here for thousands of years. When you sleep, remember this saying, that night is just a blink in the great hunt of life. Sweet dreams." All crap. All the locals were bought off with a little money, lots of drink and the promise of jobs. But of course the jobs went to others.'

They have now reached the forest of quiver trees, which have a subdued baize sheen, not unlike the colour of the deceased cobra. Some of the trees are 20 or 30 feet high. Each tree maintains a distinct distance from its neighbours, so that they look as if they have been placed deliberately in the landscape. David's idea of landscape has changed over the past weeks. Following his brother's lead, he looks forward to every new vista, every pile of distant rocks, every dry watercourse, as though they have an obligation to record, for unknown purposes, a mental map. And perhaps, David thinks, people go to art galleries out of the same impulse, to see and to assimilate unique and possibly significant images. As they walk up the slope and enter the quiver-tree forest, the forest made of green menorahs, he can see why this could well have been a place of special importance to wandering Bushmen, stepping ever so lightly on the vast plains, where not a single road or building had ever existed. Even now there are miles and miles of nothing, and it is this nullity in which David is happily losing himself with his crazy brother, who seems saner with every passing day.

Beyond the quiver trees the rocks, which at a distance seemed to have been dumped at random on to the plain, rise way above them. Close to, he sees that they are minutely pitted and coloured. They remind David of urns in country-house gardens, as though lichens have colonised them. But the colours seem to contain particles of brown quartz and red pimento and fragments of coral; in other places they look like Turkish delight, with embedded pistachio nuts. The Bushmen knew how to make their paints out of ferrous oxide and ochre, says Guy. Some of the rocks have the geological version of the noble rot you see on French cheese, little veins and squiggles, and Roquefort-blue lines, like veins in an old man's legs. Like the veins, in fact, on the inside of Guy's sturdy, indefatigable calves.

They stride up the slope. Above them the baboons have become derisive: they can see what they are up against and it's no great shakes, just two old men, unarmed, harmless. A mass attack by baboons would be terrifying, but Guy says they are impressed by height. He has in mind, of course, his own impressive stature. He's the deterrent. Throughout his life his size has given him an unearned distinction, which at last David doesn't begrudge him.

Now they are passing between two piles of enormous rocks and into a narrow valley between cliffs, which seem to have been neatly sliced on their facing surfaces. The air in here is much cooler. Guy says that this is the nave. He clearly sets some store by the cathedral comparison, as if to say look, it's not just in Europe that true spiritual values can be found. One side of the rock cleft is in deep shadow. The further in they go, the cooler it becomes. At the end of this corridor into the mountains is the entrance of a huge cave, curving away upwards, like the lip of an enormous oyster shell.

'This is the choir, I like to think. That's where they painted and made their fires. When I first came here, shit, twenty, thirty years ago, I found a small group camped. There is no sign that anyone has been here recently.'

Ahead of them is a pool of water, extending into the cave.

'We have to wade through it. Keep those fancy boots on.'

The water is very cold. Pairs of small frogs float on the dusty surface, locked in loveless sexual embraces. There is a piano sonata accompaniment of dripping water. On the other side of the water, they climb out on to a large, flat rock surface with an overhanging roof. The roof is decorated with hundreds of figures of animals: eland, in white and brown, springbok and kudu, says Guy.

'Leave your pack here.'

Guy gets a flashlight out and leads his brother deeper into the cave. He shines the light high on to the wall above them and reveals a scene of astonishing beauty and poignancy: a figure lies dying – Guy says – his cloak, properly called a *kaross*, spread out around him, while a medicine man, blood streaming from his nose, sings to him to activate his spirit. Around these two central figures is a group of men and women dancing. This is a trance dance. Some of the men wear cloaks and headdresses and at the bottom of this extraordinary scene is a huge white-and-brown picture of an eland, the biggest antelope in Africa. It has white legs and a pendulous dewlap, also white.

'Every time I see this, it gets me,' says Guy. Sometimes when he recites from Hopkins or Eliot, his eyes also fill and his voice chokes.

'Did you find this, Guy?'

'No, Dr Bleek's daughter, Dorothea, came here in 1921, but it's still not properly recorded.'

Guy has told him about Bleek and his daughter, who made it their life's work to record Bushman language and legends and to produce the first account of Bushman folklore, as well as a dictionary of sorts.

'There's a great story about Dorothea Bleek in her old age. An owl came and hooted outside her window. A

Bushman friend she told this to said that it was Dr Bleek visiting his children. Isn't that great? Actually, many African tribes, not just Bushmen, believe that owls have special knowledge. If they hear owls at night they get the elders together to decide what the message is. Why are owls so wise in so many cultures?'

'Perhaps because they look sort of dignified. Scholarly.'

'Maybe. Maybe.'

But he's not really interested in David's opinion. He gazes, with his half-closed eyes, at the vast rock face.

'It cracks me up,' he says.

David sees again that his life is an intense search for spiritual, perhaps mystic, experience. He wonders if he should tell him about interviewing the Dalai Lama, for *MidWeek Special Report*, but he suspects that his brother would not listen. Often when he pretends out of courtesy to listen to David's stories, his eyes are shifting as if they can't bear to be detained. It's a strange, feral look, a wild animal in a box, as though it is unbearable to be confined by someone else's anecdotes or theories. Most of the world, he says, is drowning in crap. And David thinks that this is certainly a concise summary of the world of television. When David does offer an opinion, Guy usually interrupts to say, 'But the interesting thing is . . .' before launching into one of his speeches about Hopkins or Bushmen. David has come to think that what his brother is looking for, what he is tormented by, is the grand unified theory that will explain everything in spiritual terms. He's some way off.

'The interesting thing is that the Bushmen of this area love the eland above all animals. It's their spirit animal. Animals to them are not a lesser form of life; in fact they think animals evolved from humans. They love animals and respect them. They are actually tender towards prey animals. Just like the American Indians.' (Guy hasn't yet caught up with the terms 'Native Americans' or 'First Nation'.) 'This is why the West thinks it loves the Bushman, because he seems to represent something in tune with nature, part of it, rather than dominating it. The great fucking joke is that it is the same people who pretend to love the Bushman and Chief Joseph and so on who are despoiling the earth. When the American Indian says, "Humankind has not woven the web of life, we are just one thread within it," I think of Hopkins: "How all's to one thing wrought." In fact sometimes it drives me mad, because I see connections everywhere.'

He does, and he tries to share them with his brother, the lackey of the international media, in the vain hope of redeeming him. Out here, Guy says he sees poor, suffering people praying in simple tin-roofed churches, and he believes that they are closer to God, a lot closer than he will ever be; there's a turmoil in his heart, and it is the turmoil of the religious person who cannot quite locate God. It's become more and more obvious to David as they walk, apparently sightseeing on a grand spiritual-artistic tour, that their true purpose is to tie the loose threads in his brother's world view. It's hopeless, but elevating.

The paintings are astonishing, but David wonders, although he doesn't say it, if they don't just record hunts and trance dances and prey animals, something like the visitors' and fishing books that posh people keep on the hall table: **Catch:** *2 x brown trout (1lb 6 oz, and 1lb 10 oz) on Priory Beat.* **Fly:** *Grey Wulff 14.* **Rods:** *Joanna and Roger Milford.* **Comments:** *Marvellous fishing and delicious food, as ever. Totally idyllic. Tons of love. Joanna and Rog.*

Yet his mind, far from being cramped by the solitary and elemental nature of their odyssey, has been freed. It's not always in tune with his brother's ramblings, but it is steadily ridding itself of anxieties and trivia. Even small tasks like getting the kettle going in the morning give him great satisfaction. As Guy tells him of the huge snake that was reputed to live in the pool of water, David does not ask if it a real snake or a spirit snake. The categories of the real and the imaginary seem to have collapsed. When Guy says it was a shaman's spirit creature, for some reason he thinks of Rosalie, naked, fervid, in his bed. He sees already, after their ten days of wandering, that there are deep and enduring longings that defy logic; in his brother's terms, Rosalie's longing for a child is surely the closest you can come to the sacramental: tiny cells producing a fully formed human being. When he left London he was planning to hide away for some months but now he sees the situation in a different light: if he has been the catalyst for a baby, he has only been the intermediary – the shaman – interceding for Rosalie with the spirits. This would be a difficult concept to explain to Ed – or to anybody else – but his anxiety and guilt have gone. What happened that night was for the best. And it is certainly true that what happened passed in something of a trance.

'The spirit animals, like the rain creatures, are often depicted in fantastical ways; look at this huge python.'

On and on he goes, and David encourages him because his brother doesn't have much time to discover the wellsprings of all life.

Rosalie sat astride him and her long, balletic hair fell all over his face when she kissed him – he was conscious of his expensive dental work, which has been going on for decades – and her exquisite and lively tongue entered his mouth avidly, as though she was seeking every possible connection in the creation of a child. *Make me immortal with a kiss.* She was Helen to his Faustus. Elizabeth to his Richard. His brother has reminded him that Richard and Elizabeth – 'your pals that you never stopped talking about' – remarried at a safari lodge some way north of here. The marriage didn't last.

As Guy outlines the role of the shaman, it is to achieve a kind of power, an out-of-body state, in order to help others. When David thinks about Rosalie that night – how much of the night she was there he never discovered – it seems to have become just that, an out-of-body experience, although he can't pretend that his intentions were selfless at the time. He hopes that Rosalie, too, sees it as having no reality in the material world, and he remembers what she said: 'It will be our secret. It will have to be, don't you think?' He didn't try to call her in the morning. An icy, constricting guilt had seized him and he had no difficulty denying himself.

Guy says that they should make a fire here. There is no fuel but they have carried some small sections of ironwood with them from the ramshackle farm ten miles off. After all these years, Guy is as strangely inept with fire-making as he is with mechanics. David has to collect more dried grass – 'I thought I told you exactly what to get the first time' – and eventually Guy gets a bright clear fire going, which gives off a surprising heat, but very little smoke. They grill some frozen kudu sausages from the butcher in Upington, a temple of meat, and drink brandy from a small bottle. The sun is going down, luridly and defiantly; it appears to hover indecisively for a moment on the low endless horizon ahead of them before dipping and sending a golden halation back as a reminder of its pomp.

'Shall we have some dagga?'

'Marijuana?'

'Weed. Boom. Durban Poison.'

'OK.'

Under the heaventree of stars they smoke dope around their small clear fire.

'David, my bro, do you want to go and see the desert elephants?'

'Why not? Where are they?'

'It's a day's drive. Maybe two if we go via the salt flats.'

'That is fine by me, bro. Where you lead, I follow. As your pal Hopkins says, I am in my ecstasy.'

Way above them in the boulders of unexplained provenance, the baboons are complaining. For some reason they become restless as night is falling. Down below, speaking more slowly now, Guy explains that the desert elephants are not a separate species, merely elephants whose emigration routes were cut fifty years ago by farming concessions, and so had to adapt to the desert. David is hardly listening; with the encouragement of the Oude Meester brandy and the Durban Poison, he finds himself back in Rome and he experiences again the kind of ecstasy, the wild joy of possibility, the sense he had then that transcendence is the only purpose of life. He remembers Richard Burton fondly, reverentially, and he sees his ambivalent gaze at Elizabeth, the impossible prize for which he sold his Welsh village soul.

'Have you ever seen anything so lovely, so otherworldly, boy?' Burton asked, and he hadn't.

'Guy.'

Guy breaks off, startled to find he has company.

'Oh, David. *Ja?*'

'I haven't been this happy for forty years.'

'I'll roll another one. You'll be even happier.'

'No, it's not the dope, Guy.'

They have a second joint; each draw reaches deep down.

'Good shit, man,' David says, only half ironically.

He sees a connection of his own between Faustus' necromancy and the Bushman shaman. Now he feels the urge to explain it to Guy: both are medicine men trying to escape the restraints of the physical world. It's a universal theme. But he's too late. Guy is talking about the cave paintings of Lascaux, which he wants to see one day.

And David thinks again, with powerful clarity, of the day when Nancy was led down the corridor to the scanner in a blue gown that fastened at the back, and as the gown parted for a moment he saw her utterly defenceless bottom in white pants. He knew then that it was going to be a death sentence.

'I loved her.'

'Who?'

'Sorry, I was mumbling.'

'You're crying.'

'It's the paintings.'

'What a pair of silly bloody arses we are.'

'True. Total arses.'

I loved Nancy, and I had to come and sit in a bloody cave to know it.

He laughs, and Guy joins him.

'What a pair of silly, fucking arses.'

Behind them, the light of their fire falls on spirit animals, shamans and Bushmen, causing them to dance.

17

JOSH HAS BEEN admitted to a psychiatric unit as a suicide risk. Ed doesn't believe he will kill himself, although he thinks that it would be a lot neater for all if he did.

Yesterday when he rushed to Lucy's flat, Ed found her shaking violently. He gave her tea with sugar, the British remedy for shock, and put her to bed. She didn't want a doctor but she wanted him to stay as long as he could. Ed gave the police a name and a description and they had him in custody within an hour. He was in his local, drunk, behaving strangely, with the pistol – a replica – still in his pocket. The landlord had also called the police.

Lucy said, 'Ed, how did I get involved in something like this?'

'It's my fault if it's anybody's. I introduced you to Josh, who I really didn't know that well. And I should have got an order on him the first time.'

'I mean, what have I done to lose my mother, be terrorised by Josh and have my father hide in the Kalahari? Have I done something?'

It wasn't rhetorical; she was genuinely puzzled. Under other circumstances this history could have sounded comical, but his sister, lying in her bed, was in deep distress.

The skin around her mouth had a purplish hue, the colour of a very new bruise, and the rest of her face was bloodless. He lay on the bed next to her, as if to share some of his surplus body heat, but in fact he too has found the sudden acceleration of their lives into chaos – Alice, Josh, Geneva, Rosalie's phantom pregnancy – deeply troubling.

Lucy said, 'Can you try to speak to Dad?'

'Dad? Dad's phone doesn't work in the desert, apparently. Look, Luce, the police will need to speak to you. Are you OK with that? I'll be with you.'

'I suppose I've got to do it.'

'They will want to press charges.'

'Of what? Pretending to kill himself?'

'No, it will be for harassment and possession of a weapon.'

'OK, but you will be here?'

'Of course.'

Within an hour a woman constable arrived, with a male colleague in body armour, to take a statement. She wanted to know if Josh had threatened her. No. He threatened to kill himself. He put the gun in his mouth. He had harassed her for weeks. The policewoman was thorough and reassuring. She wrote laboriously.

'We'll get the police surgeon to look at him. He'll probably section him. He'll be kept for observation and assessment. Don't worry, love, sign here.'

She handed over her card and mobile number.

'Call whenever you like.'

After they had gone, Lucy asked him to speak to Nick and tell him what had happened.

'Tell him not to rush round. He shouldn't feel he has to be involved. We are just part of the general madness to the police.'

*

She was right. Somehow, once the police are involved, you are conscripted into the ranks of the Untermenschen, who cause trouble, not necessarily by any specific crime, but by their generally anarchic life or because of their fractured personalities. And Ed knows that lawyers are complicit in this process.

When he got home, Rosalie told him that her Boots pregnancy test looked positive. They are going together to see Mr Smythson for confirmation. He can't help wondering if 'looked positive' was clutching at straws.

Now he is waiting for Robin. He has asked to see him, to tell him that he is resigning. As usual he has to go through the rigmarole of waiting to be admitted to the presence by Mandy, his satrap, who passes the message to Gloria; it's as if Robin is too busy, too much in demand to be available on request to an underling. In fact Robin is giving off the whiff of obsolescence: a lot of his time is devoted to legal committees and charitable causes which allow him a platform. It seems that people like Robin, as they are diminished, need these opportunities to boost themselves; by speaking portentously to captive audiences they convince themselves that they retain the vital spark. The twice-weekly meetings of the partners are so tedious, as Robin holds the floor, that Ed has begun to dread them. He calls Lucy. She's with Nick. She asks if he has heard from Dad.

'I haven't heard from him since the day he got there. He just sent me a text from Cape Town saying he and Uncle Guy were heading into the Kalahari Desert. But that was ten or twelve days ago.'

'Yes, I had a text, too. The same.'

'I've looked the Kalahari up on Google Maps. It's big. Are you OK, Luce?'

'I'm fine, and Nick has been great.'

Ed hears him in the background: 'I have, haven't I?'

'He's such a bighead. You were great, too. We spent the night at Nick's place. How's Rosie?'

'Oh she's in great form. We're off to see the gynae today. She had a Boots test and it looks positive and she wants confirmation.'

'You're going, too. Oh that's so great. Give her my love.'

The old female solidarity, often less generous than it appears, he thinks.

'Well, one way or another she's going to need me. Oops, got to go. The big man wants me. Today's the day.'

'Good luck.'

He walks over in the direction of Robin's office, past the antique maps and pictures of Robin's Cambridge college – much easier to get in then – along the hessian corridor. It's like living in a brown sack. Gloria holds him up at reception.

'Sorry, Mandy says Mr Robin says can you wait here for a moment. He's got to take a call from Moscow.'

Her eyebrows speak eloquently of a subplot.

'Those fucking oligarchs, eh, what a nuisance.'

'Mr Cross! What sort of language is that for a partner?'

She's smiling, however, because women of her age are susceptible to signs of intimacy from young men, and Ed has shared a joke with her. Human relations – he's in philosophical mood – are full of these tiny exchanges, which serve to strengthen, and sometimes to weaken, the ties between people.

'Did I say how lovely that suit looks, Gloria?'

'Now you're flattering me. I'm not a total muppet, you know. It's only M&S.'

'Looks great. Quiet elegance.'

'Ooops, it's Mandy. Yes. He's here. In you go, Mr Smoothie.'

Ed feels a kind of heaviness as he sees Robin, half-moon glasses on his nose, his paunch in a mustard shirt touching the edge of the mahogany or teak or whatever wood of his desk; while still holding the phone to his ear, he motions Ed to take a seat and swings away at forty-five degrees. In the Geneva offices of Zwingli, Robinson, Foubert et Cie, there is no brown furniture. There is no Gloria in her manky suit. Instead, there is glass, and multilingual young women, framed by views of Lake Geneva. Most important, there is no Robin. Today Robin is wearing the Garrick Club tie, the egg and cress or whatever they call it. What is it about this generation that it is so acutely taken by ties and cufflinks and test-match cricket?

'Moscow, Moscow,' Robin says sadly, putting the phone down. It is his lot to have to talk to the Slavic peasants who have no idea what the Garrick stands for. They do have money, and luckily they aren't yet aware that Robin Fennell is really a bottom-feeder.

'Now, young Edward, you wanted to see me. How's the first term been?'

'I'm deeply grateful.'

'Good, I'm glad you've come round. I thought it best to get Alice out of here. A young man's fancy and so on.'

'Actually, Robin, I wasn't talking about Alice.'

'No?'

'No. I was grateful that thanks to my father and to—'

'Where is he? I tried to ring him the other night to ask him to club night.'

'He's in the Kalahari.'

'Kalahari. Doing what?'

'I'm not sure. He's with his brother. Anyway, what I

wanted to say was that I have felt the pressure, as if Dad's help and your kindness to me – even in trying to extricate me from a situation – made me think I should stand on my own two feet more.'

'You're doing very well. As to Alice, she might at this stage have too many issues to be a serious lawyer. You can't have that sort of thing. I have no doubt at all that going forward she will have learned by the experience and at some later date she will have understood that what I did was for her benefit, as much as ours, and yours, Eddie, my boy.'

'Actually, I want to leave the firm.'

'When?'

For a moment, Ed feels sorry: Robin looks elderly and utterly confused.

'As soon as possible.'

'Where are you going?'

'Robin, it's not so much a question of where I am going, although I do have an offer from Switzerland, it's really that I think this set-up is too claustrophobic. You may have had, in fact I am sure you did have, the best possible motives, but I don't think I can stay in a place where I am not only suspected of shagging a – of having an inappropriate relationship with a trainee – but she is dismissed because, as you said, you had Rosalie's interests at heart.'

'Is it Foubert?'

'What?'

'Your job offer?'

'Laurent has offered me a job, yes.'

'And you have taken it?'

'I have agreed in principle. Yes.'

'He's a greasy little crook, operating dodgy trusts.'

'I thought he was one of our best associated firms?'

'Standards have slipped since Foubert *père* popped his clogs.'

'You said he was the sharpest lawyer in Geneva.'

'Sharp is a double-edged sword. Have you discussed this with your father?'

'No. Firstly, as I said, because he is in the Kalahari Desert and secondly the whole point is that I don't want to be discussing my career with him. I was grateful – I am still grateful – that you gave me a job, but it was to do him a favour.'

'And you proved yourself. More than. Let's look at this hypothetically. Worst-case scenario: you leave after a very short time as a partner, word gets out that you were having a dalliance, Rosalie gets to hear of it. It wouldn't be good, would it?'

'I don't mean to be rude – or ungrateful – but this is exactly the kind of conversation I don't want to have. It's better I go now before I become a full equity partner, if that is still on the cards, and move to Geneva, with Rosalie.'

'What do you want me to say to your father?'

'Please don't say anything to my father. It's not his business. Robin, I am very sorry, but I have to move on. When Dad appears from the wilderness, I will tell him I got an offer I just couldn't pass up.'

He stands up. Robin's round, reddish face is peering up at him. He looks – I am going mad – like his namesake in the avian world, reaching up for a worm from its mother.

'Are you sure?'

'I'm sure. And there could only be one possible source for any talk of my so-called dalliance, couldn't there?'

'Alice?'

'No, you.'

'Perhaps you had better go. Clear your desk by close of

play tomorrow. I'll tell the staff simply that you are going to Geneva. I have to say that your disloyalty and opportunism are a disappointment to me but because of my long friendship with your father and my affection for Rosalie we'll keep it very businesslike, going forward.'

'I'm very grateful.'

Robin swivels away towards the window. He is trying to summon his dignity and Ed now realises for the first time just how isolated he is, and he realises with a pang that Robin sets a lot of store by Dad and Rosalie: we have become his family in a way, and perhaps he really was trying to protect us by sacking Alice. His implied threat, to suggest that he has left because of an impropriety, is hollow. As in his whole life so far, his father's aura still protects him. Ed goes back to his office to write his letter of resignation, which he gives to Gloria for onward transmission, like the Pony Express, to Robin and the managing partner. Then he leaves the office to get some of those clear plastic crates for his personal files.

As he walks down towards Ryman he calls Alice's number. To his surprise, she answers.

'Hello, Ed.'

'Alice, look, I need to speak to you.'

'Why?'

'Why do you think?'

'I think you want to speak to me because I told your lovely wife why that prick Robin had fired me.'

'You spoke to Rosalie?'

'Yes. Has she forgotten to mention it?'

'Jesus, Alice, why did you do that?'

'Why? Because I was treated like shit. As if I didn't matter at all. I wanted to share the pain.'

'You didn't love me or anything.'

'I don't think you understand.'

Blood is racing dangerously towards his head.

'What don't I understand? What?'

'We were just shagging. It was fun. But Robin was insanely jealous. He fired me and gave me a miserable pay-off to get lost.'

'So you told Rosalie.'

'Yes.'

'To get at me.'

'No, not really. Just because I couldn't bear to see all that hypocrisy. Did he tell you why he was firing me?'

'No. I tried to ring you at least ten times when you went to your Scottish knees-up and also when you didn't come back. I wondered where you were. He told me two or three days later. Now, just this minute, I've told him that I'm leaving the firm.'

'Because of me?'

'Yes. Not entirely, but yes.'

'You shouldn't have.'

'I couldn't stand the idea of Robin believing he had some hold over me.'

'Ed, look, I'm sorry about Rosalie. I hope I haven't caused you too much shit.'

'So far she hasn't mentioned it.'

'She must be in denial.'

'Alice, when the dust settles, let's . . .'

'Meet? I don't think so. It's all over. So over. I told her I didn't fancy you, and that it was a one-night stand after too much drink, and that I was never ever going to see you again. And maybe that's why she's not mentioned it. You're a lovely bloke and I am very, very sorry. I just felt the red mist descending: it seemed so, so unfair. But don't call me ever again.'

'I understand. You're a wonderful girl.'

'Bye. Look after Rosie. She's special.'

'Bye.'

This strange and treacherous sisterhood. Now he sees that Rosalie is keeping quiet because she believes she's pregnant. God help me if she's not. He walks blindly around Ryman, forgetting what he's looking for. As he finds himself looking at the latest model of home shredder, he remembers what Lucy said, 'What have I done to get involved in something like this?' It's pretty damn obvious what I have done. But without Robin's prurience it would have been something unremarkable in the grand scheme of things.

A sales assistant comes over to him. He realises that he is wandering the aisles drunkenly.

'All right, sir? Can I help you?'

'I'm looking for . . .'

He can't remember what it is.

'No problem, sir, take your time.'

He is possibly Indian, with a plump, compassionate look.

'Oh so sorry, I was daydreaming. I want some of those plastic storage boxes. Six.'

'That's the Really Useful Box. They come in four sizes.'

Six of the large size are heavier than he had expected and he is sweating within his suit by the time he reaches the office. He must work out. Dad's leanness and asceticism are a reproach to him. It's funny how messages are conveyed in families. Mum was an expert at coded messages, which included slipping new clothes into his cupboard, to indicate, although she never said it, that she thought he was scruffy. For a week or two he would resist these gifts – in the way that unknown Amazonian tribespeople resist pots and pans and mirrors hung in trees by explorers who want to contact them – but, like them, he would always weaken and take them into his wardrobe, and feel perversely elegant in his new clothes, as though he had chosen them himself.

He struggles out of the lift, a light sheen on his face.

'Moving house?' Gloria asks.

'I'm leaving the office tomorrow.'

'Oh, but you've only been a partner for a few weeks.'

'Worse things happen at sea.'

He has no idea why he has uttered that phrase. To the best of his knowledge he's never said it before, and he's not even sure what it means. It must indicate that he is troubled. He puts the boxes on the loathsome green carpet, opens the door of his office and pushes them in with his foot. Down below at the bins he thinks he sees a rat. The last rat in Switzerland was liquidated in about 1897. He is due in Harley Street in an hour, but he hasn't the will to start packing. A lot is riding on Mr Smythson's verdict. He tries to occupy himself with tidying up his files; he pauses at some notes in Alice's childish handwriting. He reads them twice. He wonders if he should take the initiative by confessing to Rosalie, keeping the confession strictly in line with what Alice told her: a drunken mistake, deeply regretted by all, no human feelings of any sort involved, et cetera. But actually he thinks of Alice's breasts receiving his libation and he is saddened that she didn't love him and doesn't ever want to hear from him again. He tells himself that there is an upside and that he is relieved it is all over.

Rosalie's mother has paid for the fertility investigations and consultations with Mr Smythson. She swears by him. The meeting is at his rooms in Harley Street. Ed finds Harley Street a little creepy, a sort of necropolis. There's a steady traffic of the elderly and the decrepit, some in wheelchairs, and little groups of Arabs in full desert wear, exiting from taxis or shuffling out of the consulting rooms and clinics, often with a helper trailing suitcases on wheels. Rosalie has a look of glazed wonder as if she is at the gates of a shrine as they approach the heavily brassed front doors of the building, where Mr Smythson's soothing presence spends a part of every day.

'Don't be too disappointed if it's negative, darling,' Ed says.

She turns slowly towards him, not so much in anger as pity.

'I'm pregnant, trust me.'

'OK, way to go.'

'Why are you speaking like that?'

It would be too complicated, even impossible, to explain how he has arrived at this feverish state. He presses the heavy brass doorbell, worn by generations of nervous supplicants hoping for miracles, and holds Rosalie's hand as they wait for the summons. Even her hand is light and poised. Mr Smythson's rooms are on the second floor, and the receptionist points them to the lift.

In his waiting room, Mr Smythson's own receptionist welcomes them.

'He won't be too long, but I am afraid he is always a little late.'

She says this with an indulgent smile; in the tradition of middle-aged devotees, she is hopelessly in love with her boss.

Ed and Rosalie sit beneath some botanical prints. Over on the facing wall are prints of parrots; one is clinging to the branch of an exotic flowering tree. Rosalie is humming. Perhaps it's *Turandot*. She is serene and glances at him in a way that suggests – he fears – a new ambivalence towards him. They don't speak. Rosalie hums on tunefully, almost inaudibly.

When Mr Smythson's call comes, they start. The receptionist announces that they may go in. They stand up, he rather laboured, Rosalie en pointe.

Mr Smythson is standing in a closely cut grey suit. He waves at the seats. He has a convincing professional bonhomie. They all sit down.

'Welcome, welcome. Right, the scan. Just let me get your notes.'

He shuffles through some papers, and makes some squiggles with a chunky fountain pen.

'Ed, I'm going to take Rosalie into the next room for the ultrasound, and then I will know for certain. It won't take a moment.'

Rosalie goes out after Mr Smythson. For a moment he can hear her deferential squeaks and his deep emollient voice, until a door closes. Ed wonders if these gynaecologists are utterly blasé about seeing young women in their underwear.

He sits, redundant: the process is well past his competence. He looks out of the window at all the unglamorous pipes and waste disposal and air conditioning that hospitals need. After about ten minutes, they return. Rosie is in tears, but he can see immediately that they are the right sort of tears.

'Very good news, Ed, Rosalie is pregnant. Three and a half weeks. I suspected it was just a matter of time and diligence. Congratulations.'

Rosalie hugs Ed, and they are both in tears.

Mr Smythson offers them his hand.

'Well done. Now, Rosalie, a few routine tests, a few bloods, that sort of thing. Do you want to stay, Ed?'

'No, I'll go out. Rosie, it's the most wonderful thing that has ever happened.'

Rosalie gestures to him elegantly, her head cocked slightly in an unfamiliar way. He is not sure what she means by this. As he walks to the waiting room, he is more or less under control, but his whole body is convulsed with relief, admixed with guilt. It's been a day of shocks. Back in the waiting room the receptionist congratulates him. She seems genuinely pleased and of course she knows that he has had to give up intimate samples for examination. Medical people lead a strange double life; on the one hand they are obliged to be bland and reassuring, and on the other they are closely acquainted with death and suffering. He feels warmly grateful to the whole profession as he settles back to look at *Country Life*. Maybe, if the property market collapses as predicted, he will be able to buy himself this lovely thatched house on the Avon, with fishing rights and a staff cottage, using his solid, imperturbable Swiss francs; or what about this one in the Cotswolds, with ten acres of woods, highly suitable for pheasant rearing, and an insulated barn containing a swimming pool?

He hopes Rosie doesn't wonder, as he has, if there is any connection between his brief affair with Alice and this happy outcome.

He calls Lucy to tell her the good news.

'That's totally brilliant, Ed. This is probably not the moment to remind you that you said she was a fantasist. Women know these things.'

'God, I don't care what I said. I am so happy for her.'

'And for yourself?'

'Of course, but you know what I mean. The stakes were high. Just a sec.'

He goes out into the corridor.

'Lucy, sorry, Rosie's just having some tests, blood samples and stuff like that. Alice told Rosie about us after Robin fired her. Why do you think she hasn't confronted me?'

'Alice told you?'

'Yes, but Rosie hasn't mentioned it. My question is why not.'

'That's pretty obvious, don't you think?'

'Because she knew she was pregnant?'

'I would say so. I just wish Mum was here to see her grandchild.'

'So do I. I'll send Dad a text. Eventually he is going to come back to civilisation. Are you OK, Lucy?'

'I'm fine. You've been great, Nick's been great, and Josh is even now heavily sedated. We hope.'

'I'll check with the police. He's in for seventy-two hours but it can be extended by the shrinks. Look, Luce, if Rosie ever speaks to you about Alice, play it down. Just say this girl was after me and we once got pissed and I asked Robin to move her on. Deeply, deeply, regret it, et cetera.'

'That's not really totally straight, is it?'

'I'm going to be a dad. And you're going to be an auntie. The family must close ranks. There's only you and me.'

'True. And you're going to Geneva.'

'Anyway, Alice told me I was a mistake.'

'I doubt if she, I mean Rosie, will ever ask me, but if she does, I'll practise *omertà*. I'll lie for *la famiglia*, for Cosa Nostra, or I'll sleep with the fishes.'

'Yes, OK, OK, enough already.'

'Bye for now, my bro, and lots of love to Rosie. Tell her I'll call her later.'

He's glad Lucy's happy; when Rosie returns from Mr Smythson's consulting rooms, it's obvious that she is happy, too, luminously happy.

'All well?'

'Perfect, perfect.'

She hugs him close and he feels that she is giving him a message, which is probably that they have a higher destiny now, as parents, and that the past can indeed be forgotten. At least, he hopes this is the message.

18

MOTHERS LIE ON demand. Without realising it, children expect their mothers to lie for them and to them. Perhaps this is where it went wrong, that Mum never prepared me for the real world. Her every effort was directed to creating and preserving an ideal world. A little restricted but still trouble-free. Dad found it cloying, but her motive was always to protect them from harshness. Now Lucy wonders if this hasn't left her unable to deal with the more sombre aspects of life, which have lately been demonstrated to her. Typically, of course, she has now turned to Nick and to Ed to supply her with the untruths – or perhaps the unsaid – in order to protect herself. In her eagerness to avoid the facts, she's turning into her mother. The awful irony is that Mum could not protect herself from the one great ineluctable fact. When Ed said, only half joking, that the family must pull together, perhaps he was thinking of his soon-to-be-extended family; she and Ed, with Dad absent in the Kalahari, are hardly a family. It's not really fair to say he's absent: it's been less than four weeks, but even before he left, Dad was distancing himself in non-geographical ways. Lucy sees that already a lot of hope and expectation has been invested in the new baby, which is after all only an embryo of less than a month; it probably hasn't even acquired the egg-yolk-in-albumen look you see on scans, the baby thing looking happily stoned. And probably never this happy again. When they spoke, she found that Rosalie had quickly acquired the spirit of inclusiveness: the shared genes of this baby tied them together.

'You can come round to play with her whenever you like.'

'Her?'

'Yes. Definitely.'

'Because women know. OK. I would love to come and hang out with you and her. But I am not sure how often I will be in Geneva.'

Rosalie is not constrained by geography.

'I think a big family, masses of cousins and huge family occasions, are wonderful, don't you?'

'I have never really thought about it. But, yes, sounds good to me.'

'Ed told me about your awful incident with Josh. I'm so, so sorry. Can you and Nick come round for supper tonight?'

'I'll ask him. He works quite late putting the paper to bed. He has to show how keen he is, because they have given him a contract.'

She likes the phrase, *putting the paper to bed*. She's almost put her catalogue to bed. The proofs are in and Rachel said it was the best catalogue they had ever done.

'Good. Let me know if you can come. I'm going to miss you when we go.'

'Is Geneva definite definite?'

'I think so. Ed has resigned and he's going to sign his contract with the Swiss next week.'

'So the baby will be born Swiss.'

'Yes, with an apple on her head.'

It takes Lucy a moment to make the connection: *William Tell* the opera, and no doubt *William Tell* the ballet, too.

Rosie sees a future of mountain air, sparkling water, the Ballet du Grand Théâtre, powder skiing on Mont Blanc, and immaculately dressed trilingual children – no street grunge for these *bambini* – but still in touch with their artistic temperaments, even as they enjoy the benefits of Euro living. Ed's role, Lucy thinks, is so far less clearly imagined, but no doubt he will be leading the charge down the mountain at weekends as a reward for bringing home the bacon, *remportant les lardons*. Or perhaps *des lardons*. She never quite mastered the difference between 'all the bacon' and 'some of the bacon'. They have been sent details of a spacious apartment, Rosie says, available in a village on the lake. As soon as the contract is signed, they are going to look over it.

Nick is happy to come to supper with Rosie and Ed. He's also very keen to meet Dad, if he ever comes back. Ed said he was having his gap year; she hopes not. Dad has this effect: he has entered the affections of his viewers as insidiously as a virus. Nick, she is finding, is doing something similar to her, but she is trying to hold herself back in case it turns out that her judgement has been affected by the traumas caused her by Josh's craziness.

As she looks at the proofs of the catalogue – riddled with mistakes – she thinks of Constantine murdering his incestuous wife Flavia by parboiling her in a bath. It had all seemed quite pleasantly remote, like a horror movie, filtered of all reality, but since Josh pushed a pistol into his mouth and she imagined a fine Tarantino mist hanging in the air above her bath, composed of blood and capillaries and bone fragments, she hasn't seen the murderous history of the Constantines as something charmingly remote. What she sees now is a family of genuine Mafiosi, deranged and vengeful. And maybe this is what history is, a series of atrocities that are worn smooth by the passage of time. To calm her mind, she reads through the proofs very carefully, checking every spelling and every reference.

She must not become too attached to Nick. It's difficult, because he has said that she is the most wonderful person he has ever met. She knows that this is a tactic employed by bastards: women find it difficult to resist someone who claims to love them beyond reason. Mum spent her life devoted to her children. When she was dying she was ashamed that she had let them down, as if she had somehow lived a sham. Her head was shaved and her eyes seemed to be retreating into caves that hadn't been there before. Dad must have known early on that she was dying but the speed of it threw him completely. He didn't have time to perfect the easy lies that might have seen them through. Mum's concern was only for the children, her life's work, and this concern wasn't lessened by the fact that they were already grown up. Lucy knows that Mum was particularly concerned about her, as if she was especially vulnerable. Just before she died, she held Lucy's hand with the grip of a very small bird. The lightness of her hand spoke eloquently of the nearness of her death: it had lost all warmth and motive power. Her eyes, deep in their last retreats like Byzantine hermits in caves, retained a broad range of expressiveness, and the anguish in them was heartbreaking. It was so awful that Lucy wished she would die right there, partly because she was suffering so badly, but also because there is something contagious in death, moving backwards in time to infect the living memory.

And now Lucy thinks that she has always treated herself as a special case, someone deserving of some unique consideration. She's not a special case any more: it's gone with Josh's deranged stunt. I am not immune in any way to life's realities. If he had blown his brains out, I would never have recovered. They may be killing each other casually with knives and guns down in South London, but here, in the still-living radius of her mother, most of us are terrified of randomness. We don't want to know about every awful thing. The other day, leaving Green Park station, she saw some tourists photographing the picturesque but unused red phone boxes. Picturesque on the outside; inside they were full of bottles, cans, prostitutes' cards and – in one – a huge human turd. She felt sick with anxiety. Obviously, a few bits of litter and one sad person's faeces should not spoil anyone's day, but she seems to have assumed her mother's fastidiousness, which was close to agoraphobia. Not so long ago, before Mum died, she believed that somehow life would reveal itself evenly and predictably. All the evidence to the contrary, which, naturally, was available to her – the tsunami, earthquakes, murder, torture, betrayal – seemed real enough but impersonal, as if happening in a parallel world. Her grandfather's friend, Pavel Gersbach, had lived all his life in a small rented flat in Highgate because, after what he had seen when the Nazis arrived in Prague in 1939, he had thought it would be tempting fate to buy a house. When Dad told her this story, she had imagined that it was really just some colourful hangover of Mittel Europa; the Holocaust, she sometimes thought, should be put behind us. Now she knows that none of us is exempt.

She meets Nick later after the paper has been tucked up. He appears, running from the building.

'What would you rather be or a wasp?' he says.

'I fell out of the cradle laughing at that one.'

'Really? I've just heard it. You look great. Do you want a drink before we go to dinner?'

'Supper. Rosalie prefers the term: it's more pastoral. And yes, I do.'

'Come, I know just the place. I really need one. Any news of Josh?'

'Safely locked up.'

In the leafy opulence of Kensington, he kisses her and holds her close.

'Do you have a drink problem?' she whispers into his ear.

'Probably.'

'How little I know about you. Nada.'

'Not much to know, sadly.'

The pub has a lively, dense atmosphere, which they must break into. It's almost a natural process; the human and alcoholic vapours and gases part to admit you, and then close around you. She thinks of those microscopic shots of in vitro fertilisation. There's a gynaecological theme to her thoughts.

'Tell me about your sister-in-law.'

'As I said on the phone, she's pregnant. They've had a few problems in that department, so she's on a total high. My brother's been offered a job in Geneva, the world's dullest city, and I foresee a future of increasing prosperity and cheese consumption. Nick, I'm only going to say it once, because you will think I am babbling like a fool, but you were great last night, without you God knows . . .'

But she can't go on, and weeps in this gamy pub, where none of the regulars takes any notice as Nick holds her:

they have seen many domestic dramas. Their credo is that there is nothing a drink can't fix.

'There's nothing to be afraid of. I want you to stay with me. Just until you feel safe,' he adds, as if he imagines he has gone too far.

'Thank you.'

'Look, I'm only offering so that I can get into your knickers twenty-four seven.'

'Oh thanks,' she snuffles. 'Actually, that's fine by me.'

By the time they get to Rosalie and Ed, they are both tipsy. Ed comes to the door.

'Sorry, bro. We're both a little pissed,' says Lucy.

'No problem. So am I. We opened a bottle of champagne to celebrate my new job and our baby. But Rosie's on water.'

'The job's done and dusted?' asks Lucy.

'Just about. Nick, come in. And thanks, you have been wonderful. Lucy can't stop talking about you. To be honest, she's become a bit of a pain. Come in, come in. This is Rosalie.'

'Hi, Nick.'

'Hi, Rosalie, I hear you're pregnant, congratulations.'

'Sorry. I told him. I just couldn't stop myself,' says Lucy.

'Let's keep it in the family for the moment. But still, no harm done.'

They are so obviously happy that Lucy feels tears coming to her eyes again. Rosalie is more than happy, serene. Only now is it apparent how anxious she has been: she looks as though she has never heard of Alice and never feared being childless for ever. Lucy hasn't told Nick about Alice, because she doesn't want the family to seem too flaky, what with Dad gallivanting in the desert somewhere.

'You look sensational, Rosie.'

They embrace with unaccustomed vigour.

'Can you give me a hand for a moment in the kitchen; I've made some snacks. Ed, can you take Nick through to our enormous courtyard?'

'Are you more or less over the Josh business, Luce?' Rosalie asks as she busies herself.

'Who knows? Nick's been great and so has Ed. How do you feel? Any different?'

'I feel absolutely fine: I keep imagining things are happening. I almost believe I can feel the baby.'

'Even though it's about the size of a walnut. Or smaller.'

'Exactly. You obviously lose touch with reality when you're pregnant. Luce, I think this business, and your Mum's death, has had one good effect: it has brought us all much closer, don't you think?'

'I do. It struck me after we talked that we are the re-formed family. Like reconstituted. I'll be the spinster auntie, who makes sponge cakes.'

They take the snacks out to the courtyard, two women in domestic union. There is something about Rosalie that is curiously out of time, but at this moment Lucy loves her ethereal, slightly whacked, sister-in-law. And feels a deep kinship with her — the baby is already signalling to her aunt from the womb — a kinship she has never really felt before. It's like the meeting of passengers in a lifeboat after the ship has sunk: a certain unavoidable intensity of feeling has arisen; the life force is running strongly in Rosalie this evening and its elemental power has swept Alice away. Lucy would have liked to have met Alice, to compare and contrast.

As they bear in the tiny but fashion-conscious eats, she sees that Ed and Nick are having a fine time. Whatever story Ed was telling, he breaks off quickly: chaps have a kind of Freemasonry. She finds it reassuring to find Nick so relaxed and sociable. She has never seen him in company before. Behind them, the Moroccan snake-charmer lights cast a beguiling light. And she sees that the moribund bougainvillea has gone at last.

'Snacks?' Rosalie asks.

'Snacks?' says Nick. 'They look too beautiful to eat.'

Ed takes four.

'This is how to do it,' he says.

'You're a pig,' says Rosalie.

'Oink, oink.'

'Christ, you can be silly, Ed,' says Rosalie indulgently.

Lucy believes that Rosalie has decided once and for all to erase the conversation with Alice from her mind. She wonders how you could possibly do something like this, and she hopes that it is more than a lull in their torrential lives.

'Did you like them?' Lucy asks after they have made love.

Their lovemaking has that thrilling sense of discovery, as though they are on a reckless journey whose destination is not yet known. The intensity is extreme, almost unbearable, racked up by the knowledge that Josh, who was once her lover, is under lock and key.

'I loved them. Ed's great, and Rosalie is almost too good to be true.'

'You got her in one. She's a sort of uber-woman. She always makes me feel clumsy. But she's had her problems, as I said.'

'Your brother told me, too.'

'Crikey, you didn't waste time getting down to basics.'

'He told me in the club, man to man. He seems very relieved. It must have been a strain.'

'He is. Rosalie's instincts are strong. You can't fuck with them.'

' "You can't fuck with them." What sort of language is that from one of London's hottest and brainiest girls?'

'I'm still drunk. That's my only excuse.'

'So am I. Usually about this time I feel like death, but thanks to you I am so happy I feel like I am flying. Let's not go to sleep.'

She melds her naked body with his. The dull, sick feeling that has inhabited her since Josh pretended to kill himself – before that even – is already seeping away. Although it is at times hard to believe it, the recuperative powers of the body and the mind are strong, as everybody says.

When they arrived at the club, somewhere in Shoreditch, wrapped in a happy corporate spirit, Rosie said she hadn't been to a club for a year or more, and for a moment Lucy thought she saw desolation on her brother's face, as if he recognised the future, stuck at home in the twilight zone of marriage and babies. Who knows, this baby may be the precursor to a whole *corps de ballet*. Ed seemed to have a suspiciously wide knowledge of cocktails, but maybe that's what lawyers *en fête* do – drink cocktails with silly names to take their mind off the tedium of pushing paper. Rosalie swayed, like deep tethered seaweed, and drank mineral water. Lucy and Nick danced and kissed. Ed and Rosalie came by; dancing is a strange thing. Ed always gives the impression that it is somehow a little amusing: he smiles madly when he's at it, as if he's demonstrating that he is still in touch with the ordinary people. The trouble is, to be any good, you have to take it seriously. Rosalie was floating and Ed, sure enough, was grinning, as if to say,

Look, I'm getting down with my homies. And Lucy wondered, not for the first time, if he was a lawyer at heart. Nick danced neatly and naturally, nothing fancy, but pretty rhythmical. Like me, she thinks. Like me.

Much later, outside the club, the rain was coming down hard; a meteorological change had taken place while they were drinking lurid cocktails underground, oblivious. It was disconcerting, like waking in the night unsure of where you are. The music was incredibly loud, and now, back in Nick's flat, she can still hear its susurration and its beat, going on minutely inside her head.

They talk. They've reached that point where they want to talk about their families and their deepest wishes, although a certain editorial control is still required because the magic of the first few days must be preserved. Too much frankness could still destroy it. Nick tells her that his mother and father are divorced, which happened when he was fifteen, a bad time, and his younger brother, Simmy — Simon — suffered even more than he did. Simmy took to drugs briefly, but is now a budding academic. Their mother has married again, but his father's affair lasted only two years after the separation, and he now lives in France.

'And your famous father? How has he taken your mother's death?' Nick asks.

'That's difficult. Ed and I have discussed it. At first he was very calm, almost serene. But I don't think you ever know what goes on between your parents. He was always off somewhere, and she kind of took over at home. I think she resented him a little when he came back from Washington or somewhere, having interviewed the President or smuggled himself into Afghanistan. And I think he felt that she was a little too much the hausfrau. Now I think he's beginning to see just how wonderful she was. In less obvious ways, of course. I think he's got a woman, too, some whacko with a dog. But anyway, he's gone to the Kalahari with his brother who is dying. Uncle Guy. He lives out there.'

'Do you miss your mother?'

'I am always wanting to talk to her. Yuh, I know this sounds banal, by the way, before you think I'm one of those bitches from hell who launch into like self-obsessed psychobabble without warning, but there are moments in every day when I want to speak to her and it takes me a second or two to remember.'

She worries a little in case there isn't just a touch of the self-serving in these questions of families and loss and inchoate childhood anxieties. No one can say, *Shut the fuck up* when you are talking about your childhood and your parents, as much as they may want to.

'When my parents separated,' Nick says, 'we were sent to boarding school and I would wake up each morning thinking I was at home in my own bed and then be absolutely shattered to discover I was in a dormitory with fifteen others, all farting away. But I got to like it after a while.'

'The farts?'

'No, obviously not the farts. What I loved was the sodomy and being flicked with wet towels.'

They hold on to each other, their lives bundled together now. She strokes his chest.

'You don't have much hair on your body.'

'Oh God, I hoped you wouldn't notice. Do you mind?'

'Mind? No, no, sorry. I love it. It was a compliment.'

Josh, locked up, drugged, closely monitored, is a hairy person. He is furry, and that hirsuteness she thinks now is linked to his psychotic behaviour. She wonders exactly what

Josh was intending by putting a gun in his mouth. She can't describe to Nick the abyss that Josh opened in front of her and she can't understand how it came to this. She wonders if there isn't something about her that attracts disorder.

19

HIS BROTHER SAYS that the elephants pass by here often at this time of year. Elephants always pass: they are restless spirits, apparently never one hundred per cent content with their surroundings.

They make camp on a ridge overlooking the dried riverbed. Although it contains no water, the Huab has many recognisable attributes of a river: a line of trees follows its course in the red desert, boulders are strewn about, hurled there by forgotten floods, and the banks are sharply cut in places where the phantom river turned a corner. His brother is big on phantom rivers, which David thinks is a lovely phrase. Also, there are bright blue and carmine birds nesting in holes in the walls of the river, and there are nests of weaver birds hanging down from the trees. The weaver birds have masks of black over their eyes, like robbers in cartoons. Deep sand, beach sand, covers parts of the riverbed, rolled and sieved – presumably – by storm water. The elephants browse the trees, *Acacia erioloba*, commonly called the camel thorn, and they dig for water in places known to them. So says brother Guy.

Two nights before, they camped on a vast, barren salt flat. There was no sound and no life at all, not even insects could exist on the salt. Guy said the salt flats covered an area larger than Wales. It's curious how very large areas of the wilderness are routinely described as being bigger than Wales; Wales has become a handy yardstick. In his career David found that countries were often described as the breadbasket of Africa if they could grow anything at all, or the Switzerland of Africa if they had a functioning currency.

Guy has a mission to impress on his brother the spiritually expansive possibilities of open spaces and the limitations of life in a small wet country; he has in mind England.

'Don't you sometimes feel cramped?'

'Not especially.'

'Yah, but look at this.'

'What, this nothingness?'

'Yes. Do you know what "hermit" means?'

'Means? What do you mean, "means"?'

'The word "hermit" comes from the Greek for "desert", *eremos*. People who lived in a desert, like St Alexander of Cairo. The eremitic life came before the monastery. The point was that hermits didn't want anything or anyone coming between them and their God. Like Hopkins.'

'Particularly not women. Hopkins was gay.'

'What, a pansy?'

'Well, yes. He was gay. In a Victorian way. The Roman Catholic Church was the best place to be at that time before it was acceptable to come out. It provided a sort of deliberate separation. Like a hermitage.'

'Are you sure?'

'Of course. Does it matter?'

'No. I suppose not.'

He was uncharacteristically silent for a while.

Later he asked David to stand up.

'Now, shut your eyes. Walk for ten minutes in any direction, but keep your eyes shut.'

The night before they had heard lions, roaring with a hoarse, rumbling intensity.

'What about lions?'

'There are no lions within fifty miles, in fact. There's nothing here. No insects, no plants. Absolutely bugger all. If you shut your eyes you will experience total sense-deprivation.'

'Do I want that?'

'It opens the mind.'

'OK, I'll give it a whirl.'

He stood up. He walked for ten or maybe more minutes, meeting no resistance in this stark, magnificently dead landscape. If his brother was suggesting that deserts are places where you could shed distractions and come closer to your God, he was probably right. If you had a God.

As he walked he tried to empty his mind to create a productive space into which some important under-standing might creep. It was a hopeless task: his mind became chaotically active and was flooded with memories; it was treading water, with a hint of panic. He thought of Jenni's drowning reproach and felt again violent shame so that his face heated from within as he wandered in the nothingness. He thought of Rosalie, her hair falling on his face. But he couldn't pin his thoughts down or turn them in a contemplative, self-improving direction. His brother's mistake, he thought, has been to look for meaning out here, when in fact all around them is an unmistakable demonstration of meaninglessness and nullity.

When he finally opened his eyes he could see the campfire and the silhouette of the Toyota about half a mile away in the steel blue and ox blood dusk. He walked back and perversely the emptiness of the vista calmed his mind.

'How was that? Mind-blowing, isn't it?'

'I don't think I did it right.'

He suddenly felt irritated by his bother's assumption of spiritual authority; easily assumed but difficult to substantiate.

They had bought a stunted, fatalistic sheep at a tiny settlement a few hundred kilometres away, which was promptly and inexpertly butchered; the dismembered body parts – they returned the head to the grateful vendor – are in the electric cool box, which is powered by the vehicle's battery. Guy has decreed that it is a useful aid; in fact if his own car hadn't been occupied by poultry he would probably get one himself, he said. When David arrived back from his blind walk, Guy had a scrawny leg of this sheep on a spit over the fire. He believes that anything can be cooked on an open fire, flavoured by beer, and while this is happening you should smoke a joint. As they inhaled, David, nursing his peevishness, looked at his brother, deliberately turned away towards the more congenial mysteries beyond. His motile face suggested that he was perhaps coming to terms with the idea that Hopkins might have been gay. It was making small involuntary movements, somewhere been speech and chewing: *O my chevalier!*

David wondered what Guy had been doing all these years, in pursuit of spiritual enlightenment at the expense of his family, or families. And his health. He seems to have no concept of healthy living; for instance, on a whim he will eat a half-kilo tin of tiny wiener sausages in brine, slathered in ketchup. The day before he ate a packet of Romany Creams for breakfast. During the journey the Romany Creams had collapsed in the heat and had congealed overnight to become a sort of trifle, on to which he poured condensed milk before setting to.

When David, watching this, asked him about his health, he said, 'I've had my time. So have you. What does it matter if we go tomorrow or in five years? This is delicious, by the way; you should try some.'

Technically speaking, this must have been a general recommendation for the recipe rather than an invitation to partake, because he had eaten the lot. His face had a high colour and a softness, like a fruit that was on the turn, and David was concerned.

Later in the day, when they arrived at the great salt flats – 'This is just the very edge, they go on for hundreds of miles' – he looked better, less palpable, as he became excited by the prospect of endless space. His enthusiasm hasn't diminished once during the weeks they have traversed this space.

'I think this is what Merleau-Ponty meant when he spoke about *le regard pré-humain*. This is how the world looked in prehistory.'

His accent was shocking. David was tempted to tell him, as brothers are inclined to do, that he hadn't actually done French. Languages were David's forte.

Guy turned towards him.

'The human creature. Oh shit, ow, that hurts,' he said, sucking his fingertips, scorched as he prodded the lamb, 'the human creature is an abnormal creature forcibly removed from all connection with nature. What Hopkins saw was that sacraments don't just belong in church. We can enter a personal sacrament. This is the REAL PRESENCE, in nature. It's there. It's always there.'

'And the snake you decapitated the other day?'

'I don't think you understand what I'm saying.'

'I do. You killed a snake. You forcibly removed it from all connection with nature, and life, too.'

'I had forgotten what a competitive little monkey you are. It's all coming back.'

He shook his head sadly at the recollection of his limitless forbearance. Now they were both turned towards the immeasurable emptiness. For a while David considered taking the hire car he had paid for and leaving his brother out here to reconnect with nature in his own time. He looked at Guy: they shared the same implausibly thick hair, but little else. His brother's hair lent him a misleadingly sage look, especially now, as it was covering his ears and creeping down his collar. The family's monumental look — which has skipped Ed — had undoubtedly helped him in his television career. Guy looked at David's teeth one day soon after they set out and said, 'You know, your teeth are about as natural as a tuxedo on a baboon.' Global had paid a fortune for these teeth — six veneers and two implants — in one of their frequent rebranding exercises. Guy's teeth — there aren't that many — are crooked and grey, tending to brown. But David didn't try to explain the demands of television. He was wrong to imagine that his brother would be impressed by his celebrity. Out here it meant nothing anyway: in truth his glittering teeth were confirmation of everything his brother believed about the delusions of Europe and North America. It depends on where you are standing, of course: there on that desolate salt pan, his brother was at the centre of the universe.

And who am I to deny him?

'Do you know what moves me most about the Bushmen?' Guy asked, still in brooding profile.

'No, but I have a feeling you are going to tell me.'

If he detected the irony, Guy was above it.

'It cracks me up that they valued their own simple lives above anything. They just wanted to carry on as they had done for fifteen thousand years. They just wanted to get in touch with their god. One day I will take you to a rock painting that shows a white man firing on Bushmen. One lies dead, the others are running for their lives. It's the saddest thing I have ever seen. I've written a paper on it.'

David saw by the light that Guy was racked by the memory. Guy poked the meat again, this time with a penknife. He hacked at it, cutting off a large piece, and chewed on it; juices — surprisingly plentiful from such a skinny animal — ran down his pupate mouth.

'Perfect. Let's graze.'

David wakes very early. Because elephants are unpredictable, Guy decreed that they should sleep in the back of the Toyota. They started the night bedded down in the back on foam rubber, but Guy soon rolled over almost on top of him, and farted constantly (perhaps it was the wiener and Romany Cream diet), and then his remaining teeth began to grind alarmingly. After an hour David moved to the front passenger seat and covered himself with his grey blanket. He was very comfortable, although the dental grinding still reached him, albeit at diminished volume.

Now he hears a ripping sound. Soon afterwards an elephant appears in the riverbed below them, carrying a slender branch of acacia in its trunk. The elephant has a hide something like the colour of dark paprika, something like the colour of Rosalie's hair. It stops for a moment in the delicate business of stripping off the leaves and transferring them to its mouth and turns towards the Toyota. It shakes its head — its ears are immense — and then from deep inside it comes a rumble, a sound like the approach of a train on the Northern Line, before it walks on. Eleven more elephants, all coated with red dust, follow. Two of them are calves, perfect elephants in miniature; they are quickly screened from the Toyota by two adults, which turn towards the vehicle and raise their trunks anxiously to test the wind. David tries to wake his brother by banging on the partition. While obviously inaudible to his brother, it arouses the elephants' interest. One advances up the ridge towards the Toyota, huge, red and terrifying. It has only one, broken, tusk. In its agitated state, its legs are strangely loose as though it is doing a comedy shuffle. David sits very still, trying to be calm, although his heart begins to pound. He thinks it may be audible to elephants with their famously sensitive hearing. It is like some independently terrified animal trapped in his ribcage with no way out; it clearly knows instinctively what he knows intellectually, but this is no time for an exploration of dualism. A few feet from the Toyota, the elephant looms like a medium-sized building; it fills his vision as it shakes its head once or twice, advising him to retreat. He can't; he's trapped in the passenger seat without the keys. The elephant now advances, lowers its head and pushes the vehicle backwards. The locked tyres slide over the stony ground.

From the back of the Toyota, he hears Guy shouting.

'What are you doing? What's going on?'

'Elephant. A fucking elephant is pushing us.'

David hears the back door of the Toyota open and, to his horror, his brother appears outside the vehicle beside him. He is naked. He raises his arms in the manner of a charismatic, outstretched in forgiveness, as if to invite the elephant to reconsider its sins, and it does, retreating reluctantly in the face of this old naked fellow with the yellowed buttocks and greyish penis. It turns and follows after its fellows at a slow trot. Some way down the riverbed the other elephants emerge again, rambling along their pathways, casually harvesting the trees as they go, before disappearing suddenly between some cliffs of red stippled rock.

'It's amazing how quickly they come and go,' says Guy contentedly.

'Jesus, Guy. Have you done that before?'

'Once or twice. They're usually bluffing.'

'And if they are not?'

'Ah well, that's the chance you take.'

David sees that there is no bravado, just a sort of matter-of-factness about facing down a huge rufous elephant.

'Breakfast? Then we can follow them.'

'Do you think following them is a good idea? Don't you think they will recognise us?'

'Do you want to see them or not?'

'I have seen them. Way too close.'

'You go and get some acacia twigs and we'll brew up.'

David is too shaken to walk down to the trees. God knows, there could be more of them arriving on their mysterious migrations.

'I'll tell you what. Why don't you go down there for the wood, while I get the breakfast stuff out? Do you want wiener sausages?'

'Love some.'

His brother wanders naked down to the trees: *As he came forth of his mother's womb, naked shall he return to go as he came.* David finds a tin of sausages and some beans and pours water into the blackened kettle, which has a ritualistic importance on this journey. Soon Guy returns with some firewood.

'I'll just put on some clothes,' he says.

'Good idea.'

'By the way, you didn't tell me there were young. I saw the tracks.'

'No, for some reason it slipped my mind.'

'They can be more dangerous when they have young.'

'More dangerous? Than what? What's more dangerous than being shunted into a ravine by a 10-ton elephant?'

The fire, the kettle, the slippery little sausages, the beans with more than a suggestion of the can infusing them, the *rooibos* tea in the chipped metal cups, the weaver birds busy in the hardy trees, the bee-eaters flashing their carmine and blue as they leave their burrows, a lizard approaching with reptilian curiosity, the platoon of Maoist ants (seeking testicles), the overwhelming dryness which causes the snot in your nose to grow hard and granulated, the thin wisps from the fire (our sacred fire), as delicate as the smoke of paper money in a Buddhist temple being sent heavenwards, the sky turning from its deep morning blue – the colour of their mother's beloved willow-pattern china – to a whiter, bleached duck egg blue; the sound of crickets tuning up in the dried scrub, the whisper of a parched wind riffling the pods in the acacia trees, the immensity of the landscape already stunned by the new day – all this, David sees, with blinding clarity, is Guy's reality. What does it matter to him that his younger brother received the Royal Society of Television's Gold Award or that Gordon Brown will be forced from office or that the colours for next spring's fashions, according to the fashion experts, will see a return to the natural; in fact, intense colours like red and pink and violet will have a monochrome sheen? More than once he has reported on fashion from Milan or Paris but there was no mention of that in the elaborate calligraphy decorating his Gold Award. And yet, David knows – he has always known – we all make what we can of what is to hand.

And now, as they sip *rooibos*, which he has learned to like, he wonders if the urge for redemption isn't universal but expressed in many unconscious ways; in his brother's case (mercifully he has his rugby shorts on again) this is the mystical-poetical, the morning's minion, the crazed longing to understand, *how all's to one thing wrought*. And in the end it all does come down to one thing, death.

For himself it's the death of Nancy, which has become fixed in the pathetic image of her in the degrading hospital gown – a shroud – and her cruelly exposed buttocks. She turned to him, and waved, just once, utterly cowed, from some way down the wide, sinister corridor – a deadly boulevard – and he waved back in chipper fashion, a fool. A fucking idiot.

Death was semaphoring.

'Guy, what you did was incredible. When I saw you stark bollock naked waving at that elephant, I couldn't believe what I was seeing.'

'The elephant or my bollocks?'

'One thing's sure, the elephant didn't like your bollocks.'

They laugh. Even as he looks at his brother, the elephant man, with new respect, perhaps humility, he nonetheless sees looming that strangely complex, just-off-true nature and the stubbornness that he used to think spoke of a closed mind. The hedgehog and the fox. *The fox knows many things but the hedgehog knows one big thing*. No doubt who is the hedgehog in this brotherly relationship: all his life Guy had been striving for some way of knowing the mind of God. David remembers Richard Burton and his real anguish when Mephistopheles said, *I, who saw the face of God*. For Burton, *Dr Faustus* was not a play, but a terrifying presentiment of the hell into which he was knowingly descending.

'Shall we go and look for eles? They move deceptively fast. And could you just wash up the plates a little?' He says this with a stoical weariness. 'I've been meaning to tell you. You have to be organised on a trip like this. You're just as untidy as you were at fifteen. I'm going to take a crap.'

His diet has caused a chronic slow-down in his metabolism, but he has faith in alfresco evacuation. He heads for the trees, taking his own toilet roll.

David could point out that his brother's one and a half rooms at the back of someone's garden in Cape Town are filthy and piled with yellowing press cuttings – the pale iodine colour of his buttocks, he now realises – and cans deep in fungal growth, and that the spare bed, which he proudly revealed by hitting a sofa with a brick to release the mechanism, exposed a family of striped and understandably rattled field mice: 'Harmless little buggers, although they attract snakes, so I don't really encourage them.' He could have said many things, but of course you are saddled with the family myth and at this late stage it's probably pointless to put anyone straight, least of all his brother.

They set off along the riverbed. At first his brother had derided the air conditioning in the hired Toyota as a tragic pandering to the spoilt and decadent. After all, for tens of thousands of years man has lived without it. But now he has become a prince, the nabob, of cooled air, constantly adjusting the flow to reach those parts of his body that need attention. Actually, his body seems to be in some discomfort as though various regions of it are at war. Often a pained, preoccupied look and a high colour seize his face and he appears to be suffering; his eyes narrow as if trying to shut out memories, in the way that people shut out bright sunlight. But suddenly he is liable to jump nimbly out of the Toyota to study tracks or dung in the riverbed.

'They're about twenty minutes ahead of us,' he says. 'They've settled down, and will probably rest under the nearest big trees as it gets hotter. Jeepers, this air-con is top notch. I think I will be going to get one of these.'

'Good idea. Trade in the hen coop, chickens included in the price, as part exchange.'

'Great car, don't knock it. Do you want a beer?'

'From the icebox? The one you said was for – what was your word? – oh yes, I remember, cissies?'

They are happily adolescent, drinking beer and jeering amiably, the way they used to be, as they drive down the river course in pursuit of the elephants. It's as though the only relationship they can resume is fifty years old. Guy motions David to stop and gets out on to the riverbed to examine a large pile of dung. He pokes his finger into it.

'They're quite close. I had better drive,' he says, wiping his finger on the rugby shorts.

They find the elephants in a valley carved by flood waters and shaded by cliffs and trees.

Guy turns off the engine.

'The secret,' he says, 'is to know that you have an exit. You can never tell with eles, particularly these ones. Sometimes they can be as quiet as mice and sometimes they will charge. As we saw.'

They watch the elephants at rest. Deep in the sand is a hole they have excavated and they kneel in turn to drink. The calves are in playful mood and wrestle with their trunks.

After about ten minutes, Guy turns to his brother.

'Davey, as you already know, I am dying.'

It's the first time he has used his childhood name. He speaks awkwardly, his mouth full of unknown substances, and perhaps with regrets. And now he has a soft, collapsing mien. He's been struggling, it seems, to get to his subject.

'I knew that you weren't well. Frans told me. How long have you got?'

'A month. Six months. That's not the point. I'm not going to wait for them to take me in and pump me full of drugs.'

'What can I do?'

'Nothing. I'm a goner. But I wanted to talk to you and this is as good a place as any, the end of the line.'

David watches the elephants, unable to look at his brother.

'I've made a helluva mess of my life, in one way. Family, children and so on, total balls-up. In another, I've followed my interests. But there's nothing to show for it. None of my papers or theses has ever been accepted. I have no money to give to my kids, no home. Nothing.'

'I'll look after them.'

'Now look, I'm not asking you to do anything for my women or the youngest children or anything.'

'I will help them, whatever you say now.'

'Thanks.'

He is humiliated, because he has had to ask for help.

'Guy, you've had a fantastic life. These last few weeks have made me deeply envious. I have never been happier.'

'Thanks. I'm sorry I didn't know Nancy properly . . .'

'It's one of those things. Guy, I have had a truly incredible time with you.'

'With your crazy brother.'

'With my crazy brother.'

'That's something. Davey, I have always been very proud

of being your brother, even though you are an argumentative little bastard. All I want is that if I die before we get back you just bury me under some stones. Do you promise?'

'I promise.'

They embrace, something they have never done before. Despite his size, Guy has an insubstantial feel, as though he has been winnowed out. Even at this moment, they are unable to sustain the embrace.

'Keep your pecker up, bro,' says Guy. 'I am going now.'

'What do you mean? Where?'

'I'm just going for a walk.'

Guy climbs out of the Toyota with some difficulty. From behind he has an unsteady, old man's roll, requiring a few shuffling steps before he can get moving, placing his feet like a duck's – actually like a ballerina's, like Rosalie's – pointed outwards, flat on the sand of the riverbed to ensure steadiness. *Why have I never noticed this before?*

His brother disappears into some trees, and then appears again, walking along the riverbed towards the elephants; he has gathered a respectable speed and he does not apparently feel the need to look back.

20

SOME MONTHS LATER, IN LONDON

IT'S ANOTHER FOUR months before David gets back
from Africa. As he leaves Heathrow in a taxi, he finds that
he has adopted his brother's perspective of the metropolis,
or possibly Fritz Lang's: the terminal building is an ant's
nest; the road out of the airport is impossibly, pointlessly
busy. The skies lack . . . What do they lack, exactly? It is
winter and they are host to politely jostling, obese, grey,
dull clouds, great udders of rain. Rain is falling right now,
grudging, but persistent.

He decides that the skies lack majesty. Out in the desert,
just before he left for Cape Town, the clouds were slashed
and electrified by lightning for a few days. It was truly the
twilight of the gods. The Huab River, whose course he
was following all the way to the sea, flooded: water,
streaming red and brown – Christ's blood – roared down
in a solid wall 10 feet high. From a ridge, he watched the
river carrying away the red topsoil and a few small animals.
The elephants had spread out into the desert some time
before the rains came; elephants sense that sort of thing.
Guy's body, crushed and bruised, buried under rocks as he
had asked, would have been washed away and – he guessed
– been eaten by hyenas or jackals. Perhaps even the ants,

with their undiscriminating appetites, have joined in the recycling.

The cab driver's chubby face looks unnaturally pasty as it appears in the rear-view mirror.

'Been somewhere nice?'

'Africa.'

'Orright is it out there at the moment?'

'Yes, thanks. Lovely.'

As they approach London in the grim dawn, he feels that England is unnaturally cramped: the sky is low and the landscape is demure and he finds the buildings, particularly the new industrial parks and housing estates, tacky and presumptuous.

He is seeing things the way Guy saw them, but he thinks that is not so bad.

The Camden house has been on the market for four months, but there are no takers. Lucy has described her new boyfriend, Nick, in texts and an email; she and Nick have been looking after the house and showing the few prospects around. It doesn't look as though it will sell until the spring when things — the agent says, via Lucy — will undoubtedly pick up. The agent has also said that the house will 'show' better with less clutter. Ed and Rosalie are in Geneva. Rosalie is pregnant; the baby is due in twelve weeks. He's been away for almost exactly six months.

After what seems like hours, the cab finally approaches Camden. He thinks this is exactly what the painter Sickert saw, the scarcity of light, the oddly damp buildings, the air of apathy. Lucy has put flowers in the house. He's touched. Nancy loved flowers. He wondered exactly what they represented to her. Many people appropriate values from natural objects. His brother believed that the landscape and the wildlife out there were speaking to him: the message was never completely clear, that was the problem, but he never ceased from looking to the Bushman paintings to yield up the answers.

The elephants had dealt brutally with him. The body was horribly bruised and broken. Two of his ribs stuck right through the canoeing T-shirt. He hopes even now that it was a quick death. He dragged his brother's body out of the riverbed and laid it under a huge acacia and used the shovel from the Toyota to dig a shallow grave. He pulled the body into the grave and piled rocks on top of it, as Guy had requested. He had underestimated his length, and had to dig an extension. If he were a more practical man, he would have made a memorial, but there was anyway nothing to use for a headboard. Instead he recited the whole of his brother's beloved 'The Windhover', which he now, perforce, knows by heart.

As it happened, there was a falcon (or perhaps a hawk) hovering overhead, drifting on the thermals; for his brother's sake he hoped that it was his spirit creature arrived to accompany him. He tried to fix this spot in his mind, and took some photographs of the mound of stones under the tree. He noted the coordinates on the GPRS in the Toyota, in case there were questions from the authorities or from the family.

Lucy calls to see if he has arrived. She says she's coming over immediately. There is milk and bread and orange juice, fruit and single cartons of soup. Everything seems excessive, overorchestrated, even a little confusing. Guy believed that the West was 'spoilt' and David recognised one of their parents' favourite rebukes. Another was 'showing off': 'You're showing off,' was a devastating criticism back then. David suspected that his parents thought he was showing off when he first began to appear on the news. Later they were very proud of him. He once heard his father tell an old friend that he was afraid his son had inherited the gift of the gab from him. Looking uncertainly at all this furniture, all these things that he owns, the mountain of mail, the absurd little soups of artichoke, three types of Italian bean, and winter lentil and bacon – and bathed by the scents of perfect flowers – David thinks that he has been purged in the desert. (In the eremitic tradition, from the Greek, *eremos*, of course.) All this around him seems to be unnecessarily lavish. He thinks of Guy dipping wieners into the ketchup and inexpertly cooking anonymous chunks of meat on the fire, and farting in the back of the Toyota. Lucy has stacked his mail neatly and he rifles though it half-heartedly – hundreds of letters and bills and offers – until he spots Simon's handwriting. Strange how you can identify handwriting. He announces that the Noodle Club is invited to his bookshop, the Owl and the Pussycat Books, for a reading by Adam. Simon asks if he will drive Adam. He also says that Julian has died, from a second stroke. David thinks of him with his permafrost pubic hair in the changing room. Brian is away in the Far East but should be back in time; some of his investments are going down the tubes. The reading is just a few days away; he calls Simon immediately. Simon is relieved, because the last he heard David was in the desert somewhere.

'I'm relying on you to get Adam here, sober. We've sold a hundred tickets.'

'I'll try. I'm just back.'

'Adam's saying you're his only friend and he won't come unless you drive him as you promised.'

'He doesn't mean it. When did Julian die?'

'Five weeks ago. He was on a trip to Como with his

wife, and he suddenly had a massive stroke. She's devastated because she thought he had recovered.'

But he has other matters on his mind.

'David, do you think quails' eggs are all right? They are the thing, are they?'

'Don't ask me, I've been in the Kalahari. I'll be there with Adam, no need to panic.'

He rings Adam.

'The rover's return. How are you, my old chum? Wiser?'

'I don't think so.'

'How long have you been away? Two months?'

'Six.'

'Six. Fuck me. How time flies, et cetera.'

'I'm coming to get you next Tuesday.'

'You heard that Julian's died?'

'Yes. Was there a service?'

'There was. Utter crap.'

'What do you mean?'

'Some snivelling little shits of grandchildren read sentimental memoirs of Gramps, written by their parents, a whole fucking procession of whey-faced turds from the Foreign Office made banal remarks, a bearded rabbi and a little paedophile priest both talked ecumenical bollocks. Either you believe in all the religious mumbo-jumbo or you don't; there's no fucking point in trying to update it. Julian, in these accounts, was someone you and I didn't know. We were celebrating a total fiction. It was sickening. Still, the usual hypocrisies are maybe what you want when your time is up.'

'The necessary fictions.'

'Exactly. See you next week. Let's drive slowly, stopping at many hostelries.'

David feels cheered by this conversation.

Lucy arrives. She is happy, even overcome.

'You have a beard. You look amazing. Like a prophet. Brown as a nut, too. Baked.'

'Lucy, Lucy. It's wonderful to see you. I'm sorry I was away so long. I missed you terribly.'

She hugs him fervently and he strokes her hair.

'Oh Dad, I thought you were never coming back. Welcome home.'

'How are you, my angel? How've you been?'

'I'm so happy, Dad. You're home, that's the best thing, and also Nick and I are going to get married.'

'That's wonderful. When did that happen?'

'We only decided last night.'

'I can't wait to meet him. He sounds terrific, by text.'

'He is terrific by text, and even better in the flesh.'

He wonders if Lucy isn't a little desperate to create the family life he hasn't provided since Nancy died. At the same time some archaic instinct tells him that he's relieved to have disposed of his daughter.

'And how's Ed? And Rosalie and Geneva and all that?'

'They love it. I told you I had been to see them. All very organised and clean and lovely. Rosalie's an associate of the ballet.'

'Does Ed like his new job? I spoke to him, but I didn't really ask him.'

'You never quite know with Ed. But he seems to. He's taken up husky racing. He's also got a very French haircut. How were Uncle Guy's wives and children?'

'We've sorted things out. There was some argument about whether or not they should go and retrieve the body. I said I thought that would be difficult. I told Frans what had happened and that Guy said he wanted to be buried out there. The question of a death certificate didn't really come up, because Guy had virtually no possessions at all, so there's no need for a will. When I had to find my way back, I discovered that we had crossed borders two or three times. Lucy, sweetie, thanks for stocking up and for the flowers. It was very thoughtful. I'll make some tea. I brought back some *rooibos* – do you want to try it? I love it now, but I have to say it takes some getting used to.'

He feels a slight awkwardness.

'Dad, did you think of Mum when you were there?'

'I did. A lot.'

He can't explain to her just yet that under the Kalahari stars you see things differently. You don't, as Guy imagined, find the core of things, but you understand that many of your assumptions have no absolute truth. If the Bushmen believed that trance dancing put them in touch with the spirits, that was fine by him: it was as valid an explanation as anything he believed. In truth he is not sure exactly what he believes: I have beliefs but I don't believe in them. The strange thing was, although Guy talked about them all the time, they never met any Bushmen, apart from one silent family gathered in a few makeshift huts outside a small town of stunning inconsequence.

He makes the tea, something he did every morning on the campfire, even after Guy died. Lucy seems to have become more grown-up in six months: the student look has gone, and she is more poised. He thinks it may just be the effect of seeing her after six months: seeing her anew. Perhaps he had always thought of her as a little girl. In a way, he wishes she still were; parents cannot forget the days when their children regarded them with uncritical admiration and love.

'Do you like the tea?'

'As you said, it may take a little getting used to. What exactly did you do after Uncle Guy was killed?'

'Nothing, exactly. I travelled around in my hire car.'

'For four months?'

'When Guy died, I went to Cape Town to see the relatives, and then I took off. I just sort of followed my instincts.'

They talk for an hour or more. They arrange to meet for dinner with Nick.

'And now I have to go to Grimaldi, Dad. I'm head of my department now.'

'Why didn't you tell me? Congratulations.'

'It's not such a big deal. But I do handle the press and some clients. Being your daughter has helped. Everyone still asks me about you.'

'Do you say nice things?'

'Usually. Bye, Dad, see you at about eight. Can you handle it?'

'I hope so. I like wiener sausages and ketchup and a spot of kudu.'

'I'll see what they can do. There's loads of stuff in the cupboards and all the sheets are clean and fresh.'

'Thanks, my darling, I saw. You are an angel. Oh, Lucy, one thing: beard, on or off?'

'Leave it; it looks great. And not too grey.'

When she's gone, he rings Ed. Ed's at Geneva airport, about to board for New York.

'Ed, sorry to catch you like this: just one thing I didn't ask you. Is Lucy going to be OK with this Nick?'

'He's wonderful. They've been over to see us. You'll come soon, I hope? Skiing has started.'

'What's happened with Josh?'

'Josh? He decided he would be better off in Australia.'

'I just wanted the background before I meet Nick. I feel a little guilty about being away.'

'As long as you discovered the meaning of life. That's the main thing. There's my plane. Got to go, Pops.'

David can hear the final call in three languages.

ED CROSS SEEMS to have lost every skirmish with his wife, Rosalie, since she became pregnant. For example, he hadn't wanted this elaborate church ceremony. His father, David Cross, said don't think of it as suggesting that you believe in God, just accept it as part of the social ritual, the grease that makes the wheels go round.

'Are you talking about the wheels of marriage?'

'The wheels of marriage, and the other sort.'

Lucy Cross, Ed's sister, is a godmother and very much at the centre of things. She is soon to be married to Nick Grimczek, who is watching keenly, his face at a questing angle. She holds the silver baptismal shell with which generations — at least two — of Rosalie's family, the Brownjohns, have been doused. It's a family tradition. The child, Darcey Nancy Cross ('Darcey' was another battle lost), is strangely quiet as the priest, a positive, rather fat woman with an upbeat, demotic manner — she announced that she prefers to be called the Reverend Jacqui — takes the baptismal shell from Lucy and scoops a little water from the font. On her arm she has a deep and surprisingly fluffy white towel, the sort of towel you find in luxury hotels. She is equipped to dry the baby's almost bald head. There are signs, a russet filigree, that the baby's head is the seedbed for a magnificent growth of hair, like her mother's.

David thinks that Ed, under his floppy French haircut, looks a little moist, as though he has been caught up in the baptismal theme himself. David's role in all this is mute support. Grandfathers take a backward step as the business of life – day-to-day, essential life, including the upbringing of children – finds its natural rhythms. At this point women are promoted to the front rank. Ed is only now discovering that a marriage is a shifting alliance. Certainly while his mother was alive, she was the final authority on all family matters, the keeper of the family lore.

The baptismal service is quite short and to the point; as the vicar cradles little Darcey in one arm and says, 'I baptise thee in the Name of the Father, and of the Son, and of the Holy Ghost,' and, as the water trickles on to her forehead, David feels the tide of the numinous running at a deep level, like a rumble in a sea cave. It is not a belief in God that affects him so deeply, but the never-ending and restless human desire to make some meaning out of life. And death. 'We receive this Child into the Congregation of Christ's flock, and do sign her with the sign of the Cross, in token that hereafter she shall not be ashamed to confess the faith of Christ crucified, and manfully to fight under his banner against sin, the world, and the devil, and to continue Christ's faithful soldier and servant unto her life's end. Amen.'

David looks at Rosalie, so elegant in a long floral summer dress, which just about snags on her slim hips, and he knows that this will always be one of the great moments of her life, to be cherished for ever. Nancy was the same: the albums of photographs of Ed's and Lucy's christenings were sacred objects. Today, if she were still alive, Nancy would have known not only how to behave, but how to feel. For himself and, he thinks, for Ed, a conscious effort, a kind of sieving, is required to find the point of these social rituals. Nancy would have seen her first grandchild as a tribute, the natural reward for having carried Ed and Lucy, her contribution to keeping the show on the road. To greasing the wheels.

The vicar is giving an address about the gift of children and the need to give them a Christian upbringing. She talks of the sacred ties that bind parents and children and here, at least, David is with her. His feelings for Ed and Lucy are so acute, so bound up with his own essence, that he has no language to articulate them. He guesses that these feelings – these deep, irrational longings, fears, hopes – are really the source of all the religious stuff. These inchoate yearnings are heightened by the dread of death and, out of this potent mix, religion was born. David thinks that his own death is a small matter, but the idea of Ed or Lucy, when they were children, dying in an accident – drowning, for example – or as the result of sudden illness, tormented him in the small hours most acutely when he was in a flea-ridden guest house in the unfriendly mountains of Afghanistan or caught in the cross-fire in Soweto or utterly drained on a transport plane back from some hell-hole. Even now that they are grown-up he can't bear to contemplate such a thing. When Nancy died he wasn't immediately devastated, as he would have been if one of the children had died. But, from the moment the Reverend Jacqui poured a few drops of water on her head, he was gripped with a deep love for this baby and also for Nancy, her grandmother, even if the baby possesses none of her genes. Maybe this is the real presence, transcending the merely rational, that Guy was looking for.

The Reverend Jacqui speaks loudly and theatrically: *In the name of the Father, and of the Son, and of the Holy Ghost. Amen.*

'And Nancy,' he whispers. 'In the name of Nancy.'

SINCE HE LOST his licence for the third time, Adam has travelled in cars with a hint of condescension; he behaves as if David as a driver has a rather pointless hobby, like those rail enthusiasts who play trains at the weekend. He refuses to look at the map or to take any interest in the route: he gave up that sort of thing long ago. On the way to Simon's bookshop, the Owl and the Pussycat Books, they stop only once for a drink. Adam has a Scotch and a beer chaser. David sips a mineral water, but without any suggestion of reproach. Adam is his own man and he loves him for that.

When they finally arrive in the village, Adam is asleep, slumped deep into the passenger seat. His face is older in repose, his mouth slightly open. Older people often sleep with their mouths open and their noses pointing skywards. For some reason, Adam is dressed in green corduroys and a green Barbour. On his head is a baseball cap, with what looks like a black-and-red weaver bird on it. It is in fact the headgear of the away uniform of the Baltimore Orioles.

David wakes him gently.

'That didn't take long,' he says. 'Well driven. You should take it up professionally.'

His face is a little flushed, but otherwise he looks fine. Simon comes out to greet them and shows them into the shop.

'Simon, this is so beautiful. The Owl and the Pussycat. I've come as the pea-green boat. And look at all these books. Who would have thought it?'

The bookshop has a large fireplace and a log fire is burning gently. It looks more like Simon's private library than a bookshop. There are three comfortable old leather chairs around the fireplace – now shunted together – and in the body of the shop, at least a hundred wooden chairs lined up. In a storeroom, Simon has laid out some drinks and snacks for the Noodle Club. There are only five of them, Brian, David, Adam, Simon and Philip Entwhistle, who lives in France and drove over via the tunnel. He has a daughter who lives near by in Alfriston.

'Before we start the real business of the day, I think we should drink a toast to absent friends, and of course I am particularly thinking of Julian. Raise your glasses to absent friends, to Julian,' says Brian.

'To absent friends, to Julian,' they say, raising their glasses.

'Absent' is a curious description of Julian, David thinks. He's not coming back.

Simon says that the paying guests will be here in less than half an hour. He is nervous and keeps dashing out to see if the two volunteers are able to handle the parking, the crowd, the quails' eggs, the raffle – to be presented by David – the microphone on the lectern, where Adam will speak, and the extra chairs required; as many as six people have phoned in late saying they want to come. Adam asks if anyone has a copy of his book, as he has forgotten to bring one, although there is a copy of a P.G. Wodehouse in his Barbour. Simon rushes off to the shelves. When he comes back he asks if David will sign copies of his Afghanistan book, and whether he will make some closing remarks. Adam drinks two large glasses of red wine.

'Fabulous wine, Simon. Made mostly with grapes?'

'No, I just mix the water and the powder in a plastic bucket.'

'Hello, Philip,' David says. 'How've you been?'

'Not great. My daughter's husband has left her. Why do I care so much? She's thirty-two, but it's killing me.'

'I know the feeling. Mine's twenty-six and just about to get married. I'm terrified.'

In fact Nick is astonishingly charming and self-possessed, and also he seems very straightforward, which is the quality you most want for your daughter. What you don't want is someone like me.

'If you were a novelist, Philip,' says Adam, 'you would recycle this: you would see it as material.'

'Unfortunately I'm a retired investment banker, like Brian, so I see it as an utter fucking disaster.'

'Strictly speaking, I'm not retired. I am still chairman of four investment funds,' says Brian.

'How are they doing?'

'All going down the pan, sadly.'

David feels himself being drawn back into the life he vacated. With these battered friends he has a shared intimacy. He may be imagining it: people of our generation have never been too good at expressing real emotion. Together again, they see their true selves, which are invisible to others, emerging. It's comforting. Brian decides to help Simon, who is flustered because of the increased numbers; he goes out to assess the situation. After a few minutes he comes back into the storeroom, which now has a warm conviviality, and says that everything is under control and the place is filling up nicely. Quails' eggs and wine are being dispensed enthusiastically by the lady volunteers. Adam pours himself another large glass of red wine. He's talking to one of the lady volunteers. She is laughing.

'Will he be all right?' Simon asks anxiously.

'He'll be fine. Don't worry.'

Soon they are led out into the bookshop to take their seats. Simon follows: he goes to the podium.

'Welcome, everybody, to this very special occasion. As you know, every entry ticket has a number on it and at the end of the reading my old friend David Cross, who needs no introduction, even though he is sporting a beard, will draw one number from a hat that corresponds to a seat number, and the lucky winner will receive a book token for fifty pounds. David will also say a few words at the very end in conclusion. I thank you for coming. And now it is my very great pleasure to welcome tonight's speaker, author of the classic, *The Wise Women of Wandsworth*, and many other fine books, prize-winning scriptwriter, broadcaster and all-round national treasure, Adam Edwards.'

Adam, still wearing his green Barbour and Orioles baseball cap, in his hand a freshly filled glass of red wine, walks up to the podium. His cheeks have those familiar highlights.

'Friends,' he says, 'friends, I sometimes feel that those of us who love books, and I mean real books with long words, are a dwindling band. We're like the Bushmen of the Kalahari Desert that David was telling me about on the way here, marginalised, even despised, as though we have a secret vice or carry a contagion. My friends, I am here this evening to tell you that a country without a respect for its own literature is a country going to hell in a fucking handcart. We, the readers, are now like monks in the dark ages, keeping alive our culture. We are living in a new dark age, an age of mass ignorance; we are squeezed in the embrace of triviality and infantilism. I, for example, spend my days turning dumb ideas into dumber scripts that become even dumber mini-series. The BBC, where David and I first started our working lives all those years ago, has turned into a sink of touchy-feely mediocrity . . .'

On and on he goes. David glances at Simon, who looks pale. But the audience loves it. Adam breaks off to sing a folk ballad to illustrate some point, and then he reads a short extract from *The Wise Women*, and finally he recites from memory a large chunk of *The Waste Land*. After forty minutes, he closes saying, 'We readers have a sacred duty, to keep alive our literary tradition, to save our language from the barbarians, to read until our eyeballs burst. God bless you.'

A hundred English men and women rise to him, some a little unsteadily because of age and drink.

Now David moves to the lectern.

'I am here only to mop up. I thought Adam's talk was absolutely inspirational and I know you would want to thank him with me. Adam and I will be signing books, if you want them signed. The big event of the evening, the raffle, comes soon, but please bear with me. I have been in the Kalahari Desert, as Adam said, for the last six months. I was with my brother, who died there. I believe he wanted to die there. Before I draw the raffle, I hope you will indulge me, I would like to recite a few lines of his favourite poem, 'The Windhover', by Gerard Manley Hopkins, in his memory.

I caught this morning morning's minion, kingdom of
daylight's dauphin, dapple-dawn-drawn Falcon, in his
riding
  Of the rolling level underneath him steady air, and
striding
High there, how he rung upon the rein of a wimpling wing
  In his ecstasy! then off, off forth on swing . . .

He cannot continue alone. Adam comes and puts an arm around his shoulder and kisses him. Adam begins and they go on together to the end:

As a skate's heel sweeps smooth on a bow-bend: the hurl
and gliding
  Rebuffed the big wind. My heart in hiding
Stirred for a bird, – the achieve of; the mastery of the
thing!

Brute beauty and valour and act, oh, air, pride, plume, here
  Buckle! AND the fire that breaks from thee then, a
billion
Times told lovelier, more dangerous, O my chevalier!

  No wonder of it: shéer plód makes plough down sillion
Shine, and blue-bleak embers, ah my dear,
  Fall, gall themselves, and gash gold vermillion.

In the car, Adam says that there will never be another meeting of the Noodle Club. Then he falls asleep, as the Jaguar makes its way through the shires.

Near Hayward's Heath he wakes for a moment and says, 'We saw the face of God.'

Acknowledgements

I would like to thank my agent James Gill for his patience and diligence; all at Bloomsbury, but particularly my editor Michael Fishwick, Alexandra Pringle, and Colin Midson. Nobody, however, knows better than me that many others have played a vital part, and I thank them too. I am also deeply indebted to Liz Calder, as so many writers are.

A Note on the Type

Linotype Garamond Three – based on seventeenth-century copies of Claude Garamond's types, cut by Jean Jannon. This version was designed for American Type Founders in 1917, by Morris Fuller Benton and Thomas Maitland Cleland and adapted for mechanical composition by Linotype in 1936.

ALSO AVAILABLE BY JUSTIN CARTWRIGHT

THE PROMISE OF HAPPINESS

The Richard & Judy bestseller

Winner of the Hawthornden Prize 2005

Charles Judd wanders across a wild Cornish beach, contemplating the turns his life has taken. At home, his wife Daphne struggles hopelessly with the latest fish recipe. Two of their children are keeping it all together – just. The third, the prodigal daughter Juliet, is being released from prison in New York after a sentence for art theft. This is the day, on the face of it so ordinary, on which Justin Cartwright's explosive novel opens, as all five members of the family try to come to terms with the return of Juliet, and their deepest thoughts and darkest secrets are laid bare.

*

'A compelling and candid portrait of a family in crisis'
MAIL ON SUNDAY

'Extraordinarily bold ... This is a funny, angry, moving novel'
INDEPENDENT

'Impressive ... an intelligent, generous and unsentimental take on an English middle-class family'
DAILY TELEGRAPH

*

ISBN 9781408807071 · PAPERBACK · £7.99

B L O O M S B U R Y

THE SONG BEFORE IT IS SUNG

On 20 July 1944, Adolf Hitler narrowly escaped an assassin's bomb. Axel von Gottberg and his conspirators were hunted down and hanged from meat-hooks, and the executions filmed. Sixty years later, Conrad Senior is left a legacy of letters by von Gottberg's close friend, the legendary Oxford professor Elya Mendel, and becomes obsessed with what they reveal and finding the brutal film. Award-winning writer Justin Cartwright has conjured a masterwork that addresses the nature of friendship and what it means to be human, and it is a remarkable tapestry of passion, ideas, frailty and courage.

*

'A richly detailed evocation of one of the darkest periods in modern history, and an eloquent exploration of human fallibility and guilt'
THE TIMES

'Heart-stopping ... utterly accomplished'
SUNDAY TELEGRAPH

'A profound exploration of guilt, friendship, voyeurism and morality. A cracker'
INDEPENDENT ON SUNDAY

*

ISBN 9780747585947 · PAPERBACK · £7.99

B L O O M S B U R Y

THIS SECRET GARDEN

OXFORD REVISITED

Oxford is many things. But it has a symbolic meaning which reaches well beyond its buildings, gardens, rituals and teaching. It stands for something deep in the Anglo-Saxon mind: excellence, a kind of privilege, open-mindedness, respect for tradition.

Cartwright has spoken to many leading figures, looked at favourite places in Oxford, subjected himself to an English tutorial – he performed very poorly – attended the freshers' dinner in his old college, studied various works of art, libraries and museums, investigated the claim that dons like detective novels, and reread many Oxford classics. At the same time he has looked at some of the great debates and reforms which made Oxford what it is, as well as the most recent debate about funding reform, which ended in a resounding defeat for the reformers.

He finds that the Oxford myth, while it is at odds with reality, is as powerful as ever. This is an enchanting and intelligent look at Oxford, indispensable reading for anyone interested in the myth and reality of this famed city.

*

'A poignant meditation on youth and age'
GUARDIAN

'An attractively written book, which captures the university's mixture of the serious, the silly, the political and the picturesque ... it will appeal to both armchair tourists and homesick Oxonians'
TIMES LITERARY SUPPLEMENT

*

ISBN 9780747579618 · HARDBACK · £9.99

ORDER YOUR COPY: BY PHONE +44 (0)1256 302 699; BY EMAIL: DIRECT@MACMILLAN.CO.UK
DELIVERY IS USUALLY 3–5 WORKING DAYS. FREE POSTAGE AND PACKAGING FOR ORDERS OVER £20.

ONLINE: WWW.BLOOMSBURY.COM/BOOKSHOP
PRICES AND AVAILABILITY SUBJECT TO CHANGE WITHOUT NOTICE.

WWW.BLOOMSBURY.COM/JUSTINCARTWRIGHT

B L O O M S B U R Y